Handy Kitchen Information

Weights and Measures

3 teaspoons = 1 tablespoon
4 tablespoons = ¼ cup
8 tablespoons = ½ cup
16 tablespoons = 1 cup

1 tablespoon = ½ fluid ounce
1 cup = 8 fluid ounces
1 cup = ½ pint
2 cups = 1 pint
4 cups = 1 quart
4 quarts = 1 gallon

1 ounce = approximately 30 grams
4 ounces = approximately 120 grams
16 ounces = 1 pound

Handy Kitchen Information

Ingredients Substitutions

If you don't have the exact ingredients a recipe calls for, don't worry. You can often use alternative ingredients without any change in flavor or appearance.

2 tablespoons all-purpose flour = 1 tablespoon cornstarch

1 cup all-purpose flour = 1 cup + 2 tablespoons cake flour

1 cup buttermilk = 1 cup low-fat milk + 1 tablespoon lemon juice or vinegar (let stand for 5 minutes) or 1 cup low-fat plain yogurt

1 whole egg = 2 egg whites

1 ounce unsweetened chocolate = 3 tablespoons cocoa + 1 tablespoon butter or margarine

1 cup mayonnaise = ½ cup low-fat plain yogurt + ½ cup regular or reduced-fat mayonnaise

1 cup honey = 1¼ cups granulated sugar + ¼ cup liquid

1 cup granulated sugar = 1 cup packed brown sugar

1 clove garlic = ⅛ teaspoon garlic powder

1 small onion = 1 teaspoon onion powder

1 tablespoon prepared mustard = 1 teaspoon dry mustard powder

1 teaspoon lemon juice = ½ teaspoon vinegar

The
Pregnancy
COOKBOOK

· · · · · · ·

Easy Recipes for
Nine Months
of Healthy Eating

Marsha Hudnall, M.S., R.D.
and Donna Shields, M.S., R.D.

BERKLEY BOOKS, NEW YORK

The ideas, procedures, and suggestions contained in this book are not intended as a substitute for consulting with your physician. All matters regarding your health require medical supervision.

THE PREGNANCY COOKBOOK:
EASY RECIPES FOR NINE MONTHS
OF HEALTHY EATING

A Berkley Book / published by arrangement with the authors

PRINTING HISTORY
Berkley edition / August 1995

All rights reserved.
Copyright © 1995 by Marsha Hudnall and Donna Shields.
This book may not be reproduced in whole or in part,
by mimeograph or any other means, without permission.
For information address: The Berkley Publishing Group,
200 Madison Avenue, New York, New York 10016.

ISBN: 0-425-14883-1

BERKLEY®
Berkley Books are published by The Berkley Publishing Group,
200 Madison Avenue, New York, New York 10016.
BERKLEY and the "B" design
are trademarks belonging to Berkley Publishing Corporation.

PRINTED IN THE UNITED STATES OF AMERICA

10 9 8 7 6 5 4 3 2

Acknowledgments

To Alan, my husband, thanks for your loving and supportive ways. To Lesley and Jake, my children, whose smiling, healthy faces and love of all things sweet remind me daily of the importance of providing for plenty of pleasure in a plan for healthy eating.

— MARSHA HUDNALL

Many thanks go to my first food mentor: Mom. She was interested in nutrition long before it was fashionable and taught me that good cooking means mixing lots of love into the pot. Working on those recipes together, in snowbound Clinton Corners, generated some great food and was fun for both of us.

And thanks to my husband and number one taster, Ted, who gave me honest and valuable insight into my food. And I can't blame you for feeling pregnant after testing more than one-hundred and twenty recipes. Your witty suggestions for recipe names and chapter titles made me giggle while I slaved away in the kitchen. And you're right—*Feed Us . . . Fetus* would have been a great title!

— DONNA SHIELDS

Contents

The
Pregnancy
COOKBOOK

CHAPTER ONE

Healthy Eating for the Next Nine Months . . . and Beyond

So you're pregnant! What an exciting—and sometimes overwhelming—time this is, especially if it's your first pregnancy. So many new things are happening to your body: your breasts are enlarging, you're gaining weight, and your body is changing shape right before your very eyes. Further, your thoughts are filled with wonder and just a bit of anxiety about this new life forming within you.

While you're mentally adjusting to all these changes, you're probably learning how to take care of yourself and your developing baby from your obstetrician or nurse-midwife. You're also likely to be devouring information from magazines and books. As if all that is not enough, you may be still working outside your home, while taking care of it and perhaps other children. That's a pretty full agenda!

During this busy time, the many essential elements of a successful pregnancy almost seem to compete for your attention. But taking it one slow step at a time helps you deal with it all in a sensible and enjoyable manner.

Eating healthfully to help ensure a healthy pregnancy may be one of the most anxiety-producing concerns you have right now. How can you be certain you're eating what your baby needs? Do you need to worry about pesticides and other additives in your food? How can you avoid gaining too much weight? Do you have to quit eating your favorite foods? These are just a few of the typical questions pregnant women ask.

This book is designed to help answer those questions as they arise during each stage of pregnancy. It also outlines in a quick and easy-to-read way a rational approach to healthful eating during this important time. The nutritional guidance in this book incorporates the latest recommendations from the American College of Obstetrics and Gynecologists, the American Dietetic Association, the Food and Nutrition Board of the National Academy of Sciences, and the U.S. Department of Agriculture. In addition, it provides practical advice for enjoying eating healthfully when pregnant (and after).

This book is designed to be used by healthy pregnant women who are under the care of a qualified obstetric professional such as an obstetrician. *It does not substitute for such care, and you should always follow your health care provider's advice if it conflicts with anything you read in this book.*

Eating for Health and Enjoyment

Following the advice in this book will help you be sure you and your developing baby get the many nutrients you both need during this important time. Indeed, *eating a nutritionally balanced diet is one of the most important things you can do to ensure a healthy pregnancy and baby.*

By the same token, now is *not* the time to get paranoid about every single food you eat. Food does more than just nourish us. As an integral part of our social culture, food plays an important role in how we enjoy our surroundings and each other, whether at home or dining out. There's no reason to give up restaurant meals, parties, or having friends over for dinner just because you're pregnant.

Food also comforts us. If you have mood swings during pregnancy, you may find your favorite apple pie is just the thing to soothe your rattled nerves. Eating desserts or other favorite high-fat, high-calorie foods does not mean you've failed yourself or your baby in any way if you eat such foods within a total, well-balanced nutrition plan.

A positive outlook during pregnancy—both about what you eat and other important aspects of caring for your and your developing baby's health—goes a long way toward making the entire experience satisfying and enjoyable. This is a time of doing something good for your body, not a time of deprivation.

Changing Nutrition Habits for Your Child's Health

If your eating habits weren't so smart before you became pregnant, take this opportunity to learn about nutrition. Make important changes in your diet now so you can continue eating healthier foods after pregnancy. Indeed, your nutritional responsibility to your child does not end with delivery. If you plan to breast-feed, you'll need to remain nutrition-conscious after giving birth. After infancy, your child will look to you as a role model for developing the healthy eating habits that will help ensure his or her healthy future.

Making dietary changes, however, cannot be done overnight. In fact, research shows gradual change succeeds best. We do not suggest you wake up one morning and try to completely revamp your eating habits. Most likely, they don't need complete revamping; they just need a little adjustment.

The reality is that your diet should be appealing to you, take the amount of time you have to prepare it (which is usually minimal), and include foods that everyone else in your household will eat. This can mean incorporating into your diet calcium-rich foods other than milk because you hate milk. Or cutting back on (*not* eliminating) sugary, high-fat treats that provide lots of calories but little else nutritionally.

Also, it can mean learning how to identify the best nutritional choices on a restaurant menu. These are all small changes you can make over the course of nine months, without feeling deprived and without placing a burden on your family, and they are all small changes that can stay with you for the rest of your life to boost your and your family's health.

To get some idea of what you already know about diet and pregnancy, take this quick quiz. Our Healthy Eating for Two quiz covers some typical questions, concerns, and popular myths about eating during pregnancy. Your answers will give you an idea of whether you've got a lot or a little to learn.

Healthy Eating for Two

Answer True or False.

1. Experts recommend that you gain no more than 24 to 28 pounds when you are pregnant.
2. You need to eat an additional 500 calories each day throughout your pregnancy.
3. A vitamin and mineral supplement is a *must* during pregnancy.
4. Adequate nutrition plays a vital role in how much your baby weighs when born.
5. If you gain too much weight the first trimester, you should go on a diet and start exercising more throughout the rest of your pregnancy.
6. Food cravings result from an instinctive need for certain nutrients.
7. It's extremely difficult to eat healthy for pregnancy if you travel and are away from home a great deal.
8. Increased protein needs can only be met by eating more meat, fish, or poultry.
9. Restricting salt will prevent water retention.
10. Morning sickness can be avoided by simply not eating.

Answers to
Healthy Eating for Two

1. False. Most women should gain between 25 to 35 pounds for a healthy pregnancy. Women who are underweight should gain more, and women who are overweight may be advised to gain less.

2. False. Your calorie needs jump by about 300 calories a day if you continue your same activity level. Even then, the increase doesn't come until the second and third trimester. During the first three months, you really don't need more calories than usual unless you're underweight to begin with.

3. It depends. The absolute answer really isn't in yet. While iron appears to be the only nutrient we cannot get in sufficient amounts from food, research indicates a multivitamin supplement may help cut the risk of some birth defects. A supplement, however, doesn't negate the need for well-balanced nutrition throughout pregnancy such as is described in this book.

4. True. While many things such as genetics; prenatal care; use of drugs, alcohol, or cigarettes; and medical conditions including diabetes can result in low birth weights, an inadequate diet can also affect how much your baby weighs when born. Low birth weights in full-term infants can mean serious complications for the baby.

5. False. Regardless of how much weight you gain, you should *never* diet during pregnancy. Dieting can deprive your baby of essential nutrients critical to his or her proper development. Exercise during pregnancy should be moderate and only done with the approval of your health care provider.

6. False. Why women crave specific foods during pregnancy isn't clear, but it's usually *not* related to nutrient deficiencies.

continued

7. False. Healthy eating during pregnancy is not a particularly complicated task, and it can be done almost
   anywhere.
8. False. Dry beans and peas, nuts, eggs, milk, cheese,
   and fish are all great sources of protein. Some of
   these choices are also much lower in fat than meat
   or poultry.
9. False. While it was once a common practice, we now
   know that salt restriction can be harmful during pregnancy. Your body needs some additional sodium, although the total amount should remain moderate.
10. False. What helps relieve morning sickness is very
    individual, but not eating usually makes it worse,
    not better.

How did you do? If you're like many women, you found
you have a few misconceptions about good nutrition during
pregnancy. To help you understand it all better, the next few
pages give a brief introduction to why and how your nutritional needs change. In the following chapters, we then
guide you in meeting the particular nutritional needs and
concerns of each trimester. After reading this chapter, rely
on those chapters to guide you in healthy eating each step
of the way.

Meeting the Nutritional Needs of Pregnancy

You undergo tremendous physical changes as your body
gets ready to give birth and produce milk. Your uterus and
breasts grow, the placenta develops, your blood volume ex-
pands, and you begin to store fat. All these changes require
extra energy and nutrients to keep you at your best. After
all, food provides the fuel your body needs to do what it
has to do.

To meet your increased nutritional needs as your pregnancy progresses, you need to modify the Food Guide

Pyramid, the basic tool for healthy eating for all healthy adults. We explain the pyramid in detail in the next chapter. Then in the following chapters, we describe exactly how to modify the Food Guide Pyramid according to your nutritional needs during each trimester of pregnancy and if you breast-feed.

In addition to supplying energy and nutrients for your body, you're also supplying them for someone else. The food you eat provides a direct line of nourishment for your growing fetus.

The first trimester is an especially critical time for fetal development. During this period, vital organs and body parts form. By the end of the first thirteen weeks, most of the fetus's organs are formed, and it can move. Development is very rapid during this period, and good nutrition is important. Yet this is often a time when you least feel like eating due to morning sickness (which for many women lasts all day). Chapter 4 gives you practical nutrition tips for making it through the first trimester.

As your pregnancy progresses, the fetus further develops its organs and adds weight. Your baby's birth weight is directly related to your nutritional intake, including alcohol consumption and smoking. By eating according to the plan we've outlined in Chapters 5 and 6, eliminating alcohol, and not smoking, you increase the likelihood you'll deliver a healthy infant.

Getting Started

We've been discussing the fact that during the entire nine months of pregnancy, you need a nutritional boost to help ensure your health and that your growing baby reaches his or her fullest potential. If you always eat healthfully, that boost comes from simply adding nutritious foods and cutting back (not necessarily out) on foods that provide calories but few other nutrients. If your eating habits have long cried out for improvement, now is the time to focus on them to make important changes.

Complete the How Do You Eat? questionnaire below. Your answers provide a good starting point for assessing the changes you may need to make or the steps you need to take to help ensure the healthiest pregnancy and baby you can.

How Do You Eat?

What you eat and some of your lifestyle choices can affect both your and your baby's health now and in the future.

Eating Behavior

1. Do any of the following conditions frequently interfere with your appetite?
   Nausea   Vomiting   Heartburn   Constipation
2. Do you skip meals at least three
   times a week?   No   Yes
3. Do you try to limit the amount or
   kind of food you eat to control
   your weight?   No   Yes
4. Are you on a special diet now?   No   Yes
5. Do you avoid any foods for health
   or religious reasons?   No   Yes

Food and Drink

Answer the following questions based on what you ate yesterday. If that does not reflect how you typically eat, answer questions according to a typical day's intake.

continued

---

6. Which of these did you drink yesterday? (circle all that apply)

Soft drinks	Coffee	Tea	Fruit drink
Orange juice	Grapefruit juice	Other juices	Milk
Beer	Wine	Alcoholic drinks	Water

Other beverages (list)_____

7. Which of these foods did you eat yesterday? (circle all that apply)

Group A

Cheese	Pizza	Other foods made with cheese
Cereal with milk	Yogurt	

Group B

Carrots	Green beans	Sweet potatoes	Turnip greens
Spinach	Collard greens	Green peas	Other vegetables
Broccoli		Green salad	

Group C

Apples	Bananas	Berries	Grapefruit
Melon	Oranges	Peaches	Other fruit

Group D

Meat	Fish	Chicken	Eggs
Peanut butter	Nuts	Seeds	Dried beans

Group E

Cold cuts	Hot dog	Bacon	Sausage
Cake	Cookies	Doughnut	Pastry

continued

Chips	French fries	Other deep-fried foods, such as fried chicken or egg rolls	

Group F

Bread	Rolls	Rice	Cereal
Noodles	Spaghetti	Tortillas	

Were any of these whole grain?   No   Yes

Lifestyle

8. Do you exercise for at least thirty minutes on a regular basis (three times a week or more)?   No   Yes
9. Do you ever smoke cigarettes or use smokeless tobacco?   No   Yes
10. Do you ever drink beer, wine, liquor, or any other alcoholic beverages?   No   Yes
11. Which of these do you take? (circle all that apply)
    Prescribed drugs or medication
    Any over-the-counter products (such as aspirin, acetaminophen, antacids, or vitamins)
    Street drugs (such as marijuana, speed, downers, crack, or heroin)

Adapted and reprinted with permission from *Nutrition During Pregnancy & Lactation: An Implementation Guide.* Copyright 1992 by the National Academy of Sciences. Courtesy of the National Academy Press, Washington, D.C.

Assessing How You Eat

Compare your answers to How Do You Eat? to the discussion below.

1. Problems with nausea, vomiting, heartburn, or constipation can interfere with proper nutrition. Read the discussion on page 43 regarding nausea and vomiting during pregnancy. We discuss heartburn and constipation on page 56. If these problems persist, discuss them with your health care provider.

2. If you skip meals frequently, you may be skipping nutrients important to you and your baby at this time, or you may find yourself overeating at other meals, leading to excessive weight gain and discomfort.

3. If you try to consciously limit the type and amount of food you eat due to weight concerns, you may find it difficult to adapt to eating the additional food you need during pregnancy. Or you may find yourself susceptible to excessive weight gain because you feel set free. Be aware of your tendency and check with your health care provider if you find yourself struggling either way.

4. Tell your health care provider if you are following a self-imposed diet or one prescribed by another health professional. You may need to make specific changes.

5. If you avoid major groups of foods (see the Food Guide Pyramid on page 17), you may be missing important nutrients in your diet. Read the section on the Food Guide Pyramid to identify different food sources of important nutrients. You may also want to consider vitamin and/or mineral supplements. Discuss your diet and supplements with your health care provider.

continued

6. Beverages such as coffee, tea, fruit drinks, soft drinks, and alcoholic beverages provide few nutrients. Don't let them take the place of more nutritious beverages such as milk, the only dependable source of vitamin D, or orange juice, which is an important source of vitamin C. Although, according to the National Academy of Sciences, two or three servings of caffeinated beverages daily is not likely to have adverse effects, avoid these in larger quantities. Alcoholic beverages are not recommended for pregnant women or for women trying to conceive.

7. The foods in the various groups are all important to a healthy diet. We discuss this in more detail throughout this book. The following brief description gives you a look at the important nutrients these foods provide.

- Foods in Group A contain milk, cheese, or yogurt and are good sources of calcium (as well as many other minerals, protein, and vitamins). Many are also good sources of vitamin A. Women who do not drink milk or eat one of these foods daily may need a calcium supplement.

- Foods in Group B include vegetables most commonly eaten in the United States. Carrots, spinach and other greens, sweet potatoes, and winter squash are very high in beta-carotene (the plant form of vitamin A). Asparagus, broccoli, avocados, okra, brussels sprouts, greens, and corn provide more folate (folic acid) per serving than do other vegetables. If you do not and will not regularly eat any vegetables other than potatoes or corn, talk with your health care provider. You may also need a vitamin/mineral supplement.

continued

- The fruits listed in Group C are those most commonly eaten in this country. Citrus fruits and juices, strawberries, and cantaloupe are especially good sources of vitamin C and folate. If you do not and will not regularly eat fruits or drink fruit juices, discuss this fact with your health care provider. You may also need a vitamin/mineral supplement.
- Meat, poultry, fish, eggs, and beans—the foods in Group D—provide protein, iron, zinc, and many other minerals and vitamins that are extremely important during pregnancy and when breastfeeding.
- The foods in Group E tend to be high in fat and calories. Frequent use of these foods may crowd out better sources of nutrients. The key word here is *moderation*.
- The foods in Group F provide vitamins, minerals, protein, and energy without providing much fat. Whole grains are an important source of fiber and other nutrients not found in refined grains.

8. Staying active during pregnancy helps you feel and look your best, and it helps get you ready for all the running you'll do after the baby is born. If you regularly exercise, discuss your activities with your health care provider. If you aren't very active, increase your activity slowly, following your doctor's advice.

continued

9–11. If you smoke cigarettes, use smokeless tobacco, drink alcohol, or use street drugs, you are exposing your baby to substances that can slow growth and development and cause permanent harm. Review all medications you take with your obstetrician. Only use those that he or she prescribes, recommends, or approves.

Adapted and reprinted with permission from *Nutrition During Pregnancy & Lactation: An Implementation Guide.* Copyright 1992 by the National Academy of Sciences. Courtesy of the National Academy Press, Washington, D.C.

Putting It All Into Practice

This book doesn't stop with nutrition advice. We've developed a wonderful variety of good-tasting, healthful, and simple recipes to meet the nutritional needs of pregnancy and breast-feeding.

Indeed, putting nutrition into practice in the kitchen is the fun part. While we might certainly enjoy doing so, few of us have hours on end to spend cooking. So we've developed recipes that will give you the maximum nutrition and good taste for the least amount of effort.

The recipes in each chapter correspond to the particular nutritional needs, concerns, discomforts, or potential complications that may arise during each stage of pregnancy. For example, coffee might rate as one of your favorite beverages, but you're conscious about caffeine. You'll want to try our recipe for Coffee Colada on page 67. It's an easy way to enjoy that great coffee taste, reduce caffeine, and increase the calcium in your diet.

As you read the rest of this book, remember that eating smart is one of the best things you can do to set the stage for a healthy, happy baby. So, bon appetit!

CHAPTER TWO

Setting the Stage
for a
Healthy Pregnancy

To get a good start on healthy eating during pregnancy, it helps to understand the basics of healthy eating anytime. They are summarized in the Dietary Guidelines for Americans below. By following these guidelines, you may enjoy better health and reduce your chances of getting certain diseases. The guidelines incorporate the most up-to-date advice from nutrition scientists.

The Dietary Guidelines for Americans

- *Eat a variety of foods* to get the energy, protein, vitamins, minerals, and fiber you need for good health.
- *Maintain healthy weight* to reduce your chances of having high blood pressure, heart disease, a stroke, certain cancers, and the most common kind of diabetes.
- *Choose a diet low in fat, saturated fat, and cholesterol* to reduce your risk of heart attack and certain types of cancer. Because fat contains over twice the calories of an equal amount of carbohydrates or protein, a diet low in fat can help you maintain a healthy weight. *Don't restrict fat in the diets of children under two years of age;* they need an adequate amount of fat for proper growth and development.

continued

- *Choose a diet with plenty of vegetables, fruits, and grain products.* They provide needed vitamins, minerals, fiber, and complex carbohydrates—and can help you lower your fat intake.
- *Use sugars only in moderation.* A diet with excessive amounts of sugars has too many calories and too few nutrients for most people and can contribute to tooth decay. Moderate amounts of sugars, however, can help people cut fat intake and contribute to the enjoyment of healthy diets.
- *Use salt and sodium only in moderation* to help reduce your risk of high blood pressure.
- *If you drink alcoholic beverages, do so in moderation.* Alcoholic beverages supply calories but few or no nutrients. Drinking alcohol is also the cause of many health problems and accidents and can lead to addiction. It's not recommended at all during pregnancy.

The Food Guide Pyramid

In 1992, nutritionists at the U.S. Department of Agriculture designed a graphic to help put the Dietary Guidelines into action. It's called the Food Guide Pyramid. Today it's the most widely used nutrition education tool there is. It can help you choose nutritious foods without getting too many calories or too much fat, saturated fat, cholesterol sugar, sodium, or alcohol. Copy the picture of the Food Guide Pyramid and post it on your refrigerator for quick and easy reference.

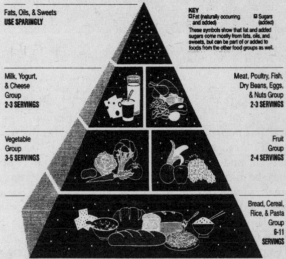

Food Guide Pyramid

A Guide to Daily Food Choices

Fats, Oils, & Sweets
USE SPARINGLY

KEY
☐ Fat (naturally occurring   ◪ Sugars
   and added)   (added)
These symbols show that fat and added
sugars come mostly from fats, oils, and
sweets, but can be part of or added to
foods from the other food groups as well.

Milk, Yogurt,
& Cheese
Group
2-3 SERVINGS

Meat, Poultry, Fish,
Dry Beans, Eggs,
& Nuts Group
2-3 SERVINGS

Vegetable
Group
3-5 SERVINGS

Fruit
Group
2-4 SERVINGS

Bread, Cereal,
Rice, & Pasta
Group
**6-11
SERVINGS**

SOURCE: U.S. Department of Agriculture/U.S. Department of Health and Human Services

Use the Food Guide Pyramid to help you eat better every day. . .the Dietary Guidelines way. Start with plenty of Breads, Cereals, Rice, and Pasta; Vegetables; and Fruits. Add two to three servings from the Milk group and two to three servings from the Meat group.

Each of these food groups provides some, but not all, of the nutrients you need. No one food group is more important than another — for good health you need them all. Go easy on fats, oils, and sweets, the foods in the small tip of the Pyramid.

To order a copy of "The Food Guide Pyramid" booklet, send a $1.00 check or money order made out to the Superintendent of Documents to: Consumer Information Center, Department 159-Y, Pueblo, Colorado 81009.

U.S. Department of Agriculture, Human Nutrition Information Service, August 1992, Leaflet No. 572

About the Food Guide Pyramid

The following information explains important concepts about the Food Guide Pyramid. They can help you use it to develop a healthful daily eating plan.

- The pyramid has been constructed around the concepts of variety, balance, and moderation. In other words, the pyramid calls for eating a variety of foods in appropriate amounts to get the nutrients you need and to keep fat and calorie intake in line. See What's a Serving? on page 20 to learn more about what constitutes an appropriate amount.
- For best success in adopting the recommendations of the Food Guide Pyramid, understand that it is an outline of what to eat each day—not a rigid prescription. It guides you in choosing healthful foods. The pyramid recommends a range of servings from each group to meet the nutrient and calorie needs of all healthy adults, whether they be highly active or extremely sedentary, large or small, young or old. In general, more sedentary, smaller, older people should eat from the lower range of servings. See How Many Servings Should you Eat? on page 21 to learn more about what's right for you.
- The pyramid emphasizes five food groups, beginning with a base of healthful, low-fat grain foods such as cereals, breads, rice, and pasta. Vegetables and fruits complete the foundation of the pyramid. Other vital food groups include the milk and meat groups. Choosing Smart from Each Food Group on page 23 also lists nutrient-dense choices in each group or items that pack the greatest nutritional punch. Choose low-fat and lean items from all groups most of the time to help guarantee a diet low in fat.
- The tip of the pyramid represents fats, oil, and sweets— foods with plenty of calories but few other nutrients. These foods make up only a small part of a healthy diet. You do need some fat, however, for good health.

- Each of the food groups provide some, but not all, of the nutrients you need. Foods in one group can't replace those in another, and no one food group is more important than another. For good health, you need them all. (The single exception is for strict vegetarians who avoid all animal foods, including those from the milk group. For proper nutrition, they must choose other foods wisely. See page 52 for more information on vegetarian eating during pregnancy.)
- The guidelines of the pyramid can be applied to any ethnic diet. For example, rice and tortillas count as servings from the bread group. You don't need to change your traditions to eat healthfully although you may need to use less fat in your frequently eaten traditional foods.
- The Food Guide Pyramid is a guide for choosing foods, not pills, to provide the nutrients you need. At this point, scientists are far from understanding everything about how different foods contribute to good health. For example, we're just learning about substances like phytochemicals in grains, fruits, and vegetables that may be important in warding off disease. You can't find phytochemicals—or other substances we may need—in a pill. Still, there is some research to suggest that a multivitamin supplement may provide extra safeguards for pregnant women. Several studies have shown mothers who take multivitamins cut their babies' risk of various birth defects including neural tube defects. Don't take a vitamin/mineral supplement, however, without the approval of your health care provider. Too much of certain nutrients can cause as much harm as too little.

If you would like to learn more about the Food Guide Pyramid, contact the USDA Human Nutrition Information Service, 6505 Belcrest Road, Hyattsville, MD 20708; 301/436-5724.

What's a Serving?

Bread, Cereal, Rice, and Pasta

1 serving averages 80 calories.

1 slice of bread
1 ounce of ready-to-eat cereal
½ cup of cooked cereal, rice, or pasta

Vegetable

1 serving averages 25 calories.

1 cup of raw, leafy vegetables
½ cup of other vegetables, cooked or chopped raw
¾ cup of vegetable juice

Fruit

1 serving averages 60 calories.

1 medium apple, banana, orange
½ cup of chopped, cooked, or canned fruit
¾ cup of fruit juice

Milk, Yogurt, and Cheese

1 serving of skim milk averages 90 calories; 2 percent milk = 120 calories; whole milk = 150 calories. Skim and part-skim cheeses average 75 calories per ounce, and regular cheeses average 100 calories per ounce.

continued

1 cup of milk or yogurt
1½ ounces of natural cheese
2 ounces of processed cheese

Meat, Poultry, Fish, Dry Beans, Eggs and Nuts

1 ounce lean meat averages 55 calories; 1 ounce of medium-fat meat such as regular ground beef, roasts, most steaks, lamb, poultry with skin, and eggs average 75 calories; high-fat meats like spareribs, luncheon meats, and sausage average 100 calories per ounce. Peanut butter has about 100 calories per tablespoon. Cooked, dried beans average about 120 calories per ½ cup.

2 to 3 ounces of cooked lean meat, poultry, or fish
½ cup of cooked dry beans, 1 egg, or 2 tablespoons of peanut butter count as 1 ounce of lean meat

Fats, Oils and Sweets

1 teaspoon butter, margarine, or oil or 1 tablespoon full-fat salad dressing averages 45 calories.

There are no specific serving sizes for these foods. They should be eaten in moderation, which for most people means only in small amounts.

How Many Servings Should You Eat?

The Food Guide Pyramid lists a range of servings for each food group. The number you need depends on your calorie requirements, which depend on your activity level, age, sex, and size. Most people should eat at least the lowest number of servings recommended for each food group.

The following chart indicates servings for three calorie levels.

- Sedentary women and some older adults generally need about 1600 calories a day.
- Most children, teenage girls, active women, and sedentary men need about 2200 calories a day. Women who are pregnant or breast-feeding generally need more.
- Teenage boys, many active men, and some very active women need about 2800 calories a day.

Calorie guidelines aren't so clear for young children. Generally, they may eat the same number of servings as the rest of the family, but the serving sizes are smaller. They should have the equivalent of two cups of milk a day, however.

What's Right for You When You're Not Pregnant or Breast-feeding?		
About 1600 calories	*About 2200 calories*	*About 2800 calories*
Bread group servings		
6	9	11
Vegetable group servings		
3	4	5
Fruit group servings		
2	3	4
Milk group servings*		
2–3	2–3	2–3
Meat group (ounces)**		
5	6	7

*Teenagers and young adults to age twenty-four need three servings.
**Meat group amounts are in total ounces. See What's a Serving? on page 20 for information on how to count foods like dry beans, eggs, and peanut butter.

Choosing Smart from Each Food Group

Each food group contains a wide variety of foods. Nutrient-dense choices—foods with plenty of nutrients compared to the calories they contain—top the list as the smartest choices. Study the following information to learn how to choose smart for your and your family's best health.

Bread, Cereal, Rice, and Pasta
- Of the six to eleven recommended servings from this group, experts say we should eat three or more servings of whole-grain foods each day. To meet this requirement, try:

  Whole-grain breakfast cereals like Wheaties, Cheerios, or Whole Grain Total
  Whole wheat breads (they must say *whole* wheat on the label)
  Brown rice
  Bagels
  Whole grain pasta (Many people swear this is taking it too far—they just don't like the taste! But remember, only three servings need to be whole grain. This leaves plenty of room for regular pasta.)

- Choose low-fat foods most of the time. Muffins, pancakes, waffles, doughnuts, biscuits, nut breads, and other specialty items contain extra fat.

Fruits and Vegetables
- Choose at least one serving rich in vitamin A each day. Go for dark yellow-orange and deep green items such as cantaloupe, peaches, spinach, brussels sprouts, broccoli, and green peppers.
- Choose at least one serving rich in vitamin C each day. Try citrus fruits, strawberries, green peppers, cantaloupe, tomatoes, and cauliflower.
- Eat cruciferous vegetables several times a week. These vegetables are packed with substances that help keep you

healthy. Choose cauliflower, broccoli, brussels sprouts, cabbage, and kale.
- Season vegetables with lemon and herbs; go lightly on added fats. Try broth-based vegetable soups instead of creamy versions; they're full of vitamins and minerals and a great source of fluid.

Milk, Yogurt, and Cheese
- Choose skim milk and nonfat yogurt often—they're the lowest in fat in this food group. Choose part-skim and low-fat cheeses when available.
- 1½ to 2 ounces of cheese contain the same amount of calcium as 1 cup of skim milk or nonfat yogurt, but the cheese has a lot more fat. Cottage cheese contains less calcium than other cheeses; 1 cup has only as much calcium as ½ cup of milk.
- Look for lower-fat ice cream, frozen yogurt, and other low-fat frozen desserts to enjoy in place of high-fat ice cream.

Meat, Poultry, Fish, Nuts, Eggs, and Dry Beans
- Lowest-fat choices from this group include lean meat, poultry without skin, fish, dry beans, and peas. Try round or sirloin steaks, pork tenderloin or ham, all cuts of veal except ground veal, leg of lamb or loin, all poultry and fish (fish canned in oil is higher in fat).
- Trim all the fat you can see from meats and remove skin from poultry before cooking. Then broil, roast, or boil instead of frying these foods.
- Eat nuts and seeds in moderation; they're high in fat. Egg yolks are high in dietary cholesterol, but recent studies indicate most people can eat them without affecting their blood cholesterol levels. Egg whites are low in fat and cholesterol; enjoy them freely.
- Bacon and luncheon meats like bologna are high in fat and low in vitamins and minerals. Try sliced chicken, turkey, beef, or ham instead.

Snacks

While we wouldn't advise counting snack foods like chips as servings from any food group, you can still make smart choices. Consider unbuttered popcorn and pretzels instead of high-fat potato or corn chips, or look for low-fat versions of your favorites; stores are beginning to stock more baked chips these days. Try calcium-rich pudding instead of cake or sweetened gelatin desserts. Stock your pantry shelves with nutrient-rich foods such as raisins to satisfy the munchies.

A Special Focus On . . .

Water

Water makes up about 60 percent of our bodies and ranks as the most important nutrient. Without it, we can only live for a few days while we can potentially live for several weeks without food. Water plays a vital role in virtually all our bodily functions: digestion, absorption, circulation, excretion, transporting nutrients, building tissue, and maintaining temperature. Yet we tend to forget about water when talking good nutrition.

We need about 8 cups of water every day, and pregnant women are often advised to drink about 10 cups. That may sound like a lot to swallow and, fortunately, we get water from many sources other than the tap. One to two cups comes from the food we eat; think about all the fluid in watermelons and other fruits and vegetables. Then there's the fluid/water in juices, milk, and other beverages. Even more water forms during the process of using fats, protein, and carbohydrates in our bodies; water is a by-product of that process.

To guarantee plenty of fluids to keep your body processes functioning smoothly, drink enthusiastically whenever you're thirsty. In warm, humid weather, drink frequently. Nursing mothers, in particular, should remain very aware of fluid intake. You need more when breast-feeding because a lot of what you take in goes out in the form of breast milk.

Fiber

If you enjoy breakfast cereal, you're probably tuned into the benefits of fiber. It's a favorite subject of cereal companies because many of their products are great sources of the stuff.

Rather than a single substance, dietary fiber is a mix of things that act together to provide health benefits ranging from a lower risk of colon cancer to potentially lower blood cholesterol levels, and risk for heart disease.

Insoluble fiber is the material that remains after plant foods pass through the intestinal tract. It is found in foods such as wheat bran, whole-grain cereals, dried beans and peas, vegetables, and nuts. This type of fiber is most helpful in preventing constipation and is linked to lower colon cancer risk.

Soluble fiber is classified as such because it absorbs water, and turns into a gummy-like substance that may have beneficial health effects. It is found in whole-grain oats, oat bran, some fruits, dried beans, and other legumes. This fiber appears to help lower blood cholesterol levels when it's part of an overall diet low in fat. It may also help control blood sugar levels in people with diabetes.

In a healthy diet such as that outlined in the Food Guide Pyramid, you get plenty of both types of fiber, particularly if you eat whole grains and don't peel your fruits and vegetables. Fiber is particularly important to relieve constipation, a problem that haunts many women during pregnancy.

If you're increasing your intake of fiber, however, remember that you need to drink plenty of fluids along with it. And go slowly. Jumping from a low-fiber to a high-fiber intake too quickly may cause cramping and gas.

Fat

The very word *fat* doesn't sound too good these days. With concerns ranging from fat bodies to fatty foods (which definitely have a connection—fat contains double the calories of protein or carbohydrate), many people would just prefer to avoid the subject altogether.

The problem is, most of us can't seem to do that. Fat tastes too good. Indeed, it is to a large extent responsible for the rich, creamy taste of favorite foods like ice cream and the satisfying flavor of a great steak.

Fortunately, contrary to what it may seem like when reading the latest article about fat, we don't need to avoid it entirely. Indeed, we need some fat, but not nearly as much as we eat. Today's nutrition goal is to just cut back on it a bit from our current average of about 36 percent of calories to about 30 percent of calories.

In particular, we need to cut back on saturated fat, the kind that primarily comes from animal foods like meats, whole milk, and cheese made with whole milk. Too many of these fats may lead to heart disease. That doesn't mean we have to give up these foods entirely; just watch portion sizes. Decorate your dinner plate with only three ounces of cooked, lean meat (about the size of a deck of cards); that's significantly less than many Americans now eat. See page 24 for a list of lean meats.

If skim milk just doesn't make it for you, try 1 percent. If that's still too much of a taste jump, try 2 percent initially. When you've firmly established that habit, try to make the switch to 1 percent. If you don't ever go all the way to skim, don't worry; 1 percent still qualifies as low-fat.

Good-tasting, reduced-fat cheeses line grocery store refrigerator cases today. Try a few. You may be pleasantly surprised at their taste, especially if you haven't tried them recently. They've been improved. Also try mixing low-fat and regular cheeses for your favorite lasagna or other cheesy casseroles. You'll get the same great flavor with a lot less fat.

Unsaturated fat, the kind found in oils such as olive oil and corn oil, tops the list as the most desirable kind of fat for today's healthy diets. Just remember, you can go overboard on these, too. When using any kind of fat, go lightly. It doesn't take a lot to add great flavor and do whatever else you're using the fat for, such as to stir-fry vegetables or dress a salad.

Some more tips for cutting fat include:

- Limit your intake of fried foods. Bake, broil, sauté, or poach foods instead.
- Trim all visible fat from meats and remove skin from poultry.
- Chill soups, broths, or chili to harden the fat that rises to the top, then remove it before reheating.
- Add herbs, lemon juice, and other seasonings instead of butter or margarine to vegetables.
- Sprinkle oils like sesame, walnut, or extra-virgin olive oil in or on soups, salads, and vegetables. Just a little adds a lot of flavor.

Eating Safely

If you get most of your information about food and nutrition from the media, one question may really be bothering you right now. You may wonder how you can eat healthfully for a healthy pregnancy when there seem to be so many questions about the inherent safety of our food. That is, with all the pesticides, food additives, and other things in and on the foods we eat, do we really have the personal power to eat healthfully?

You also may have heard before that Americans enjoy one of the safest food supplies in the world. Regardless of what you read or hear to the contrary, believe it! We're not saying that potential health risks from food don't exist, but they're much less than we have been led to believe in recent years.

Food additives are rigorously tested before they are allowed in our foods. In addition, their use is closely monitored to guarantee they are used properly and in amounts that are safe. Still, a small percentage of people are sensitive to some additives such as sulfites. If you're sensitive or allergic to any food additive, you're likely to have learned this long before you became pregnant, and you should continue to avoid any substances that previously affected you negatively. Food labels list all additives used in a food.

Many pregnant women also question whether they should be using additives like low-calorie sweeteners. In its recent position paper on these sweeteners, The American Dietetic Association states that such sweeteners can safely be used in moderation by most pregnant women. However, those with phenylketonuria (a rare disorder in which the amino acid phenylalanine cannot be metabolized) should avoid the sweetener aspartame, which contains phenylalanine.

Perhaps your biggest worry is pesticides. Certainly, there's been a great deal of discussion about the safety of the fruits and vegetables we eat, even as nutritionists plead for us to eat more of these nutritional powerhouses. Seems a bit conflicting, doesn't it? It's not. Experts agree that the potential benefits of eating fruits and vegetables far outweigh any potential risks. If you're still concerned, however, there are a few steps you can take.

- Wash fruits and vegetables in water (not soap) and scrub them with a brush or peel them.
- Eat a variety of foods to reduce your exposure to any one pesticide.

There are some soaps especially produced for washing produce. The manufacturers of these products claim they remove more dirt and pesticides from produce than scrubbing with water alone can do. The soaps are expensive, and we don't believe you need them; a good scrubbing will suffice. But if you feel more comfortable using such products, go ahead.

Contaminants in seafood such as methylmercury and polychlorinated biphenyls (PCBs) are another story. Medical experts caution pregnant women to limit consumption of any fish that may contain excessive levels of these contaminants.

Methylmercury accumulates in fish with long life spans, such as swordfish, shark and tuna. As a result, the National Fisheries Institute states that pregnant women should not eat swordfish and shark more than once a month. Studies show canned tuna, however, does not contain excessively high levels of methylmercury. The National Fisheries Institute cites seafood safety experts who "see no harm if a pregnant woman wants to eat canned tuna as often as several times a week."

Some freshwater lakes, rivers, ocean bays and harbors are polluted with PCBs. Fish living in these waters can also contain excessively high levels of this substance. Therefore, you should avoid fish from areas such as the Great Lakes or waters near other industrial areas. (If you live near areas that may be so polluted, you've likely heard a lot about them already.) According to the National Fisheries Institute, most of the commercial fish supply is harvested deep at sea where waters are much cleaner. That's certainly good news since the many varieties of fish are great additions to a healthy eating plan.

Caffeine is another subject that makes the worry list for many pregnant women. Again, if you read the newspapers, you could find yourself changing your mind almost daily about whether to continue drinking coffee or colas. As with most nutritional concerns, the bottom line with caffeine is *moderation.* If you don't overdo it, there appears to be no harm associated with the substance to you or your developing baby. According to a National Academy of Sciences Committee on Nutritional Status during Pregnancy and

Lactation, drinking two to three servings (cups) of caffeinated beverages a day is unlikely to have adverse effects.

There is one absolute food no-no for pregnant women, and it's good advice for the rest of us, too. Avoid raw meats, fish, and eggs at all costs. They can contain bacteria or other organisms that are destroyed when we cook these foods, yet if we eat them raw, they will make us sick. So stay away from sushi, raw oysters, steak tartare, and Caesar salads made with raw eggs.

As far as raw foods go, there's another risk called toxoplasmosis. Toxoplasmosis is a parasite infection that may cause birth defects. You may be exposed to it by eating raw or rare meats. When pregnant, cook all meats well-done (to an internal temperature of 160° F). The parasite is also found in cat feces, so stay away from the cat litter box and wear gloves when gardening if there are cats in the area. Thoroughly wash fruits and vegetables, too.

While it's not food, one more subject bears discussion in this section concerning the safety of the things you put into your body. That's the use of harmful or potentially harmful substances like cigarettes and alcohol during pregnancy. We've certainly heard about many of the health risks associated with smoking when we're not pregnant, but you may not know that cigarette smoking is also a major cause of low birth weight and other health problems for infants. And we just don't know how much alcohol in pregnancy is safe, so the best course is to avoid it altogether. The same advice holds true when you're breast-feeding.

Handling Food Safely

If there is one major food safety problem today, it's in how we handle our food. As many as 80 percent of the food-related illnesses that occur each year result from the improper handling of food. While potentially harmful bacteria is often on food when we buy it, it's how we handle it—whether we store or cook it properly, whether we properly wash utensils that touch raw foods—that makes us sick.

Pregnant women should be especially careful about handling food properly because any illness you contract affects your unborn child. Unborn children don't have a developed immune system and can't fight the bacteria as well.

Protect yourself and your developing baby by storing and preparing food properly. Refrigerate food as soon as you arrive home from the grocery story (and don't make any long stops on the way home). Also, don't leave food sitting out after you've finished eating. Use a cooler to store items for a picnic, and keep it in the shade, not sitting out in the hot sun. Wash all utensils and cutting boards that have been used to prepare raw meats, especially poultry, in hot, soapy water before using them to prepare other foods. And remember the golden rule for food safety: When in doubt, throw it out.

For more information, contact the USDA's Meat and Poultry Hotline at 800/535-4555. They can send you a copy of *A Quick Consumer Guide to Safe Food Handling*. The Food and Drug Administration also operates a Seafood Hotline to answer your questions about seafood safety. You can reach it at 800/332-4010.

CHAPTER THREE

About the Recipes

As you know by now, sound nutrition is important throughout your entire pregnancy, but some specific nutrient needs vary as you move through each trimester. To meet those particular needs and provide foods that meet other healthy eating guidelines, we have developed recipes nutritionally appropriate for each trimester. There is also a section of recipes designed for post delivery, to help meet the nutritional needs of breast-feeding moms.

Nutritious Fast Food

We've developed these recipes to fit all occasions by providing a wide range of flavors and ingredients, different cooking methods, and an assortment of colors and textures. Since many of you may be too busy or tired to fuss with complicated recipes, we have made all the recipes quick and easy to prepare, using a minimal number of ingredients, the simplest methods, and the least amount of equipment. You may cook for a family, just you and your husband, or perhaps just yourself. To accommodate different family sizes, we purposely varied the number of servings for each recipe. If you are cooking for a family, these recipes are ones that everyone can enjoy. Some recipes, especially the soups and one-dish meals, freeze well and we have noted those for you. If you cook for a large family, most recipes can be easily doubled to produce a larger quantity of food.

Cooking Techniques

You will notice that we do not add any oil, butter, or margarine to a pan when browning meat. This is not an oversight. Using fat to brown meat is something many of us automatically do just because that's the way we always cooked. Instead, use the technique known as *dry sauté*. It really works. Place the meat in a preheated pan and let the meat sit until well browned. Don't try and turn it right away, because it will stick. The meat's own fat is released and allows browning to occur (called caramelization) and allows you to turn it without any problem. Although this process only takes a few minutes, the key to browning without any added fat is patience.

Ingredients

You will notice we make liberal use of reduced-fat and nonfat dairy products. This helps boost the calcium content of certain recipes while controlling fat and calories. We also use small amounts of dairy foods that have more fat, such as cheddar or blue cheese, to provide flavor. By using small quantities of higher-fat ingredients, recipes will taste good but still meet nutritional guidelines.

You may be wondering why we use butter rather than margarine in our recipes. We are using such small quantities that, on a per serving basis, butter is not contributing a significant amount of cholesterol. We would rather have butter's rich flavor make a dish taste good than save a few milligrams of cholesterol by switching to margarine. Don't forget: butter and margarine have the same amount of calories and fat; the only difference is in the cholesterol content. If you choose to use margarine in the recipes, it will not adversely affect the results.

In baked goods, we use whole wheat flour when it will make a significant contribution to the dietary fiber value of each serving. Whole wheat flour also adds many other important nutrients, such as magnesium and iron, that make it an important ingredient for healthy eating.

We call for dried herbs and spices for convenience' sake, but fresh ones can be substituted without altering the nutritional profile. Generally, use twice as much of a fresh herb as you would the dried herb.

Nutritional Benefits

After each recipe is a section that shows the contribution each serving provides toward the RDA (Recommended Dietary Allowance) for pregnant women. We have listed only those nutrients contained in significant amounts or those pertinent to the particular trimester. The recipes, however, often contain many other important nutrients in smaller amounts. Selecting a variety of these recipes will provide you with necessary nutrients, although they may not be listed on the recipe page. The recommended recipe options, listed for each recipe, may or may not slightly alter the nutritional values. Some alternative recipe options are for convenience' sake; others may alter flavor; and some reduce the fat, cholesterol, or sodium content and are so noted.

Pyramid Servings

The number of Food Guide Pyramid servings has been calculated for each recipe. This can serve as a handy device for you in planning a balanced diet. Keep in mind, however, that because recipes contain fats, oils, sugars, and small quantities of other ingredients, the calories per serving may be higher compared to adding up food group servings alone.

For example, Cherry Rice Pudding, on page 174, has 240 calories per serving and contains 2 bread group servings, which alone would add up to 160 calories. So where did the additional 80 calories come from? The eggs, evaporated skim milk, and sugar in the recipe do not provide enough nutrients on a per serving basis to be counted as a significant pyramid serving, yet they do contribute calories and other important nutrients.

A similar example would be the bean recipes. Beans are listed in the meat group because of their protein content. Yet they contain more calories than an equivalent amount of meat due to their high carbohydrate content. Therefore, bean recipes often have a higher calorie value than lean meat recipes. We point this out just so you won't be confused by what may seem like a discrepancy in the numbers. As we've explained in the chapters, don't get hung up on calorie counting. Let your hunger and the Building a Healthy Baby Nutrition Plan guide you.

Food Moods

Another important piece of information provided with each recipe is the food mood indicator. This has nothing to do with nutrition, but has everything to do with enjoying the right food at the right time. Food does much more than provide good nutrition. What you feel like eating will depend on your mood, the setting, your energy level, whether you're eating alone or with your family—a whole host of factors. The food mood indicator should make it easy for you to find a recipe that suits your specific taste needs. For example, if you feel like having something cold and icy to drink but can't put your finger on it, just thumb through the book. Look at the food mood indicator; perhaps the Motherita on page 64 will do the trick.

There's probably no other time in your life when food likes and dislikes are going to have such an effect on you. You need to eat what tastes good to you. By offering a wide assortment of healthful recipes in this book, we believe there's something in here for everyone. Enjoying the foods you eat is just one more way to enjoy your pregnancy.

CHAPTER FOUR

The First Three Months: Oh, What a Feeling!

It's hard to imagine a more contradictory time than the first few months of pregnancy. You're excited, full of anticipation about this new life within you, yet you may be nauseous and vomiting frequently. You've probably quickly learned that some smells can instantly turn your stomach, and just the thought of some foods can send you running for the bathroom.

If you're lucky enough to avoid the common first-trimester problems with nausea, you may be watching the needle climb on the scale when your doctor is already warning you about excess weight gain. Or you may be plagued with other concerns including heartburn, constipation, and worries about your diet.

Stop, take a deep breath, and read this chapter. It tells you what you need to know about nutrition during the first trimester of pregnancy. It gives you useful tips for managing the nutrition and eating challenges you may face. Further, it contains some great recipes for satisfying your very specific taste bud demands and nutritional needs during the first three months of your pregnancy.

Nutritional Investments

It's really easy to meet both your and your developing baby's nutritional needs at this time. All you need to do is eat according to the Building a Healthy Baby Nutrition Plan for the First Trimester of Pregnancy. Copy it and post it on your refrigerator for quick and easy reference.

As you'll see, the plan for these first three months uses the Food Guide Pyramid as the basis for healthy eating during this time (as it does at any time). It's important, however, to pay close attention to getting enough folic acid, and while your need for protein may rise only slightly during the first trimester, now is the time to start making certain you choose the right kinds of protein.

---

*The Building a Healthy Baby Nutrition Plan
for the First Trimester of Pregnancy*

The Food Guide Pyramid serves as your basic guide. Review the information on pages 16–21. Then:

- Eat a variety of nutrient-dense foods from the five food groups—breads and cereals, vegetables, fruits, milk, and meat—each day. Choose at least the minimum number of servings from each group, with the exception of those groups discussed below. Realize you'll probably need and want more than that. Review Choosing Smart from Each Food Group on page 23.
- Choose plenty of foods rich in folic acid, such as fortified cereals, green leafy and other vegetables, beans, fruits, nuts, and liver.
- Consume at least four servings each day from the milk group.
- Eat at least three servings each day from the meat group (6–7 ounces total).
- Eat enough food to gain weight at the rate recommended by your health care provider. (See page 46 for information about gaining weight during pregnancy.)
- Choose low-fat and lean items from each group to keep fat and calorie intake in line.

continued

- Eat small to moderate-size, nutritious meals and snacks every three to four hours.
- Salt your food to taste unless your health care provider advises otherwise.
- Drink plenty of fluid, about 8 cups a day. Try water, juice, milk, and soup. Limit coffee and other caffeinated beverages (cola, tea, etc.) to two to three servings or fewer daily.
- Do not drink alcohol.
- Stay, or get, active. See page 50 for more information about healthy exercise during pregnancy.

Getting Enough Folic Acid

Neural tube defects (NTDs), which include anencephaly and spina bifida, account for about 5 percent of all U.S. birth defects each year. Infants born with anencephaly are missing most or all of their brain and die shortly after birth. Most babies born with spina bifida, in which the spinal cord is exposed, grow to adulthood but suffer severe paralysis or other disabilities.

According to a recent report from the Centers for Disease Control and Prevention, the incidence of these painfully crippling defects could be cut in half in this country if all women of childbearing age consumed adequate amounts of folic acid (also called folacin and folate), a B vitamin.

The average American woman consumes about one-half the amount of folic acid recommended for pregnancy. Because many women do not know exactly when they get pregnant—and neural tubes start forming immediately—the U.S. Public Health Service recommends that all women capable of becoming pregnant take a daily supplement of 400 micrograms of folic acid, which is the Recommended Dietary Allowance (RDA) for pregnant women. The American College of Obstetricians and Gynecologists recommends high-dose supplements of 4 milligrams daily for women who have previously had an infant with an NTD, starting at least four weeks prior to conception through the first three months of pregnancy. This, however, should only be done under a doctor's supervision. Indeed, avoid using any medication or supplement unless it is prescribed or approved by a physician who knows you are pregnant.

Whether you take a supplement is something to be decided by you and your health care provider. Regardless of your decision, safeguard your baby's health by making certain you get plenty of folic acid from the foods you eat. (In fact, we hope you read this before you get pregnant so you can start eating this way now, since adequate folic acid is important from the very beginning.) Eat some foods from the following list every day.

* Fortified cereals
* Green leafy vegetables, especially spinach
* Other vegetables such as green beans, broccoli, brussels sprouts, asparagus, okra, and corn
* Beans, including lentils, kidney beans, and black beans
* Fruits and their juice, including oranges, grapefruit, strawberries, and cantaloupe
* Nuts such as peanuts and almonds
* Liver, especially chicken liver

Recent research also suggests a diet rich in fruits and vegetables may reduce the risk of infants developing certain types of brain tumors. Scientists speculate these protective benefits of fruits and vegetables may result from their folic acid content more than any other nutrient. But the lack of a definite answer underscores the wisdom of eating nutritiously even if you're taking vitamin/mineral supplements.

Getting the Protein You Need

Adequate protein is essential for growth—something that's occurring with both you and your baby right now. Protein is needed for your developing placenta and expanding blood volume as well as your baby's growing tissues. An adequate protein intake also helps you fight illness.

Your actual need for protein may increase only slightly during the first trimester. During the second and third trimesters, your protein needs increase to the equivalent of an additional 1½ ounces of meat, fish, or poultry a day.

You're probably already eating enough protein, however. That's because in our land of plenty, where protein-rich foods are not scarce, most of us eat much more than we need. You don't need to worry about eating enough protein if you eat according to the Building a Healthy Baby Nutrition Plan. If you're a vegetarian who avoids protein-rich animal foods such as meat, fish, poultry, eggs, or milk, you need to make sure you're getting all the essential amino acids that come from protein by paying close attention to the type of the protein you eat.

Complete proteins are one type, and they are found in meat, poultry, fish, eggs, milk, yogurt, and cheese. Complete proteins contain all the essential amino acids our bodies need for good health. We must get essential amino acids from foods we eat because our bodies cannot make them.

Beans, nuts, and grains also contain protein, but it's *incomplete*. That means these foods do not contain all the essential amino acids. By eating these foods in combinations that together provide all the essential amino acids—such as beans and tortillas, or tofu and rice—we can meet our nutritional needs. (By the way, we do not have to eat these complementary foods at the same meal as was once believed. Aim to eat such foods in the course of one day to meet your protein needs.) Pregnant women who are vegetarian must take care to make certain their diets provide adequate amounts of essential amino acids. For more information about vegetarian eating, see page 52.

We can also meet our protein needs by eating smaller amounts of foods that contain complete proteins in combination with foods that provide incomplete protein. For example, we could eat a smaller portion of meat with rice and beans on the side. This practice helps control your intake of total fat and saturated fat. Some foods that contain complete proteins, such as fatty meats, cheese, and whole milk, contribute much of the total fat and most of the saturated fat in our diets. Choosing lean meats, poultry without skin, skim and 1 percent milk, and low-fat and skim milk cheeses and yogurt also helps keep total fat and saturated fat consumption within recommended limits.

You don't need special high-protein supplements, powders, or beverages to meet your protein needs during pregnancy. As mentioned above, Americans generally eat plenty of protein, and there is evidence that suggests special protein preparations may be harmful during pregnancy.

But I Don't Even Feel Like Eating!

It's called *morning sickness,* but millions of women suffer from it all day long—and even during the night. Just lifting their heads off the pillow in the morning turns their stomachs, and starts another day-long bout with nausea that makes them wonder if they'll be able to make it through the day.

Morning sickness affects as many as nine out of ten mothers-to-be. Even worse, as many as one out of five pregnant women continue to suffer with the problem throughout their entire pregnancy. Some even end up in the hospital due to dehydration and other problems.

Traditional—but usually inadequate—advice ranges from "eat a few saltines" before you rise in the morning to getting plenty of bed rest. Worse, some health professionals call morning sickness a psychological problem and even claim it is a subconscious effort to terminate a pregnancy!

While no one is exactly certain why some women suffer morning sickness, we are clear that it is not "all in your head." One of the most popular theories is that it is related to the increase in hormone levels that occurs during pregnancy. In fact, research shows women who experience no morning sickness have a higher rate of miscarriages than women who do. (If you aren't suffering from morning sickness, don't worry. Plenty of women carry healthy babies to full term without ever experiencing one bout of nausea.)

Whatever the reason for morning sickness, it is a real problem, and we have only recently been able to offer some truly effective advice for managing it. Registered dietitian Miriam Erick has worked for over a decade with pregnant women suffering severe morning sickness. Her book *No More Morning Sickness: A Survival Guide for Pregnant Women* details an approach to quell nausea and provide vital fluid and growth-sustaining calories for a pregnant woman and her fetus.

If you suffer mild morning sickness—it's worse in the morning and lying down helps, but you can still eat between attacks of nausea—try the following advice. But be assured that women who occasionally are not able to eat or drink well due to morning sickness run little risk of problems.

If you're suffering severe morning sickness such as frequent nausea and vomiting throughout the day, and you have difficulty drinking or eating at any time, contact your health care provider. You run the risk of dehydration and other problems. Also read Miriam's book. Don't try to go it alone; it's too debilitating, and it can be dangerous.

Managing Morning Sickness

Try these tips for easing your morning sickness, no matter what time of the day it occurs. They may help to satisfy your very particular taste-bud demands and provide much needed fluid and calories.

continued

- Eat frequent, small meals. Go for fluids if you can't handle solids.
- Ask yourself what beverage or food sounds good. Think of the tastes of different foods: sweet, salty, sour, bitter, etc. Would different textures help? How about consistency or temperature? Or the flavor of a food—spicy, aromatic, bland? Don't be overly concerned about perfect nutrition. Keeping down fluids and calories is the important thing right now. Miriam has found that lemonade and potato chips do the trick for many women. Then they can eat more healthfully when they feel better.
- Keep a food diary in which you identify foods with certain characteristics that appeal at different times. Look for patterns to discover when a particular food may help. Remember, one food may help at one time but not at another.
- Smells, light, noise, movement and other stimuli—even hot, humid weather—may bring on queasiness, too. Also record in your food diary specific things you know will make you sick (like grocery store smells). Then avoid those stimuli at all costs.

SOURCE: *No More Morning Sickness, A Survival Guide for Pregnant Women* by Miriam Erick, MS, RD. Plume, Penguin Group, New York, 1993.

Expecting to Gain Weight

In today's weight-obsessed society, women face undeserved scrutiny about weight from others as well as themselves, even during pregnancy. Many women worry about gaining *any* weight at all, even though it's absolutely necessary for a healthy pregnancy. Indeed, an inadequate weight gain increases the risk that your baby will not weigh enough when he or she is born—and that potentially means serious health complications.

How much weight should you gain, however, varies according to the individual. See the following guidelines, but be certain to discuss with your health care provider the right weight gain for you. Additionally, if you are preoccupied with your weight, if you exercise constantly to keep your weight in control, or if you have a history of eating disorders, bring it to your health care provider's attention. He or she will want to work with you to make certain your eating or exercise habits do not negatively affect your pregnancy.

Weight Gain During Pregnancy

Guidelines for weight gain during pregnancy, with a few exceptions, depend on your prepregnancy weight.

- If your weight was normal before pregnancy, you should gain between 25 and 35 pounds during your pregnancy.
- Women who are underweight should gain more (about 28 to 40 pounds).
- If you're overweight, you should gain less (15 to 25 pounds). Obese women should gain at least 15 pounds.

If you're carrying twins (or more), you should gain more weight (check with your health care provider). Young teenagers and African-American women should strive for gains at the upper end of each range. Short women should strive for gains at the lower end of each range.

Expect to gain about 10 pounds during the first twenty weeks of pregnancy and about 1 pound per week after that. Alert you health care provider if you experience quick and excessive weight gains. They may be due to fluid, not fat, which may signal a need for other types of intervention.

Also check with your health care provider if you fail to gain at least 2 pounds in any one month.

Although extra pounds during pregnancy are necessary, as those pounds add up, you and others may worry you're gaining too much, or you worry whether you will ever be able to take it all off after you deliver. Understanding what's going on in your body, however, may make it easier to accept these changes.

The following section tells you where the extra weight of pregnancy ends up.

Where Does the Weight Go?

- Your bodily changes—growth of your uterus, breast, blood volume and body fluid—make up about 12 of the 25 to 35 pounds it is recommended you gain. Your body also stores about 7 extra pounds of fat, protein, and other nutrients you may need when breast-feeding.
- About 6 to 8 pounds will be your baby's weight, a healthy weight for a newborn. Eat healthfully and avoid harmful habits such as smoking and drinking alcohol to help guarantee a healthy weight for your baby. Babies with low birth weights face more health problems, and a smaller baby does not mean an easier delivery.

Eating Your Way to a Healthy Weight

You need an extra 55,000 calories or so to provide the energy you and your developing baby need during the nine months of pregnancy. Rather than try to divide those calories into a daily number of extra calories to strive for, it's best to focus on eating healthfully and let your hunger guide you in eating more.

Women who struggle with extra pounds when they're not pregnant, however, often have trouble identifying when they are truly hungry for food or if they're eating to soothe themselves. If this is true for you, and you're struggling to meet the weight goals recommended by your health care provider, start by eating at least the minimum number of recommended servings from each food group as specified in the Building a Healthy Baby Nutrition Plan for the first trimester. Aim for at least six servings of breads and cereals, five servings of fruits and vegetables, three servings of milk products, and three servings from the meat group. If you find you're still hungry, eat more breads and cereals first, then work your way up the pyramid.

It's best to regard this minimum amount of food as a true minimum. That is, don't eat any less on a regular basis. An occasional day where you don't eat at least six servings of grains or five fruits and vegetables is fine. But to ensure you get the nutrients you and your baby need, make certain you meet these guidelines a very large majority of the time.

Also, keep calories to a minimum and nutrition at a maximum by choosing low-fat, high-nutrition foods from each group most of the time. Study page 23 to learn the wide variety of nutrient-dense foods available in each food group.

Finally, limit the amount of foods you eat from the fats, oils, and sweets section of the pyramid. Remember that some fat is important to a healthy diet, however, so you don't want to try to eliminate it entirely. Choose unsaturated fats like olive, corn, or safflower oil when possible.

Don't prohibit sweet foods, either. You may find yourself overeating these foods as a result. Feelings of deprivation can send us off the deep end when it comes to foods. If you've struggled with your weight before, you probably realize that already.

If you are overweight or obese when you become pregnant, and your health care provider advises a more limited weight gain for you, see a registered dietitian to devise a healthful and realistic eating plan that will ensure you and your baby get the nutrition you both need.

Gaining Enough Weight

It may be hard for some women to believe, but there are women who struggle to gain enough weight during pregnancy. Oddly, the recommendations to help these women are much the same as for women who are struggling not to gain too much. Whether you're overweight, underweight, or just the right weight, it basically comes down to this: Eat regularly, eat well-balanced, high-nutrition meals and snacks according to the Building a Healthy Baby Nutrition Plan, and stay active. These three elements combine to help you feel good and provide the nutrients, including the right amount of calories, you and your baby need at this most important time.

Underweight women, however, may need to eat from the upper range of servings recommended from each food group. To do this, it may help to include more snacks in your daily meal plan. By the way, lack of weight gain is usually not a major problem in the first trimester. Later on, however, it does become one.

Weight-Conscious Tips for Pregnant Women

- Concentrate on eating the right foods, not on how much weight you gain. Your baby needs a wide range of nutrients you can only get by eating healthfully. Continue to eat well even if you think you are gaining too much weight. Then discuss it with your health care provider.
- Never try to lose weight during your pregnancy, even if you are overweight.
- Eat nutrient-dense foods, i.e., those that contain plenty of nutrients compared to the calories they contain. See page 12 for a list of smart choices from each food group.
- Eat at least three meals a day, starting with breakfast. Include snacks, too. Regular meals and snacks are important in controlling your hunger. Breakfast gives you the energy and nutrients you need to start the day feeling good.
- Stay active. Read the following section on appropriate physical activity during pregnancy.

Even If You Look Like a Potato, You Don't Have to Spend Your Time on the Couch

Active women can take heart that pregnancy doesn't have to mean an end to physical fitness. If your doctor says it's okay, you can continue a moderate level of activity and enjoy all the physical and mental benefits to be derived. If you didn't exercise much before you became pregnant, start out slowly, no more than fifteen to twenty minutes at a time. If you were active previously, up to thirty minutes is fine. See the following for recommendations for exercise during pregnancy from the American College of Obstetricians and Gynecologists.

Staying Active When You Are Pregnant

- Exercise regularly, at least three times a week.
- Brisk walking and swimming top the list as great ways to stay in shape when pregnant. Or seek out exercise classes especially designed for pregnant women. (If you already regularly attend exercise classes, make certain your instructor knows you are pregnant. Also, make certain he or she knows the type of exercises that are safe for pregnant women.) Check with your health care provider if you have questions about other exercises.
- Avoid jerky, bouncy, or high-impact movements as well as full sit-ups, double leg raises, and straight-leg toe touches.
- After the first trimester, avoid exercises that require you to lie on your back. The weight of your uterus presses on blood vessels and may decrease blood flow.
- Stop exercising when you are tired; don't keep going until you are exhausted.
- Drink plenty of fluids and don't get overheated.

continued

• If you have any of these symptoms when exercising, stop and contact your doctor: pain, dizziness, shortness of breath, a feeling you will faint, vaginal bleeding, rapid heartbeat when resting, difficulty walking, uterine contractions, no fetal movements (although you generally won't notice fetal movements until the end of the second trimester). Even moderate exercise may not be wise for women carrying twins or more, or who have incompetent cervixes or other problems of pregnancy.

*Solving Common Nutrition Problems
During the First Trimester*

If you need it, copy and tack this chart on your refrigerator for easy reference.

Problem	*Solution*
Nausea and vomiting	Eat what you like—in frequent, small meals. Try fluids if you can't handle solids.
High need for folic acid	Eat plenty of fortified cereals, green leafy vegetables, beans, fruits, and nuts. Ask your health care provider about a vitamin supplement.
Gaining too much weight	Eat healthful foods in amounts recommended in the Building a Healthy Baby Nutrition Plan. Choose lean, low-fat, and skim foods whenever possible. Stay active according to advice from your health care provider. *Don't diet!*
Not gaining enough weight	Eat regular, well-balanced meals and snacks according to the Building a Healthy Baby Nutrition

continued

	Plan. Eat from the upper range of recommended servings. If the problem is due to nausea and vomiting, check with your health care provider. Lack of weight gain in the first trimester is usually not a problem.
Heartburn	Eat frequent, small meals. Don't overfill your stomach. Drink fluids between meals. Limit spicy and high-fat foods. Wear loose-fitting clothing. Don't lie down immediately after eating or drinking.
Constipation	Eat plenty of fiber and drink 2–3 quarts of fluid each day. Never use a laxative without the permission of your health care provider.
Too tired to cook	Forget cooking. Try sandwiches on whole-grain bread, whole-grain cereals, raw fruits and vegetables from grocery store salad bars, low-fat or skim milk, sliced turkey from the grocery deli. Or try healthy frozen meals from the grocer's freezer.

Special Concerns

I'm vegetarian. How do I modify the Building a Healthy Baby Nutrition Plan to fit my needs? Many women eat vegetarian today for a variety of reasons ranging from personal health to environmental concerns. In general, vegetarianism can be a healthy way to go. Studies show vegetarians may suffer from less of the chronic diseases that afflict many nonvegetarians in the United States.

According to The American Dietetic Association, vegetarian diets can be adequate for pregnant and breast-feeding women *if* they are well planned. That's an important *if*. Many people go vegetarian by just cutting out animal products, but they fail to consider carefully how they will meet their protein needs (see discussion on page 42). As mentioned previously, adequate protein is vital during pregnancy.

There are several different types of vegetarian diets, ranging from those that include fish, milk, cheese, and eggs to those that exclude all animal products. This latter is also called a *vegan* diet. If you're a more liberal vegetarian who eats animal foods such as milk and fish, nutrition planning according to the Building a Healthy Baby Nutrition Plan is simple. Just choose foods appropriately from the five food groups.

If you're a vegan, make certain you eat the recommended number of servings from the meat group in the form of dry beans and peas, tofu, soy milk, nuts, and meat analogs. Since you would also avoid dairy products as a vegan, meet your calcium needs by eating other high-calcium foods (see page 112).

Watch your intake of zinc, too. Eat plenty of whole grains, wheat germ, nuts, and dried beans to make certain you get enough.

Like nonvegetarians, pregnant vegetarians are generally advised to take iron and folic acid supplements during pregnancy (see pages 110 and 40). A regular source of vitamin B_{12} is also recommended for vegans. Try fortified breakfast cereals (check the label to make certain B_{12} is added), fortified soy beverages, and ask your health care provider about taking a supplement. Be aware that spirulina, seaweed, tempeh, and other fermented foods are not reliable sources of vitamin B_{12}.

In addition, a vitamin D supplement is recommended for

pregnant and breast-feeding vegans who are not adequately exposed to sunlight (your body can make its own vitamin D if you're out in the sun enough).

Both vegetarian and nonvegetarian infants older than four to six months who are solely breast-fed should get iron supplements and vitamin D if exposure to sunlight is limited.

If you're not absolutely certain you know how to eat a healthful vegetarian diet, check with a registered dietitian. He or she can help you eat vegetarian while guaranteeing the nutrition both you and your baby need.

I'm pregnant with twins. Any special advice for me? Your biggest challenge may be to eat enough to gain the proper weight. The average goal is 35 to 45 pounds, and meeting that goal is extremely important with multiple pregnancies. Low birth weight is a concern, and inadequate maternal weight gain contributes to low birth weight. Experts suggest you need anywhere from 500 to 1000 calories more each day than when you were not pregnant. Also make sure your food choices count nutritionally. Eat from the upper ranges of the servings recommended from each food group, and choose high-nutrition, high-calorie treats such as ice cream, pudding, and oatmeal cookies if you need to. Limit low-nutrition extras like soda, chips, and candy. A prenatal supplement is probably a good idea, too. Check with your health care provider about getting the proper nutrition and to set your goal for weight gain.

Do I need to take a vitamin supplement if I'm eating according to the Building a Healthy Baby Nutrition Plan? According to the National Academy of Sciences Subcommittee on Dietary Intake and Nutrition Supplements During Pregnancy, prenatal vitamin supplements are not generally needed. Nutritionists also usually recommend you get your nutrients from food, not pills, because there is little concern about getting excessive amounts of nutrients that way. Too much of some vitamins and minerals can cause harm. Also, we aren't certain we know all there is about what's in our food that contributes to good health. Therefore, we can't put it all in a pill.

Some research, however, suggests a multivitamin supplement during pregnancy may cut your baby's risk of birth defects. Further, there's little risk of harm from a supplement approved by your health care provider—which usually does not contain more than 100 percent of the Recommended Dietary Allowance (RDA) for vitamins and minerals during pregnancy.

There are a few more reasons you may want to consider supplementation, too.

- If you cannot eat as recommended due to reasons ranging from economic concerns to just the fact that you can't seem to make the dietary changes necessary (Let's face it—there are plenty of women who fit this description, and they should seriously consider supplements.)
- If you are a smoker
- If you are a teenager
- If you avoid any major food groups for reasons including intolerance or religious/cultural practices
- If you are a strict vegetarian
- If you restrict your diet to control your weight (something that is not recommended at all during pregnancy)
- If you eat nonfood substances such as laundry starch or clay
- If you are substantially under- or overweight
- If you are pregnant with twins or more
- If you are anemic

All pregnant women, however, are advised to take an iron supplement beginning in the thirteenth week of pregnancy, as discussed previously in this chapter. It's also advised that vitamin A supplements be avoided during pregnancy unless a woman is known to be deficient in vitamin A. Otherwise, talk to your health care provider if you believe you may need a supplement. Don't prescribe one for yourself; it's too dangerous. For best absorption, supplements should be taken between meals or at bedtime.

I'm having difficulty eating because I have heartburn all the time. What can I do? Many pregnant women experience heartburn—a burning feeling in the center of their chest—due to the pressure of baby's weight against their stomachs. Early in pregnancy, however, it may be more the result of hormones that tend to relax the muscles of the esophagus. The best nutritional approach is to eat frequent, small meals and avoid overfilling your stomach at any one time. Drink fluids between meals most of the time. Also try to relax, eat slowly, and go easy on spicy or high-fat foods. Don't lie down after eating or drinking, and wear loose-fitting clothing. If you continue to suffer from heartburn, discuss it with your health care provider.

I'm constipated all the time, and it's making me terribly uncomfortable. Is there anything I can eat to make it better? Constipation affects many women during pregnancy. It probably results from a combination of factors: the normal relaxation of intestinal muscles during pregnancy, the pressure of your baby on your lower intestine, and an increased need for fluids. Iron supplements also cause constipation in some women. To help prevent it or get rid of it, try eating a diet rich in fiber (see page 26), drinking plenty of fluids (2 to 3 quarts daily; this includes water, milk, juice, and soup), and staying active. Warm or hot fluids may be especially helpful right after you get up in the morning. If you continue to have problems, discuss it with your health care provider. Never use a laxative (or any other medication) without first checking with her or him.

I have this craving for bagels and lox; I could eat them all the time! Does this mean my diet is missing nutrients found in these foods? The reasons why women crave specific foods during pregnancy aren't clear, but it's usually not a sign of any nutritional deficiency. The reasons are more likely to be related to desires for specific tastes at this time, as described in the section on morning sickness on page 43. Later in pregnancy, cravings may be the result of changing hormones that stimulate your appetite. Tell your health care provider about unusual cravings, including a desire to eat ice, clay, cornstarch, laundry starch, or other nonfood items. This kind of craving—called pica—can be harmful and could be related to nutrient deficiencies. Otherwise, go ahead and indulge in your cravings as long as you continue to eat a well-balanced diet and are not experiencing any potentially related problems, such as excessive weight gain.

I'm so tired. How can I eat healthfully without having to cook a lot? Eating healthfully doesn't have to mean a lot of work. Whole grain breads and cereals provide wholesome convenience food straight out of the package. Raw fruits and vegetables may contain even more of some nutrients than their cooked counterparts, and they're ready to eat at many grocery store salad bars and produce sections. Low-fat and skim milk, of course, is just a glass or straw away, and you can enjoy fresh turkey and other lean meats and low-fat cheeses sliced for you at the grocery deli. In other words, if simple will satisfy, it's waiting for you at the grocery.

While eating like this may suffice much of the time, most of us would occasionally like a hot, cooked meal, too. That's when advance planning comes in handy. Over the weekend when you have more time, prepare stews, soups, casseroles, and other dishes you can freeze. Then, when time is short and energy low, just pop them into the microwave or oven for a quick and nutritious meal. Or try some healthy frozen meals from your grocer's freezer. They're nutritionally balanced and may be just what you need to get you through at times.

Finally, don't forget the great-tasting recipes we've pro-

vided at the end of the chapters in this book. They're designed to satisfy your taste buds and be easy to prepare
while providing many of the special nutrients you need at
each stage of your pregnancy.

I'm on the road quite a bit. How can I eat properly?
Again, the key is planning. Where will you eat—at fast-
food restaurants or their full-service cousins? Many fast-
food restaurants now offer a range of healthy food choices,
including salads, carrot sticks, baked potatoes, and grilled
chicken items. To control fat, ask them to hold the butter on
the baked potato, the mayonnaise on the chicken sandwich,
and go easy on the salad dressing you add.

In these challenging economic times, most full-service
restaurants are only too happy to prepare meals to meet
your special requests. If you're worried about weight gain,
remember the restaurant rule: The more elaborate the dish,
the more fat and calories it probably contains.

For between-meal snacks or when you're staring down
an airplane meal that just doesn't appeal to you, carry a
stash of healthy snacks with you. Nuts, dried and fresh
fruits, and cut-up vegetables travel well. By the way, don't
forget to order special airline meals ahead of time. They
have a variety of special meals that may satisfy your taste
and nutritional needs, but you have to arrange for them at
least twenty-four hours before your trip.

Meeting your daily requirement for milk, yogurt, or
cheese is one of the most frequently mentioned challenges
for travelers. But it's really very simple if you just remember to make an effort. Order yogurt for breakfast—most varieties are low-fat. MacDonald's serves 1 percent milk,
making that choice easy to find in most places. Or just stop
by the convenience store and pick up a small carton of milk
or yogurt for a quick and nutritious snack. Enjoy frozen yogurt for a delicious and nutritious snack, too.

*I've had diabetes for several years, and just got pregnant.
How can I make certain I deliver a healthy baby?* First of

all, you should be working very closely with your physician to tightly control your diabetes during pregnancy. He or she will prescribe specific blood sugar ranges for you to aim for and work with you to reach them, to reduce the risk of your diabetes affecting your baby in any way. Because each person is highly individual in this case, you should meet with a registered dietitian (RD) to devise a nutrition plan to help control your blood sugar levels. The RD should also work closely with your physician.

Some women who did not have diabetes before pregnancy develop what is called gestational diabetes. This is probably due to an increased need for insulin, which helps your body use the sugar in your blood. If you don't make enough insulin, the sugar builds up in your blood and results in diabetes. Your health care provider will watch for this as you progress through your pregnancy. Should it occur, we recommend you see an RD to help devise a nutrition plan to meet your needs.

I'm 17 years old and pregnant. Do I have any special nutritional needs? You're probably still growing yourself, so your nutritional needs are likely even higher than those of older pregnant women. For example, you may need more protein, calcium, and calories, particularly during the second and third trimesters. Meet those needs by eating according to the Building a Healthy Baby Nutrition Plan. But increase your intake from the meat group to 7 to 8 ounces a day. And go for at least five servings from the milk group. You probably don't need to be as concerned about choosing low-fat foods as older pregnant women because you need more calories (if you're not overweight to begin with).

You may also need a vitamin/mineral supplement. Iron; zinc; vitamins A, D, and B_6; riboflavin; and folic acid are among the nutrients most likely deficient in the typical teenage diet. Check with your health care provider.

In general, try to make all your food choices count to provide the nutrition you need. That means severely limiting foods that provide plenty of calories and few nutrients. It also probably means changing your food habits quite a bit if you're a typical teenager. The teenage diet of irregular meals that contain lots of soft drinks, French fries, and chips but few fruits, vegetables, and milk just doesn't provide needed nutrition, either for you or your developing baby.

In addition, being excessively concerned about your weight—a problem for many young girls and women—can stand in the way of providing your baby a good start in life. In fact, you can gauge your success at eating for a healthy baby to some extent by your weight gain. Research indicates pregnant teenagers need to gain at the highest rates recommended for the second and third trimesters. Reread the section on page 46 to learn more about how adequate weight gain is critical to the health of your baby.

One of the most effective steps you may take to ensure a healthy baby is to work with a registered dietitian. You can find one through your health care provider or, if cost is an issue, through government programs such as WIC (the Special Supplemental Food Program for Women, Infants, and Children).

While ill-advised at any time, smoking, alcohol, and other substance abuse—practices not uncommon among teenagers—are certainly taboo when pregnant.

Nutrition Checkup for the First Trimester of Pregnancy
Copy and use this chart often to quickly assess whether you're meeting your nutritional needs during the first three months of your pregnancy. Then fill in the blanks following each question with strategies for improving your nutritional habits if they need improving. (Answer the questions based on how you ate yesterday.) Set realistic goals, one change at a time or small changes, for best success.

1. Did you skip any meals?   Yes   No
   How I can improve this habit:

   _____

   _____

2. Did you eat the minimum recommended number of servings from all five food groups (6+ breads and cereals, 5+ fruits and vegetables, 4+ milk, 3+ meat)?
                                                 Yes   No
   How I can improve this habit:

   _____

   _____

3. Did you eat several good sources of folic acid (fortified cereal, green leafy vegetables, green beans, broccoli, brussels sprouts, asparagus, okra, corn, lentils, black beans, peanuts, almonds, liver, fruit such as oranges, grapefruit, strawberries, and cantaloupe)?
                                                 Yes   No
   How I can improve this habit:

   _____

   _____

continued

4. Did you eat a good source of vitamin A (deep or-
   ange-yellow and dark green fruits and vegetables,
   fortified milk)?   Yes   No
   How I can improve this habit:

   _____

   _____

5. Did you eat a good source of vitamin C (citrus
   fruits, green peppers, strawberries, melon, broccoli,
   cabbage)?   Yes   No
   How I can improve this habit:

   _____

   _____

6. Did you eat at least three servings of whole grain
   foods?   Yes   No
   How I can improve this habit:

   _____

   _____

7. Did you choose more low-fat foods than high-fat
   items?   Yes   No
   How I can improve this habit:

   _____

   _____

                                              continued

8. Did nausea, vomiting, heartburn, or constipation frequently interfere with how well you ate?

    Yes   No

    What I can do to make these problems better:

    _____

    _____

9. Did you smoke, drink alcohol, or use an unprescribed drug (including self-prescribed vitamin/mineral supplements)? Yes   No

    How I can improve this habit:

    _____

    _____

10. Did you get plenty of appropriate exercise?

    Yes   No

    How I can improve this habit:

    _____

    _____

Recipe Focus: The First Trimester

The key nutrient for the following first trimester recipes is folic acid. As you have read on page 40, folic acid is critically important during the few weeks prior to conception and during the early stages of pregnancy. Start enjoying these recipes even before you know you're pregnant. They taste great and will help you get a jump start on laying a sound nutritional foundation for the next nine months.

Motherita

This mock margarita is a refreshing drink for summer barbecues and cocktail parties. If you find tart flavors help quell your nausea, make up a batch of this drink, and keep it ready to go in the freezer.

6 tablespoons lime juice, bottled or fresh
4 tablespoons frozen orange juice concentrate
1 teaspoon sugar
2 tablespoons water
  Fresh lime wedge, if desired
  Salt, if desired

Prior to preparing this drink, pour lime juice into an empty ice cube tray and freeze. It should make 3 cubes. When frozen, put lime cubes in a blender and process with the orange juice concentrate. Add sugar and water; process again for a slushy consistency. If salting your glass, run lime wedge round the rim of the glass and turn glass upside down in a plate of salt. Pour drink into center of glass without disturbing salt. Garnish with lime wedge.

Serves 1 (¾ cup)

Nutritional Benefits	Food Pyramid Serving
Calories 125	*Each recipe portion =*
	1 fruit group serving

Percent RDA for Pregnant
Women

Folic acid	23 percent	Food Mood
Potassium	22 percent	Frozen beverage
Vitamin C	120 percent	Party beverage
		Tart lime flavor

Orange-Vanilla Cream

This will remind you of the frozen vanilla-orange ice cream pops you probably ate as a kid.

½ cup orange juice
2 ice cubes
¼ cup low-fat vanilla ice cream

Combine juice and ice, on high speed, in blender. Process until ice is a slushy consistency. Add ice cream and process until well blended. You can eat this with a spoon or drink it.

Serves 1 (1 cup)

Recipe Option
Instead of orange juice, use grape, cherry, lime, or your other favorite fruit juice.

Nutritional Benefits
Calories	60

Percent RDA for Pregnant Women

Folic acid	13 percent
Vitamin C	69 percent

Food Pyramid Servings
Each recipe portion =
½ fruit group serving
¼ milk group serving

Food Mood
Nostalgic, comfort food
Frozen beverage
Milkshakelike

Mulled Cranberry Juice

Drink this in the mornings as an alternative to coffee or tea; also nice as a warm, bedtime beverage. Make up a batch and heat as you need it.

4 cups cranberry juice
½ teaspoon ground or whole cloves
½ teaspoon ground cinnamon or cinnamon stick
¼ teaspoon ground allspice or whole allspice

Combine all ingredients in a saucepan. Heat to boiling, then simmer for 5 minutes. If desired, strain for a clear beverage. If using whole spices, put them in a cheesecloth bag and remove before serving.

Serves 4 (each 1 cup)

Recipe Option
Instead of individual spices, use spice sachet bags.

Nutritional Benefits
Calories   145

Percent RDA for Pregnant
Women
Vitamin C   61 percent

Food Pyramid Servings
Each recipe portion =
2 fruit group servings

Food Mood
Warm beverage
Tart cranberry flavor
Mulled spice flavor

All beverages are important because they provide much-needed fluid for the body, especially if you don't drink water. Adequate fluids, combined with a high fiber diet, can be particularly helpful during bouts of constipation, relieving discomfort without the use of laxatives.

Coffee Colada

Get the sensation of a morning cup of coffee, but pack it with more calcium. Coffee bars are all over the country now, so you can have your coffee made to order, which is especially handy when traveling. Names such as latte, cappucino, au lait, *and* colada *all indicate there is heated or foamed milk. Most cafés can make coffee drinks with low-fat or skim milk.*

½ cup skim milk
½ cup hot coffee

Microwave milk in a mug at 50 percent power for 2 minutes or heat just to boiling. Add hot coffee to the milk and stir. If you have an espresso machine at home and can steam milk, use that and top with a dollop of foam.

Serves 1 (1 cup)

Recipe Options
Top with cinnamon.
If caffeine is a concern, use decaffeinated coffee.

Nutritional Benefits
Calories   45

Percent RDA for Pregnant Women
Calcium   12 percent

Food Pyramid Serving
Each recipe portion =
½ milk group serving

Food Mood
Hot beverage
Cup of coffee

Strawberry Banana Muffins

Moist muffins with pockets of strawberry will hit the spot for breakfast or snack time. They'll keep for several days and easily add complex carbohydrates to your diet.

1¼ cups all-purpose flour
 ¾ cup whole wheat flour
   1 teaspoon baking powder
   1 teaspoon baking soda
   1 small banana, mashed
 ¼ cup vegetable oil
 ½ cup sugar
 ½ cup skim milk
   1 egg
   1 teaspoon almond extract
   1 cup strawberries, chopped

Preheat oven to 375° F. Coat 12-cup muffin tin with non-stick vegetable spray.

Combine flours, baking powder, and baking soda in a large bowl. Set aside. In a food processor or with a mixer, process the banana and then alternately add the oil and sugar. Add the milk, egg, and extract, and process until thoroughly blended. Stir liquid ingredients into dry ingredients and carefully stir in the berries last. Fill muffin cups with an equal amount of batter and bake for 25 minutes or until golden.

Serves 12

Recipe Options
*Instead of strawberries, use blueberries or raspberries.
Instead of fresh, use frozen fruit, unthawed.*

Nutritional Benefits
Calories   230

Percent·RDA for Pregnant
Women
Dietary fiber   10 percent
Folic acid   7 percent
Iron   9 percent
Thiamine   10 percent
Vitamin C   11 percent
Vitamin K   16 percent

Food Pyramid Servings
Each recipe portion =
2 bread group servings

Food Mood
Home-style muffin
Strawberry flavor
Something sweet and
    starchy

Cheddar Breakfast Squares

Prepare this in the evening so it's ready for the oven when you wake up. Eaten hot or at room temperature, this is an easy, make-ahead breakfast.

    3 eggs
1½ cups skim milk
 ¾ cup (6 ounces) cheddar cheese, finely shredded
    2 tablespoons fresh parsley, minced
 ½ teaspoon dried sage
 ½ teaspoon dried thyme
 ½ teaspoon mustard powder
    6 slices whole wheat bread, cut in ½" cubes
    Black pepper to taste

Coat 8" square or round baking pan with nonstick vegetable spray.

Combine all ingredients, except bread, in a bowl. Spread bread cubes in the pan and pour in egg mixture. Cover and refrigerate overnight. When ready to eat, preheat oven to 350° F. Bake, uncovered, for approximately 40 to 45 minutes until golden. Cool for 5 minutes and cut into 6 squares.

Serves 6

Recipe Options
Instead of 3 eggs, use 2 eggs and 2 egg whites or egg substitute product to reduce cholesterol.
Instead of cheddar, use Swiss, Muenster, or Monterey Jack cheese.

Nutritional Benefits

Calories　　195

Percent RDA for Pregnant Women

Calcium	10 percent
Folic acid	10 percent
Iron	6 percent
Potassium	33 percent
Protein	18 percent
Riboflavin	26 percent
Zinc	10 percent

Food Pyramid Servings

*Each recipe portion =
½ milk group serving
1 bread group serving*

Food Mood

Hot breakfast

Cheesy flavor

Crunchy French Toast

Using raisin bread to make French toast adds a natural sweetness, so you're not inclined to need as much syrup.

1 egg
2 tablespoons skim milk
⅛ teaspoon pineapple extract
4 slices raisin bread
¼ cup Grape-Nuts cereal

Spray large skillet with nonstick vegetable spray.

Whisk egg, milk, and extract in a shallow bowl. Soak both sides of bread in egg mixture, remove, and pat cereal onto each side of the bread slices. Cook in skillet over medium heat until browned on both sides. Top with warmed syrup, flavored or plain yogurt, fruit preserves, or warmed, cut-up fruit.

Serves 2 (each serving 2 slices)

Recipe Option
Instead of pineapple, use vanilla or almond extract.

Nutritional Benefits
(based on 2 slices, no topping)
Calories   230

Percent RDA for Pregnant Women
Folic acid	19 percent
Magnesium	6 percent
Niacin	25 percent
Riboflavin	34 percent
Vitamin A	29 percent
Zinc	6 percent

Food Pyramid Servings
*Each recipe portion =
2½ bread group servings*

Food Mood
Crunchy coating
Raisin flavor

Creamy Asparagus Soup

Made in a food processor or blender, this soup couldn't be easier. If you like the texture contrast of a smooth soup with something crunchy, try a few croutons sprinkled on top.

1 tablespoon butter
2 tablespoons onions, chopped
1 garlic clove, minced
1 tablespoon flour
1 12-ounce can reduced-sodium chicken broth
2 cups canned asparagus spears, drained
1/3 cup evaporated skim milk

Heat butter in a large saucepan and sauté onions and garlic. When soft, stir in flour. Add broth and asparagus. Bring to a slow boil, stirring constantly, until slightly thickened. Pour into a food processor or blender and process on high speed until you have a smooth consistency. Add milk and process again to thoroughly blend. Return to pan and, over low heat, warm soup to desired temperature.

Serves 5 (each serving 3/4 cup)

Recipe Options
Use fresh, cooked asparagus if available.
Rinse canned asparagus to reduce sodium content.

Nutritional Benefits
Calories 55

Percent RDA for Pregnant Women
Folic acid 23 percent
Vitamin C 28 percent

Food Pyramid Serving
Each recipe portion =
1 vegetable group serving

Food Mood
Smooth, creamy
consistency
Mild asparagus flavor

Gazpacho

Meant to be eaten as a cold soup, try also using it as a warm topping for baked potatoes, chicken, or fish. This is ideal for summer months when tomatoes are ripe and plentiful. We leave the vegetable peels on for added fiber.

  ½ medium cucumber, unpeeled, washed, seeded
  ½ medium green pepper, seeded
  1 large celery stalk
  1 small onion
  1 garlic clove
1½ teaspoons ground cumin
  4 cups fresh tomatoes, seeded
  1 cup tomato juice
  2 teaspoons balsamic or red wine vinegar
1½ teaspoons ground coriander
  Black pepper to taste

Process cucumber in a food processor or blender at medium speed until almost pureed. Gradually add pepper, celery, onion, garlic, and cumin. How long you process the vegetables will depend on whether you like your gazpacho very smooth or with tiny, visible chunks of vegetable in it. Gradually add tomatoes, tomato juice, vinegar, and coriander. Season with pepper. Cover and refrigerate at least 2 hours to allow flavors to develop.

Serves 4 (each serving 1 cup)

Recipe Options
Use low-sodium tomato juice to reduce sodium content. Omit spices if they disagree with you.

Nutritional Benefits
Calories   65

Percent RDA for Pregnant
Women
Dietary fiber   20 percent
Folic acid   11 percent
Vitamin C   60 percent
Vitamin K   54 percent

Food Pyramid Servings
*Each recipe portion =
2 vegetable group servings*

Food Mood
Chilled soup
Fresh vegetable flavor
Smooth consistency

Black Bean Soup

This is such a low-fat soup that a dollop of sour cream on top is just fine. Adding vinegar at the end helps heighten the flavors without adding too much salt. Freeze in individual containers for quick lunches or dinners.

  1 pound dried black beans, rinsed
2½ quarts water
  1 cup onion, minced
  1 teaspoon cumin
  1 teaspoon dried oregano
  1 lemon slice
  1 teaspoon Tabasco sauce
  1 teaspoon salt
  2 tablespoons balsamic or red wine vinegar
  ½ tablespoon per serving of sour cream

Rinse beans, place in a large pot, and cover with 2" of water. Cover and boil for 2 minutes. Remove from heat and let sit for 1 hour. Drain and add 2½ quarts of water, onion, spices, lemon, and Tabasco. Bring to a boil and simmer, partially covered, for approximately 45 minutes or until beans are tender. Puree ⅓ of the soup in a blender and return to pot. Stir in salt and vinegar and heat thoroughly. Serve in bowls and garnish with a dollop of sour cream.

Serves 12 (each serving 1 cup)

Recipe Options
Add diced tomato and jalapeño pepper.
Add more or less Tabasco to suit your taste.

Nutritional Benefits
Calories 120

Percent RDA for Pregnant Women

Dietary fiber	20 percent
Folic acid	32 percent
Magnesium	19 percent
Protein	12 percent
Zinc	6 percent

Food Pyramid Serving
*Each recipe portion =
⅓ meat group serving*

Food Mood
Hearty soup
Cuban-style flavor
Slightly spicy

Cajun Spice Blend

While spices don't provide any nutritional value, a spice blend is a lower-sodium option for seasoning popcorn, vegetables, meats, and poultry while still adding more flavor. Also try using it on a snack mix of raisins, dry cereal, and nuts.

4 tablespoons ground thyme
4 tablespoons paprika
2 tablespoons garlic powder
2 tablespoons onion powder
2 teaspoons cayenne pepper
2 teaspoons black pepper
1 teaspoon salt

Combine all ingredients and store in an airtight container or spice jar. Use sparingly.

Makes ¾ cup or 36 1-teaspoon servings

Recipe Option
Reduce both peppers by half to make a milder version.

Nutritional Benefits
(Based on 1 teaspoon)

Food Mood
Hot, spicy flavor

Percent RDA for Pregnant Women

Sodium	2 percent

Salt and spices do not provide nutrients or calories, so there is no pyramid contribution, but they are fat-free flavor enhancers that complement many other nutritionally sound dishes. When used with popcorn or potatoes, you are then getting contributions from the pyramid bread group. When used on meats or poultry, you are getting contributions from the pyramid meat group. Similarly, when used on vegetables, you are getting contributions from the pyramid vegetable group.

Avocado Vegetable Spread

Use as a spread for bagels, crackers, or pita bread, all of which are good sources of complex carbohydrates.

½ cup avocado, mashed
½ cup fat-free cream cheese
¼ cup scallion, minced
¼ cup red pepper, minced
 1 teaspoon dried dill weed

Combine avocado and cream cheese in a small bowl until thoroughly blended. Stir in remaining ingredients, cover, and refrigerate for at least 1 hour to allow flavors to develop.

Serves 16 (each 1 tablespoon)

Recipe Options
Instead of scallion, use onion.
Instead of red peppers, use green peppers.

Nutritional Benefits		Food Mood
Calories	30	Creamy consistency
		Avocado flavor
Percent RDA for Pregnant Women		Dill flavor
Folic acid	8 percent	
Iron	4 percent	
Vitamin A	10 percent	
Vitamin C	20 percent	

This spread does not provide a pyramid contribution in the serving size listed, but is a lower-fat treat to complement many other nutritionally sound foods. Especially when used with carbohydrate-rich items like bread and crackers, you are then getting contributions from the pyramid bread group.

Broccoli and Carrot Salad

The sesame and soy flavor combination tastes great, whether you chill this salad or eat it warm. Makes a nice lunch, side dish, or if it's dinner, shred cheese on top for some protein.

3 cups broccoli, flowerets and stalks, washed
1 cup carrot, sliced in long matchsticks
3 tablespoons reduced-sodium soy sauce
1 tablespoon rice wine vinegar
1 teaspoon sesame oil

In a medium pot, steam broccoli and carrots for 2 to 3 minutes until tender but crisp. Combine remaining ingredients and, in a serving bowl, toss with vegetables until well coated. Serve immediately. If serving as a chilled dish, rinse cooked vegetables under cold water and drain. Toss with dressing, cover, and refrigerate for several hours.

Serves 4 (each serving 1 cup)

Recipe Options
Instead of soy sauce, use reduced-sodium tamari sauce.
Instead of rice wine vinegar, use regular white vinegar.

Nutritional Benefits
Calories   50

Percent RDA for Pregnant Women
Dietary fiber	14 percent
Folic acid	14 percent
Potassium	20 percent
Vitamin A	190 percent
Vitamin C	94 percent

Food Pyramid Servings
Each recipe portion =
2 vegetable group servings

Food Mood
Chilled and crisp
Warm and crisp
Soy/sesame flavor
    combination

Roasted Marinated Peppers

Roasting the peppers gives them so much flavor that there's no need for lots of oil (which is how they're often served). Use these marinated peppers in a salad, on a slice of crusty bread or crackers, or all by themselves.

4 red peppers, whole
1 tablespoon balsamic or red wine vinegar
1 garlic clove, minced
  Black pepper to taste

Preheat oven to 500° F.

Place whole peppers directly on bottom rack in oven. As skins begin to blacken, turn peppers so they char evenly. This should take 10 to 15 minutes. Remove from the oven and place in a brown paper bag, allowing them to cool and skins to loosen. When peppers are cool enough to handle, peel skins and remove seeds, catching any juices. Cut peppers into strips and toss with juices, vinegar, garlic, and black pepper. Serve at room temperature or chilled. Cover, if refrigerating.

Serves 4 (each serving ½ cup)

Recipe Option
Instead of red peppers, use green or yellow peppers or eggplant.

Nutritional Benefits
Calories   35

Percent RDA for Pregnant Women
Dietary fiber	8 percent
Folic acid	8 percent
Vitamin B_6	13 percent
Vitamin C	145 percent

Food Pyramid Serving
Each recipe portion =
1 vegetable group serving

Food Mood
Roasted flavor
Marinated vegetables

Roasted Beets and Onions

If you're not in the mood for a meat-laden dinner, enjoy this as an entrée with a salad and some good bread. You can also serve it as a warm or chilled side dish.

1 bunch (4–5) fresh beets, stems and greens removed, washed, cut in half
1 large onion, quartered
1 teaspoon white wine vinegar
1 tablespoon olive oil
1 teaspoon Dijon mustard

Preheat oven to 350° F.

Coat a 9" round or square baking pan with nonstick cooking spray.

Place beets and onions in pan and cook for 30 to 40 minutes, until beets are tender. Mix vinegar, oil, and mustard together. Place vegetables in a serving bowl and toss with dressing. Serve warm or chilled.

Serves 3 (each serving 1 cup)

Recipe Option
Instead of making a vinaigrette, use a bottled, reduced-fat Italian dressing.

Nutritional Benefits
Calories   110

Percent RDA for Pregnant Women

Folic acid	37 percent
Magnesium	11 percent
Potassium	24 percent
Vitamin C	12 percent

Food Pyramid Servings
Each recipe portion =
2 vegetable group servings

Food Mood
Something with a deep, red-purple color
Fresh beets
Light vinaigrette flavor

Chicken with Asparagus

Asparagus is a great source of folic acid. Make this dish whenever you can get fresh, tender asparagus. Canned asparagus just won't substitute.

½ tablespoon olive oil
4 4-ounce chicken breasts, boneless, skinless
1 cup reduced-sodium chicken stock
1 tablespoon lemon juice
2 teaspoons tarragon
1 pound asparagus, stalks trimmed

In a large skillet, heat oil and lightly brown chicken on both sides until almost cooked. Remove chicken from pan. Reduce heat, add stock, lemon juice, and tarragon, scraping browned bits and bringing to a simmer. Layer asparagus in pan, place chicken on top, and cover. Lightly simmer for approximately 10 minutes or until asparagus are tender but still crisp. If chicken is not thoroughly cooked, remove asparagus and continue cooking chicken until juices run clear. To serve, spoon juices over chicken breast and asparagus.

Serves 4

Recipe Options
Instead of chicken, use lean, boneless pork loin cutlets.
If using fresh tarragon, increase amount to 3 teaspoons.

Nutritional Benefits
Calories   165

Percent RDA for Pregnant
Women
Folic acid   34 percent
Niacin   74 percent
Vitamin C   40 percent
Vitamin K   96 percent
Vitamin B₆   30 percent
Zinc   10 percent

Food Pyramid Servings
Each recipe portion =
1 meat group serving
2 vegetable group servings

Food Mood
Fresh asparagus
Light, clear sauce
Lemon/tarragon flavor

Roast Pork with Braised Apple and Cabbage

The apples and cabbage provide an interesting flavor contrast without adding any fat. During the warm months, you can also prepare this using a covered grill instead of an oven.

  1 pound boneless pork loin, trimmed
  4 cups green cabbage, shredded
  1 apple, unpeeled, sliced
  2 teaspoons fennel seeds
  ½ teaspoon salt
  ½ teaspoon pepper
  ½ cup water

Heat oven to 350° F.

On the stove top, heat a large ovenproof or cast-iron skillet. Add pork loin and brown all sides. Let each side brown well before attempting to turn the meat. Reduce heat and add remaining ingredients, mixing well. The cabbage may barely fit in the pan, but will quickly reduce in size while cooking. Cover with foil or a lid and heat in the oven for 20 to 25 minutes. If meat is cooked to desired level, remove pork loin and continue cooking cabbage, if necessary, until tender. Slice meat and serve with cabbage-apple mixture.

Serves 4

Recipe Options
Instead of green cabbage, use red.
Instead of fennel seeds, use ground fennel.

Nutritional Benefits
Calories   265

Percent RDA for Pregnant
Women
Folic acid   14 percent
Niacin   33 percent
Potassium   29 percent
Protein   49 percent
Thiamine   63 percent
Vitamin C   34 percent

Food Pyramid Servings
Each recipe portion =
1 meat group serving
1 vegetable group serving

Food Mood
One-dish meal
Savory/fruit flavor contrast

Hummus

This Middle Eastern–style dip can be used as a nourishing snack or in place of lunch. Tahini is a ground sesame seed paste, fairly high in fat, which accounts for the calorie content. Because it's rich tasting, 2 tablespoons, with a pita bread, can really satisfy you.

 1 cup chickpeas, canned, drained
¼ cup tahini
¼ cup lemon juice
 1 tablespoon water
¾ teaspoon ground cumin
¼ teaspoon salt
 2 garlic cloves
 8 rounds small pita bread

In a food processor, puree chickpeas until smooth. Add remaining ingredients, except for bread, and process to a smooth, creamy texture. Spread on the pita bread or cut bread into wedges for dipping.

Serves 8 (each serving 2 tablespoons; 1 cup total)

Nutritional Benefits
Calories   270

Percent RDA for Pregnant Women

Dietary fiber	10 percent
Folic acid	11 percent
Niacin	19 percent
Riboflavin	14 percent
Thiamine	33 percent

Food Pyramid Servings
Each recipe portion =
2 bread group servings
⅓ meat group serving

Food Mood
Creamy texture
Bean/lemon/garlic flavor

Lamb Stew

Lamb's distinct flavor makes this simple dish a very tasty one. This one-pot meal can be easily reheated for lunch or a leftover dinner.

1 pound boneless lamb loin or shoulder, cut into ½" cubes
1 tablespoon tomato paste
2 cups potatoes, unpeeled, cut into ½" cubes
⅔ cups water
2 garlic cloves, minced
2 teaspoons rosemary
1 10-ounce box frozen peas and carrots

In a large pot or deep skillet, over high heat, brown lamb on all sides. Remove meat and stir in tomato paste, scraping up any browned bits from bottom of pan. Add meat, potatoes, water, garlic, and rosemary. Bring to a boil, cover, and simmer for 35 to 40 minutes or until meat is tender and potatoes are cooked. Add peas and carrots and cook another 10 minutes.

Serves 4 (each serving 1½ cups)

Recipe Options
Instead of lamb, use lean, boneless pork or beef.
Instead of peas and carrots, use frozen mixed vegetables.

Nutritional Benefits
Calories   340

Percent RDA for Pregnant Women
Dietary fiber   20 percent
Folic acid   16 percent
Iron   15 percent
Protein   56 percent
Vitamin A   73 percent
Vitamin C   49 percent
Zinc   40 percent

Food Pyramid Servings
Each recipe portion =
1 meat group serving
1½ vegetable group serving

Food Mood
Hearty stew
Lamb flavor
Rosemary flavor

Meatball Sandwich

*If an old-fashioned meatball sandwich sounds good, make
your own meatballs and freeze any leftovers for future use.*

12 ounces ground round or extra-lean ground beef
¼ cup plain bread crumbs
  2 tablespoons fresh Italian parsley, minced
  2 garlic cloves, minced
  1 egg
  1 cup spaghetti sauce, plain or marinara style
  4 hard rolls

In a bowl, combine all ingredients except for sauce and
rolls. With clean hands, mix the ingredients and form 8
meatballs. Heat a large skillet and brown meatballs on all
sides. Do not attempt to turn them until you're sure they're
browned and crusty; otherwise they'll fall apart. Remove
meatballs from pan and drain any fat. Heat both meatballs
and sauce in the same pan. Slice rolls, cut meatballs in half,
and layer on roll. Spoon sauce over top.

Serves 4 (1 roll, 2 meatballs, and ¼ cup sauce per serving)

Recipe Option
Instead of Italian parsley, use dried Italian seasonings.

Nutritional Benefits
Calories   375

Percent RDA for Pregnant
Women

Folic acid	8 percent
Iron	13 percent
Magnesium	14 percent
Niacin	34 percent
Protein	32 percent
Riboflavin	25 percent
Vitamin C	27 percent
Zinc	22 percent

Food Pyramid Servings
Each recipe portion =
2 bread group servings
⅔ meat group serving
½ cup vegetable group
   serving

Food Mood
Italian-style meatballs
Tomato sauce

Spinach, Orange, and Red Onion Salad

When making salads, keep in mind that a small amount of dressing will go much farther if you toss the salad in a large bowl rather than pouring the dressing on individual servings. All ingredients should be lightly coated without a pool of dressing in the bottom of the bowl.

1 10-ounce bag fresh spinach, washed, dried, torn
2 medium oranges, peeled, sectioned
½ cup red onion, thinly sliced
3 tablespoons olive oil
2 tablespoons water
2 teaspoons orange *or* grapefruit juice
1 teaspoon Dijon mustard

Place spinach, oranges, and onion in a large bowl. Prepare dressing by shaking remaining ingredients in a small jar. Pour dressing over salad and toss.

Serves 6 (each serving 1½ cups)

Recipe Option
Instead of oranges, use grapefruit sections.

Nutritional Benefits
Calories   105

Percent RDA for Pregnant Women

Dietary fiber	12 percent
Folic acid	25 percent
Vitamin A	41 percent
Vitamin C	60 percent
Vitamin K	194 percent

Food Pyramid Serving
Each recipe portion =
1½ vegetable serving

Food Mood
Crisp leafy greens
Citrus flavor
Mustard vinaigrette flavor

Niçoise Salad

This is based on the classic salad served in the south of France. It can easily be carried to work in a tightly covered container. It's also a nice, light dinner for the family, served with rolls or French bread, on a hot, summer night.

  4 cups romaine or butterhead lettuce, washed, dried, torn
  1 cup tomato, washed, cut in wedges
¾ cup onion, thinly sliced
  2 eggs, hard-boiled, cut in quarters
  1 6-ounce can tuna, water-packed, drained
12 black olives, pitted
  4 anchovies, packed in oil, patted dry
  4 teaspoons olive oil
  2 teaspoons lemon juice
    Salt and pepper to taste

Using a dinner-size plate for each portion, mound equal amounts of lettuce on plate and evenly distribute remaining ingredients except for oil, lemon juice, salt, and pepper. Shake remaining ingredients in a small jar and pour over salad. This is a lightly dressed salad, so don't expect there to be lots of dressing.

Serves 4

Recipe Options
Omit anchovies, if desired.
Add steamed, chilled green beans.
Use only hard-cooked egg whites to reduce cholesterol content.

Nutritional Benefits
Calories   195

Percent RDA for Pregnant
Women
Folic acid   14 percent
Niacin   40 percent
Protein   28 percent
Vitamin C   25 percent
Vitamin K   135 percent

Food Pyramid Servings
Each recipe portion =
⅔ meat group serving
1½ vegetable group
   servings

Food Mood
Fresh, chilled salad
Tuna or anchovy flavor

Grilled Chicken Salad with Pears and Roquefort Cheese

The sweet, juicy flavor of the pears contrasts nicely with the strong cheese flavor. This makes a nice luncheon salad or a light dinner.

1 4-ounce chicken breast, boneless, skinless
2 cups romaine lettuce, washed, dried, torn
¼ cup carrots, shredded
¼ cup onion, thinly sliced
1 medium pear, peeled, cored, sliced
2 tablespoons Roquefort or blue cheese, crumbled
Light vinaigrette salad dressing to taste

Grill or broil chicken and cut into ¼"-thick slices on an angle. Set aside. Using dinner-size plates, arrange lettuce on plate, add carrots, onion, and alternate slices of pear with chicken in a circular arrangement. Sprinkle cheese over top. Use 1 to 2 teaspoons of your favorite dressing; we think a light vinaigrette tastes best.

Serves 2

Recipe Option
Instead of blue cheese, use blue cheese dressing and omit any additional dressing.

Nutritional Benefits
(Without dressing)
Calories   215

Percent RDA for Pregnant Women

Folic acid	23 percent
Niacin	50 percent
Potassium	123 percent
Protein	37 percent
Vitamin A	117 percent

Food Pyramid Servings
Each recipe portion =
1¼ vegetable group servings
½ meat group serving
½ fruit group serving

Food Mood
Crispy leafy greens
Light salad entrée
Fruit and cheese flavor combination

Crispy Sweet Potato Wedges

We like these as an accompaniment for dinner or all by themselves as a snack.

2 cups sweet potatoes, unpeeled, washed, cut into wedges
2 teaspoons vegetable oil
1 teaspoon cinnamon
½ teaspoon ground ginger
¼ cup walnuts, finely crushed

Preheat oven to 400° F. Coat baking sheet with nonstick vegetable spray.

Drizzle oil over potatoes and rub in with your fingers. Sprinkle spices over potatoes, toss, and place on the baking sheet. Bake for 25 to 30 minutes or until potatoes are done. Transfer to a bowl and toss with walnuts.

Serves 4 (each serving ½ cup)

Recipe Options
Instead of sweet potatoes, use white potatoes and other seasonings, such as rosemary thyme, sage.
Instead of walnuts, use almonds, pecans, unsalted peanuts.

Nutritional Benefits
Calories   145

Percent RDA for Pregnant Women

Dietary fiber	15 percent
Folic acid	12 percent
Vitamin A	241 percent
Vitamin C	36 percent

Food Pyramid Serving
Each recipe portion = 1 vegetable group serving

Food Mood
A lower-fat French fry
Finger food
Cinnamon/walnut flavor

Vegetable Potpourri

This colorful dish can be part of a dinner or a meal in itself, especially if you're not in the mood for meat.

1 head escarole, coarsely cut
1 tablespoon olive oil
2 cups potatoes, unpeeled, washed, sliced
1 garlic clove, minced
1 cup tomato, diced
2 tablespoons grated Parmesan cheese
   Black pepper to taste

Boil a quart of water in a large pot. Add escarole, cover, and cook over high heat for 5 to 10 minutes or until wilted. Drain and set aside. Heat oil in a large skillet and sauté potatoes over medium heat until almost cooked, about 15 minutes. Add escarole, garlic, and tomatoes until heated. Sprinkle cheese over top and season with pepper, if desired.

Serves 6 (each serving 1 cup)

Recipe Option
Instead of escarole, use chicory, mustard greens, or kale.

Nutritional Benefits

Calories 115

Percent RDA for Pregnant Women

Dietary fiber	16 percent
Folic acid	24 percent
Vitamin A	41 percent
Vitamin B[6]	11 percent
Vitamin C	55 percent

Food Pyramid Servings

*Each recipe portion =
2 vegetable group servings*

Food Mood

No meat and lots of veggies
Colorful dish
Slightly strong flavor of
    greens
Mediterranean-style flavors
    of olive oil/Parmesan
    cheese

Potato Onion Pizza/Spinach Tomato Pizza

Pizza doesn't have to have cheese or meat on it to taste good. Kids will love this as a snack or a quick dinner and might even come up with some nutritious topping ideas of their own.

    1 pound frozen bread or pizza dough, thawed
    1 tablespoon olive oil
1½ cups potato, unpeeled, washed, cut into paper-thin
    slices
1½ cups onion, cut into paper-thin slices
 ½ tablespoon dried oregano
 ½ tablespoon dried basil

Or
instead of potato and onion, substitute:

    3 cups fresh spinach, lightly steamed to approximately
1½ to 2 cups
1½ cups plum tomatoes, diced

Preheat oven to 400° F.

Working the dough with both hands, slowly stretch and pull the dough into a rectangular shape so it will cover an 11" x 15" baking sheet or jelly roll pan (a pan with a lip). Drizzle oil over dough and spread the oil over the dough with your hand. Lay potatoes and onions (or spinach and tomatoes) evenly over dough. Sprinkle with herbs. Bake for approximately 15 minutes until browned around edges. Cut into squares.

Serves 12

Recipe Option
Use other vegetables, making sure they are cut very, very thin so they will cook within 15 minutes' baking time.

Nutritional Benefits
Potato Onion
Calories   130

Percent RDA for Pregnant Women
Folic acid   9 percent
Niacin   7 percent
Thiamine   10 percent
Potassium   7 percent

Spinach Tomato
Calories   120

Percent RDA for Pregnant Women
Magnesium   3 percent
Vitamin A   10 percent
Vitamin C   12 percent
Vitamin K   52 percent

Food Pyramid Servings
Each recipe portion =
1 bread group serving
½ vegetable group serving

Food Mood
Vegetarian meal
Crispy crust

Two-Bean Picadillo

Beans added to this traditional Cuban dish make for a high-fiber meal. The interesting flavor contrasts of the raisins, olives, and capers will surprise you. Freezes well; divide and store in small containers for a tasty, nutritious, and quick meal when you're pressed for time.

  2 cups dried white and red kidney beans, rinsed
1½ pounds lean ground beef
  1 cup onions, chopped
  1 cup green peppers, chopped
  2 garlic cloves, minced
  1 12-ounce can tomato paste
  ½ cup green olives, pitted, sliced
1–2 cups water
  1 cup raisins
  1 teaspoon capers
  1 tablespoon dried oregano
    Tabasco to taste

Put beans in a large pot and add 2" of water. Cover and bring to a boil. Remove from heat and let sit for at least 1 hour. Drain and cover beans again with same amount of fresh water. Bring to a slow boil, cover, and simmer for about 1½ to 2 hours or until beans are almost cooked.

Meanwhile, in a skillet, brown beef, drain excess fat, and set meat aside. When beans are almost cooked, add beef, onions, peppers, garlic, tomato paste, olives, and enough water (about 1 cup) for a thick stew consistency. Cover and cook over low heat for 30 minutes. Stir in raisins, capers, and oregano (adding more water to maintain consistency) and heat thoroughly. Picadillo can be eaten with a spoon or fork and should not be too soupy. Season with Tabasco if desired.

Serves 8 (each serving 1 cup)

Recipe Options
For a vegetarian version, omit beef and reduce water by half.
Omit garlic if it disagrees with you.

Nutritional Benefits
Calories   470

Percent RDA for Pregnant Women

Dietary fiber	46 percent
Folic acid	49 percent
Iron	26 percent
Magnesium	35 percent
Niacin	36 percent
Potassium	69 percent
Protein	55 percent
Vitamin B_6	30 percent
Vitamin C	71 percent
Zinc	39 percent

Food Pyramid Servings
Each recipe portion =
1½ meat group serving
1 fruit group serving
½ vegetable group serving

Food Mood
Hearty, filling meal
One-dish meal
Cuban food
Sweet/salty flavor contrast

Pork and Green Beans in Tomato-Basil Sauce

This colorful dish has a rich basil flavor. It requires only one pot, which makes preparation and cleanup a snap.

1 pound boneless pork loin, trimmed, cut into ½" cubes
1 teaspoon olive oil
2 cups potatoes, unpeeled, washed, cut into ½" cubes
1 15-ounce can tomato sauce
1 tablespoon dried basil
1 garlic clove, minced
2 cups fresh green beans, washed, cut in 1" pieces

Heat a large saucepan over high heat. Brown pork on all sides, remove from pan, and set aside. Heat oil and cook potatoes for about 5 minutes until lightly browned, adding a tablespoon of water, if necessary, to keep the potatoes from sticking. Loosen any browned bits on the bottom of the pan and add tomato sauce, basil, and garlic. Cover, reduce to a simmer, and cook 30 minutes until potatoes are almost done. Add beans, pork, and ¼ cup water if it appears you need more liquid in the pan. Cover and cook about 10 minutes or until beans are tender. If desired, serve with a crusty Italian bread for dipping in the sauce.

Serves 4 (each serving 1½ cups)

Recipe Options
Instead of fresh green beans, use frozen french-style.
Instead of pork, use boneless loin of lamb.
Use low- or reduced-sodium tomato sauce to decrease sodium content.

Nutritional Benefits

Calories	340

Percent RDA for Pregnant Women

Dietary fiber	23 percent
Folic acid	14 percent
Iron	18 percent
Niacin	49 percent
Potassium	70 percent
Protein	61 percent
Vitamin B_6	47 percent
Zinc	19 percent

Food Pyramid Servings
Each recipe portion =
1 meat group serving
2 vegetable group servings

Food Mood
Hearty stew
One-dish meal
Tomato sauce flavor

Chocolate-Cranberry Biscotti

These cookies are perfect for dunking in coffee or tea. Keep them stored in an airtight container.

1⅓ cups all-purpose flour
 ½ cup unsweetened cocoa powder
  1 teaspoon baking powder
  2 eggs
 ⅔ cup sugar
 ½ cup dried cranberries

Preheat oven to 350° F. Line a baking sheet with foil and coat with nonstick vegetable spray.

Combine flour, cocoa, and baking powder in medium bowl. Cream eggs and sugar in a small bowl with an electric beater or in a food processor. Stir wet ingredients into dry, forming a sticky dough. Stir in the cranberries. Divide the dough in half and shape each half into a 10" log. Place on the lined baking sheet and bake for approximately 30 minutes. Remove from the oven and transfer logs onto a cutting board. With a serrated knife, cut into 32 pieces, slicing crosswise on a slight angle. Place biscotti, standing upright, on baking sheet and bake another 10 minutes until crisp.

Makes 32 cookies

Recipe Option
Instead of dried cranberries, use sliced almonds.

Nutritional Benefits
Calories   45

While these cookies do not contribute any significant amount of nutrients in the serving size listed, they are practically fat-free. If you eat more, they will contribute thiamine, riboflavin, and niacin to your diet.

Food Pyramid Serving
One cookie =
½ bread group serving

Food Mood
Crisp, dry cookie
Slightly bittersweet chocolate flavor

Blueberry Crisp

Served warm or at room temperature, this dessert is delightful with a bit of whipped cream, vanilla yogurt, frozen yogurt, or ice cream on top. Desserts that use oats, cereals, and other grains are a sweet-tooth way to add complex carbohydrates to your menus.

Filling
   2 cups fresh or frozen, unthawed blueberries
1½ tablespoons all-purpose flour
 ¼ cup sugar
 ¼ teaspoon cinnamon
 ⅛ teaspoon nutmeg

Topping
   2 tablespoons all-purpose flour
 ½ cup old-fashioned oatmeal, uncooked
 ¼ cup Grape-Nuts
   3 tablespoons brown sugar, packed
 ¼ teaspoon cinnamon
   1 tablespoon butter

Preheat oven to 350° F. Coat 9" round or square pan with nonstick vegetable spray.

To prepare filling, combine all ingredients in a medium bowl. Pour into the pan. To make topping, combine all ingredients, cutting butter in with two knives or pastry blender, in a small bowl. Evenly distribute over fruit mixture. Bake for 35 to 40 minutes until fruit appears bubbly. Serve warm or at room temperature.

Serves 8

Recipe Option
Instead of blueberries, use raspberries or strawberries.

Nutritional Benefits

Calories	120

Percent RDA for Pregnant Women

Dietary fiber	10 percent
Folic acid	9 percent
Vitamin A	8 percent

Food Pyramid Servings

*Each recipe portion =
½ fruit group serving
½ bread group serving*

Food Mood

Comfort dessert
Crunchy topping
Slightly sweet blueberry
   flavor

Glazed Rum Pineapple

This is a dessert on its own, but you can also use it as a topping for angel food cake, frozen yogurt, or ice cream.

    2 teaspoons sugar
    1 20-ounce can pineapple rings, drained (reserve juice)
    2 teaspoons honey
    ½ teaspoon rum-flavored extract

Sprinkle sugar on one side of rings. Combine reserved pineapple juice, honey, and extract in a small bowl. Heat a shallow skillet until very hot and place pineapple, sugared side down, into pan. Leave in place for about 1 minute until sugar browns. Turn, cook fruit on other side, and remove from pan. Over low heat, add juice mixture to skillet and simmer for 10 minutes. Place pineapple in serving dishes, on ice cream or cake, or however you plan to use it. Pour juices over top of fruit. Serve immediately. If you're not using all of it at once, cover, refrigerate, and slightly heat before serving.

Serves 4

Recipe Option
Instead of rum extract, use almond for a slightly different flavor.

Nutritional Benefits
Calories   105

Percent RDA for Pregnant
Women
Folic acid   3 percent
Vitamin C   19 percent

Food Pyramid Serving
*Each recipe portion =
½ fruit group serving*

Food Mood
Tart and sweet flavor
    contrast
Warm and cold temperature
    contrast when served over
    ice cream or frozen yogurt

CHAPTER FIVE

The Second Three Months:
Isn't Life Wonderful?

For many women, the second trimester of pregnancy is the most pleasant. Many of the uncomfortable physical symptoms of the first three months have disappeared, and the awkwardness that comes during the last trimester has yet to arrive. Parading in your new, stylish maternity clothes adds to the fun. Toward the end of these three months, you may even begin to feel your baby move.

Some of you, however, may continue to experience many of the same symptoms as the first trimester—or you may be dealing with them for the first time. Your nausea may linger, you may be frequently constipated or troubled with heartburn and indigestion, or you may feel bloated. You may occasionally experience mild swelling of your ankles and feet.

You want to now start following the Building a Healthy Baby Nutrition Plan for the Second and Third Trimesters of Pregnancy. Copy it now and post it on your refrigerator door for quick and easy reference.

It's slightly different from the first three months because your needs change a little. In particular, you need more iron. This chapter explains all about iron and a few other nutrients important during this time, and it guides you in meeting your need for these nutrients. It also gives you insight into what you can do nutritionally to deal with some of the physical symptoms you may experience. And it gives you more great-tasting, high-nutrition recipes to help you satisfy your needs and desires as your pregnancy progresses.

Nutritional Investments

The Building a Healthy Baby Nutrition Plan for the Second and Third Trimesters of Pregnancy remains very similar to that for the first trimester. That's great, because you've been practicing for three months now and, we hope, have established some very healthy eating habits.

Specifically, because you begin to require more iron at this stage of pregnancy than you did before, we've added a focus on this important mineral. Still, it's almost impossible to get enough iron from the foods you eat. In fact, your health care provider has probably advised you to start taking iron supplements, and even given you a prescription for them. Start taking them now. The section on iron explains just how important this nutrient is to your and your baby's health and well-being. It also lists iron-rich foods to help guarantee you get enough.

We've also included a section on calcium. If you've been eating the recommended number of servings from the milk group as specified in the Building a Healthy Baby Nutrition Plan, you're getting plenty of calcium. We discuss it here to help motivate you to meet your requirement for this critical nutrient.

Because you need more protein when you're pregnant—something we discussed in the last chapter—you also need more vitamin B_6. Again, although you can get plenty by eating according to the Building a Healthy Baby Nutrition Plan, we include a brief section to tell you more about this important nutrient.

*The Building a Healthy Baby Nutrition Plan for the
Second and Third Trimesters of Pregnancy*

The Food Guide Pyramid continues as your basic guide.
Review the information on page 16–21. Then:

- Eat a variety of nutrient-dense foods from the five
  food groups each day. Choose at least the minimum
  number of servings recommended with the exception
  of those groups discussed below. Realize you'll probably need and want more. Review Choosing Smart
  from Each Food Group on page 23.
- Consume at least four servings each day from the
  milk group.
- Eat at least three servings each day from the meat
  group (6 to 7 ounces total).
- Include some meat, poultry, fish, or vitamin C–rich
  foods (such as orange juice, cantaloupe, or cabbage)
  in every meal to increase iron absorption.
- Choose plenty of foods rich in vitamin B_6, such as
  fortified cereals, leafy greens and other vegetables,
  poultry, meat, fish, beans, nuts, bananas, watermelons, and prunes.
- Eat enough food to gain weight at the rate recommended by your health care provider. (See page 46
  for information about gaining weight during pregnancy.)
- Choose low-fat and lean items from each group to
  keep fat and calorie intake in line.
- Eat small to moderate-size, nutritious meals and
  snacks every three to four hours.
- Salt your food to taste unless your health care
  provider advises otherwise.
- Drink plenty of fluids, about 8 cups a day. Try water,
  juices, milk, and soup. Limit coffee and other caffeinated beverages (cola, tea, etc.) to 2 to 3 servings
  or fewer daily.

continued

- Do not drink alcohol.
- Stay, or get, active. See page 50 for more information about healthy exercise during pregnancy.

Iron Essentials

Did you know that iron plays a primary role in carrying oxygen from your lungs to your cells to produce the energy you need? This is done by your red blood cells (indeed, iron is what makes blood red).

When you're pregnant, your need for iron increases as your blood volume increases and as your baby develops his or her own blood supply. Without enough iron, you're tired and listless. Infants of iron-deficient mothers also run a higher risk for low birth weight, prematurity, and even death.

Iron is a curious mineral because it's difficult for a woman, before menopause, to eat as much as she needs without taking a supplement—and that's especially true during pregnancy. Your need for iron *doubles* from 15 to 30 milligrams a day in the second and third trimesters of pregnancy. The general recommendation for women who are not iron-deficient to begin with is to start taking a daily supplement that contains 30 mg of iron in the thirteenth week of your pregnancy. Choose supplements that contain elemental iron, such as ferrous gluconate, ferrous sulfate, or ferrous fumarate. If you have any questions about when and which supplement to take, ask your health care provider. Also be certain to store iron supplements in a childproof bottle out of reach of children.

If you didn't have enough iron reserves before you got pregnant, you may need even more iron (from 60 to 120 mg daily) and other minerals, such as zinc (15 mg a day) and copper (2 mg a day). Women who rarely eat meat, had heavy menstrual bleeding before pregnancy, give blood frequently, are carrying more than one baby, or were recently pregnant with another baby may be low in iron. Check with your health care provider before taking additional iron or other nutrients. In particular, large doses of iron can irritate your stomach if you are not iron-deficient, and high amounts of iron, zinc, and other minerals can be toxic. Once your iron reserves are built up, you should switch to a regular dose supplement.

Even at lower doses, iron supplements can cause a few problems, including nausea, cramps, constipation, and diarrhea in some women. Fortunately, these side effects only last a few days for most women. If they persist, try taking the iron twice a day instead of a single dose, or try a slow-release preparation. Experiment with taking it at different times of the day, such as before bedtime. To enhance absorption, take iron supplements between meals and with a good source of vitamin C, such as citrus fruits or juices, cantaloupe, strawberries, green peppers, cabbage, and broccoli.

Don't take iron supplements with milk, tea, or coffee. The calcium in milk and tannic acids in tea and coffee can bind or change the iron and prevent your body from absorbing it.

Taking iron supplements does not eliminate the need for iron-rich foods. Eat foods such as fortified breakfast cereals, clams, oysters, liver, meat, and eggs. Fruits and vegetables also contain varying amounts of iron and as a group contribute significant amounts. In particular, try spinach, beans, peas, potatoes, raisins, dates, prunes, and whole grains.

The Calcium Connection

Our bodies contain more calcium than any other mineral—over two pounds in a 120-pound woman. There's good reason why. Calcium works in every cell in our bodies, from bones to teeth to muscles and nerves. It helps blood clot and plays an important role in immune function.

Women who don't get enough calcium risk osteoporosis in later years. Research even links an inadequate calcium intake to high blood pressure. In short, you don't want to fall short when it comes to eating enough calcium.

When you're pregnant, your requirement for calcium increases. You need to get at least 1200 milligrams a day in your diet. How do you do that? Just eat at least four servings a day from the milk, yogurt, and cheese group as specified in the Building a Healthy Baby Nutrition Plan. Choose skim and low-fat items to keep fat and calories down and nutrition high. You'll get more, too, from other good sources of calcium, such as foods made with milk, yogurt, and cheese, including puddings or pizza, or foods such as collard greens, turnip greens, kale, corn tortillas, tofu made with calcium sulfate, and fish canned with bones, such as salmon or sardines.

If you have trouble digesting milk—it gives you gas or diarrhea and makes you uncomfortable—you may be lactose intolerant. That means you can't digest the sugar (lactose) in milk. But there's hope. First, try yogurt with live, active cultures (check the label) and aged, hard cheese (such as cheddar). Many lactose-intolerant people find these calcium-rich foods easier to digest. Also try lactose-reduced milks available in most supermarkets. You may also find you tolerate regular milk and other milk products better if you eat them in small doses, such as a half glass at a time, with other foods.

As a last resort, you may want to try calcium supplements. We discuss that on page 120.

Getting Enough Calcium

Try these quick and easy ideas to increase your calcium intake.

- Start the day with a breakfast of fruit, cereal, and milk: ½ cup of milk gives you half a milk serving from the Food Guide Pyramid. Choose a fortified cereal that's also a good source of fiber to make your breakfast a truly great one.
- Enjoy yogurt as a midmorning snack. One cup is one milk serving. Again, go for the nonfat or low-fat varieties.
- Blend a cup of skim milk with a frozen banana and some vanilla extract for a great-tasting low-fat milkshake at lunch—and another serving from the milk group. Blend in some nonfat dry milk to increase the calcium content even more.
- Add nonfat dry milk wherever you can: in pancake mixes, cream soups, puddings, cream sauces.
- Try a toasted cheese sandwich or go south of the border. Fill a corn tortilla with 1½ ounces shredded part-skim mozzarella cheese, top with salsa, and microwave for a nutritious taste treat.
- Make a creamy soup with evaporated milk. It has twice the calcium of regular milk. Look for the skim milk variety to avoid the fat.
- Enjoy puddings, custards, and frozen yogurts. They're all great sources of calcium.
- Try some of the great-tasting calcium-rich recipes at the end of this chapter.

About Vitamin B_6

Also known as pyridoxine (one of those strange words you often see on food ingredients lists), vitamin B_6 helps you metabolize protein and is involved in energy production. It's especially important for the development of your baby's brain and nerve tissues and red blood cells.

Your need for vitamin B_6 increases in proportion to your intake of protein. That is, as you consume more protein, you also need more of this important vitamin. Unfortunately, Americans often don't get enough vitamin B_6 in their diets even when they're not pregnant. Make certain to meet your needs by choosing wisely. Frequently eat:

- Fortified cereals
- Leafy greens and other vegetables such as spinach, mustard greens, cauliflower, cabbage, white potatoes and sweet potatoes
- Meat, poultry, and fish
- Dried beans and peas
- Peanuts and walnuts
- Prunes
- Watermelons
- Bananas

Weight Gain Revisited: Where's It Coming From?

By now, you've probably gained between 3 and 8 pounds. Given the weight worries of so many American women, you may be concerned that you're gaining too much. You may also be troubled by your changing shape, wishing you could skip all this business of bulging tummies and bigger bra sizes.

If you find yourself in this situation, take a few moments to review pages 45–47 in Chapter Four. It's extremely important that you do not allow any previous concerns about weight to affect the quality of your diet while you are pregnant. That is, even if you feel bloated, fat, and unsightly, *resist all temptations to diet.* Continue eating according to the Building a Healthy Baby Nutrition Plan, choosing low-fat and lean choices to keep calories down and nutrition high. Remind yourself that *weight gain during pregnancy is necessary for a healthy baby.*

If you're gaining excessive weight, make certain it's not a problem with edema, or water retention (see the following section). Check with your health care provider. It could even be due to the fact that you're carrying more than one baby.

Even if you have already gained more than recommended, aim to continue to gain at the recommended rate. While you may not need to gain additional weight, your baby does.

If there seems to be no physical reason for your excessive weight gain, examine what you are eating. For three days, keep a food diary in which you write down what and how much you eat, when, and what you feel like when you do it. Then study your diary for patterns. Are you eating too many high-fat, high-sugar (and often low-nutrient) foods? Do you see lots of cookies, cakes, and ice cream listed? If so, what can you eat instead? Will naturally sweet fruits satisfy your sweet tooth at times, too? Are there low-fat, good-tasting alternatives to some of the rich foods you enjoy?

Look at how you feel when you eat. Are you bored, angry, tired? Does it appear you're eating as a way to make yourself feel better in some way? If so, make a list of activities other than eating that you find enjoyable. Turn to another activity when the urge to nibble strikes. Would taking a bubble bath, talking on the phone with a good friend, or taking a walk make you feel good, too? It might, in fact, make you feel better than overeating.

Examine when you eat. Are you eating breakfast—or eating enough breakfast? Are you skipping other meals, too, and just snacking along? Many people find it easier to manage how much and what they eat when they eat three balanced meals and a couple of snacks each day. Skipping meals can increase hunger and lead to overeating.

Whatever you discover, don't compensate by cutting back so much that you don't eat the minimum amount of foods necessary to supply the nutrients you need for a healthy pregnancy. In the long run, it's better to gain too much weight then to deprive yourself and your developing baby of essential nutrition.

A very high weight gain, however, can lead to complications during pregnancy and after. If your weight seems to be getting out of control, seek the help of a registered dietitian (RD). An RD can help you devise a personalized plan to address your individual needs and desires, which can help you better deal with the troubles you may be experiencing.

But I'm Having Trouble Gaining Enough!

Again, while it may seem illogical, the same dietary advice goes for women who struggle with inadequate weight gain as for those who struggle with excessive weight gain. Check with your health care provider that nothing physical is affecting your weight gain, such as an illness or infection. Then make certain you're eating according to the Building a Healthy Baby Nutrition Plan. You may also try using more fat; it has double the calories of protein and carbohydrates. Choose unsaturated fat such as olive and corn oil most of the time. If you have to have a few more snacks each day to work in enough food, devise a schedule of times you will eat. If you plan ahead, it's easier to do it.

Also check for the following:

- Are you smoking? Smoking can dull your appetite. What's more, cigarette smoke is extremely unhealthy for your baby. Join a smoking cessation class if you have to.
- Alcohol and illegal drugs can also interfere with your appetite. They, too, are extremely dangerous to the health of your unborn child.

• Are you exercising excessively, or do you have a history of eating disorders that is standing in the way of your weight gain? If so, talk it over with your health care provider. It's absolutely essential that you understand the relationship between your weight gain and your baby's growth and health.

The bottom line is to do the best you can. Eat healthy, avoid tobacco and drugs, and follow your health care provider's advice about what to do about your weight gain. The personalized guidance of a registered dietitian can help here, too.

Oh, Those Swollen Ankles

Edema, or swelling, particularly in your hands, ankles, and feet, happens to many women during pregnancy. It's normally no cause for concern; it's just the retention of water related to the changes of pregnancy that go on in your body. But when it is accompanied by high blood pressure (hypertension), protein in your urine, and other symptoms, edema may be a sign of preeclampsia (pregnancy-induced hypertension). At its worst, preeclampsia can lead to eclampsia (a condition that involves convulsions and coma).

Normal edema and the more serious condition of preeclampsia were once thought to be related to eating too much salt or sodium. Today we know that normal edema is more the result of hormonal changes during pregnancy; we still don't know the cause of preeclampsia.

While doctors once restricted salt or sodium and water in an attempt to manage both conditions, we now know that salt or sodium restriction not only does not benefit pregnant women, it can even be harmful. The additional fluid your body needs during pregnancy (as part of your increased blood volume, amniotic fluid, and the baby's fluids) actu-ally increases your need for sodium (found in salt).

Unless your doctor advises otherwise, continue to salt your food to taste. Be aware, however, that a healthy diet includes salt and salty foods only in moderation. Try the following strategies to help alleviate normal edema.

• Sleep on your left side with a pillow between your legs. Try resting several times during the day in this position. It improves blood circulation in your legs and kidney func-tion, which permits better elimination of excess fluids.
• Avoid tight shoes. Wear those that allow your feet to ex-pand. You may even find you need to buy a larger size. Also remove tight rings.
• *Do not* take diuretics (water pills) unless advised to do so by your doctor.
• Continue to get good prenatal care and to eat according to the Building a Healthy Baby Nutrition Plan. This tip is your best insurance against preeclampsia.

Solving Common Nutrition Problems During the Second Trimester

If you need it, copy and tack this chart on your refrigera-tor for easy reference.

Problem	*Solution*
Milk upsets stomach	If lactose intolerant, choose yogurt with live, active cultures, aged, hard cheese (like cheddar), lactose-re-duced milk. Eat in small amounts at any one time. Try high-calcium foods such as broccoli, kale, collard greens, corn tortillas, fish canned with bones. Ask health care provider about cal-cium supplements.

continued

High need for iron	Eat fortified breakfast cereals, clams, oysters, liver, meat, eggs, spinach, beans, peas, potatoes, whole grains. Take iron supplement as recommended by health care provider.
Iron supplements upset stomach	Take iron twice a day instead of single dose, or try slow-release preparation. Try before bedtime instead of in morning.
Gaining too much weight	Check with health care provider that it's not edema. If it's not, keep a diary to determine if and why you are overeating. Eat healthful foods in amounts recommended in the Building a Healthy Baby Nutrition Plan. Choose lean, low-fat, and skim foods whenever possible. Stay active according to advice from your health care provider. *Don't diet.* See a registered dietitian if you need help.
Not gaining enough weight	Check with your health care provider that some physical problem is not causing the trouble. Eat regular, well-balanced meals and snacks according to the Building a Healthy Baby Nutrition Plan. Eat from the upper range of recommended servings. Try using more fat such as olive oil or corn oil. Stop smoking, drinking alcohol, or using illegal drugs if you do. Don't exercise too much.

continued

Swollen ankles	Sleep and rest several times a day on your left side with a pillow between your legs. Avoid tight shoes. Eat according to the Building a Healthy Baby Nutrition Plan. Continue to use salt in moderation unless your health care provider advises otherwise.
Heartburn	Eat frequent, small meals. Don't overfill your stomach. Drink fluids between meals. Limit spicy and high-fat foods. Wear loose-fitting clothing. Don't lie down immediately after eating or drinking.
Constipation	Eat plenty of fiber and drink 2 to 3 quarts of fluid each day. Never use a laxative without the permission of your health care provider.
Have to eat out a lot	Ask restaurant to prepare foods especially as you request. Don't eat all that is served—it's often twice as much as you need.

Special Concerns

I just don't like milk and other dairy products. What can I do to get enough calcium? Go for calcium-rich vegetables such as broccoli, collard greens, kale, and mustard and turnip greens. Spinach also contains a lot of calcium, but the oxalates in spinach may bind the calcium and make it unavailable for absorption. Also try corn tortillas, tofu made with calcium sulfate, and fish canned with bones (such as salmon and sardines).

If you still think you're not getting enough calcium, talk to your health care provider about supplements. If you are advised to take them, choose calcium carbonate or calcium citrate. Avoid supplements that contain oyster shell calcium or dolomite, which may be contaminated with heavy metals or lead. Take calcium supplements at mealtime; food helps you better absorb it.

If you do avoid most milk products, you need to ensure you get enough vitamin D and riboflavin. Riboflavin is found in many foods such as enriched and fortified breads and cereals, broccoli, turnip greens, asparagus, spinach, meats, poultry, and fish. Vitamin D is harder to get. While your body makes vitamin D when your skin is exposed to the sun, your physician may recommend a vitamin supplement. Don't take extra vitamin D on your own; too much can be poisonous.

My gums bleed every time I brush my teeth. I've heard that can be due to a vitamin C deficiency. Once again, it's those pregnancy hormones at work. They can lead to swelling of the gums, which may become sensitive and bleed easily. The condition generally has nothing to do with the quality of your diet, but eating a well-balanced diet that contains plenty of vitamin C–rich foods, such as citrus foods, berries, green peppers, and potatoes, helps keep your gums in good condition. Be certain to visit your dentist at least once during your pregnancy, too, to ensure healthy teeth and gums. (Let him or her know you're pregnant before your visit.)

I eat in restaurants constantly as part of my job. How can I eat healthfully? You're in luck. Today more than ever, restaurant chefs are willing to prepare foods to meet their patrons' special needs and desires, so don't feel you're necessarily tied to the menu. Peruse it to get an idea of the types of food available in the kitchen, then ask for foods prepared how you want them. For example, if pasta smothered in cheese sauce is featured, ask for pasta with a lighter topping, such as a fresh marinara. Be aware, though, that many restaurants buy partially prepared foods, so be flexible. It may not be possible, for instance, to get a baked chicken breast if fried chicken fingers are on the menu. The restaurant may have bought the chicken fingers ready-to-cook.

If you frequently eat in the same restaurants, talk to the chef to get an idea of the foods he or she can prepare for you on a moment's notice. Planning ahead is the best way to get what you want.

You also don't have to forgo the regular menu. Look for lighter items, and tell the waiter or waitress to ask the chef if he or she can go easy on the added fat. A sole almondine that's normally served swimming in butter can easily be served with just a touch of that flavorful fat instead.

Watch portion sizes, too. American restaurants are famous for quantity, serving at least twice the amount most of us would serve at home. If you find you just can't stop when it's in front of you, ask the waiter or waitress to serve you only half the meal. Put the other half in a doggie bag *before* it comes to the table, or try sharing a dish with your meal partner. You'll probably have to pay a plate charge, but you may decide it's worth paying for it now, rather than later in the form of excess fat and calories.

I seem to lose my balance quite a bit when I'm exercising. I don't want to stop exercising, though. What can I do? As your baby grows and your tummy enlarges, you may find your center of balance somewhat affected. For safety's sake, forgo exercises that require good balance, such as biking or bowling or skiing, or that require sudden stops, such as tennis or softball. Instead, try walking or swimming (no diving).

Nutrition Checkup for the Second Trimester of Pregnancy

Copy and use this chart often to quickly assess whether you're meeting your nutritional needs during the second trimester of your pregnancy. Then fill in the blanks following each question with strategies for improving your nutritional habits if they need improving. (Answer the questions based on how you ate yesterday). Set realistic, small goals for best success. Look back on previous Nutrition Checkups to see how far you've come in meeting some goals. Give yourself plenty of pats on the back for making some important changes.

1. Did you skip any meals?   Yes   No
   How I can improve this habit:

   _____

   _____

2. Did you eat the minimum recommended number of servings from all five food groups (6+ breads and cereals, 5+ fruits and vegetables, 4+ milk, 3+ meat)?
                                       Yes   No
   How I can improve this habit:

   _____

   _____

continued

3. Did you eat several good sources of iron (fortified cereal; clams; oysters; liver; meat; eggs; fruits and vegetables, especially spinach, dried beans, peas, potatoes, raisins, dates, prunes; whole grains)? Are you taking your iron supplement?   Yes   No
How I can improve this habit:

_____

_____

4. Did you eat several good sources of vitamin B_6 (fortified cereal, bananas, poultry, meat, fish, potatoes, sweet potatoes, spinach, prunes, watermelon, nuts)?
                                    Yes   No
How I can improve this habit:

_____

_____

5. Did you eat a good source of vitamin A (deep-or-ange yellow and dark green fruits and vegetables, fortified milk)?   Yes   No
How I can improve this habit:

_____

_____

6. Did you eat a good source of vitamin C (citrus fruits, green peppers, strawberries, melon, broccoli, cabbage)?
                                    Yes   No
How I can improve this habit:

_____

_____

continued

7. Did you eat at least three servings of whole-grain foods?   Yes   No
How I can improve this habit:

_____

_____

8. Did you choose more low-fat foods than high-fat items?   Yes   No
How I can improve this habit:

_____

_____

9. Did you smoke, drink alcohol, or use an unprescribed drug (including self-prescribed vitamin/mineral supplements)?   Yes   No
How I can improve this habit:

_____

_____

10. Did you get plenty of appropriate exercise?
                                                    Yes   No
How I can improve this habit:

_____

_____

Recipe Focus: The Second Trimester

By now, we hope any nausea you may have had has passed, and you're really able to enjoy eating and cooking.

During this second trimester, the nutritional spotlight is on calcium, iron, protein, and vitamin B_6. Your baby's bones, tissues, and blood supply are taking shape, which requires sufficient amounts of all these important nutrients. Although these nutrients are plentiful in animal-based foods such as dairy products and meats, we have included plenty of nonanimal-based recipes to help vegetarians or those who are just turned off to animal products during this time to meet their nutritional requirements. So, even if you are not a milk drinker or a meat eater, there are plenty of creative and tasty ways to get these important nutrients into your diet.

Peanut Banana Milkshake

If you're not in the mood for traditional breakfasts in the mornings, this is a nourishing alternative.

½ medium banana, mashed
1 tablespoon creamy peanut butter
½ cup skim milk
3 ice cubes

Puree banana and peanut butter in a blender until smooth. Add milk and ice and continue blending until you get a creamy consistency. This will not be a frozen slushy drink, but more like a smooth, thick milk shake.

Serves 1 (each serving 1 cup)

Recipe Option
Instead of skim milk, use low-fat chocolate milk.

Nutritional Benefits
Calories 170

Percent RDA for Pregnant Women

Calcium	13 percent
Magnesium	22 percent
Protein	12 percent
Vitamin B_6	19 percent
Vitamin D	26 percent
Vitamin E	35 percent

Food Pyramid Servings
Each recipe portion =
½ milk group serving
1 fruit group serving

Food Mood
Chilled beverage
Creamy, thick beverage
Banana/peanut butter flavor combination

Hot Mocha Float

Enjoy this beverage as a snack, in place of dessert, or even at breakfast. Who says you can't have a bit of ice cream in the morning?

1 teaspoon instant coffee
1 teaspoon instant cocoa mix
1 cup hot skim milk
1 tablespoon vanilla or chocolate ice cream or frozen yogurt

Combine coffee and cocoa in a large mug. Pour in milk, stirring constantly, until thoroughly blended. Float ice cream on top.

Serves 1 (each serving 1 cup)

Recipe Option
Instead of cocoa mix, use unsweetened cocoa and add 1 teaspoon sugar.

Nutritional Benefits
Calories   125

Percent RDA for Pregnant
Women
Calcium   27 percent
Potassium   25 percent
Protein   13 percent
Riboflavin   25 percent
Vitamin D   26 percent

Food Pyramid Serving
Each recipe portion =
1 milk group serving

Food Mood
Hot and cold temperature
   contrast
Mocha flavor

Creamy Virgin Mary

If you like cream of tomato soup, you'll enjoy this chilled beverage version. The seasonings are like those found in a Bloody Mary, so this is a good party drink. Use it at breakfast with or without seasonings.

½ cup tomato juice
¼ cup skim milk
⅛ teaspoon horseradish
  Dash of dry mustard, celery seed, and ground black pepper

In a glass, combine juice and milk until thoroughly blended. Stir in seasonings.

Serves 1 (¾ cup)

Recipe Option
Use low- or reduced-sodium tomato juice to reduce sodium content.

Nutritional Benefits
Calories   40

Percent RDA for Pregnant Women
Calcium   7 percent
Potassium   18 percent
Vitamin C   14 percent

Food Pyramid Servings
Each recipe portion =
1 vegetable group
¼ milk group serving

Food Mood
Chilled beverage
Tomato flavor
Bloody Mary–type
    seasonings

Raisin Pecan Scones

Scones are perfect for dunking in morning coffee or tea. Baked goods with less fat will dry out more quickly, so be sure to wrap them tightly.

  1 cup all-purpose flour
  1 cup whole wheat flour
¼ cup brown sugar
  2 teaspoons baking powder
  1 teaspoon cinnamon
  2 tablespoons margarine
⅔ cup raisins
¼ cup pecans, coarsely chopped
  1 cup skim milk
  2 teaspoons powdered sugar

Preheat oven to 400° F. Coat baking sheet with nonstick vegetable spray.

Combine flours, sugar, baking powder, and cinnamon in a large bowl. Use 2 knives or a pastry blender to work in margarine until texture becomes crumbly. Stir in raisins and nuts. Pour milk into center and stir to a slightly sticky texture. On a lightly floured surface, knead the dough for a minute until it loses its stickiness, adding more flour if necessary. Divide the dough into 2 pieces. Flatten each piece into an 8" circle and cut into 8 pie-shaped wedges. Place on the baking sheet and bake for 8 to 15 minutes until lightly brown. When done, sprinkle with powdered sugar.

Makes 16 scones.

Recipe Option
Instead of raisins, use other dried fruits such as blueberries, cherries, or apricots.

Nutritional Benefits
Calories   110

Percent RDA for Pregnant
Women
Dietary fiber   8 percent
Iron   3 percent
Magnesium   6 percent
Potassium   6 percent

Food Pyramid Servings
Each recipe portion =
1 bread group serving
½ fruit group serving

Food Mood
Not-so-sweet breakfast
   bread
Slightly crumbly, dry
   texture

Apple Cheese Griddle Cakes

If you're not using all of these at once, store cooked cakes in a freezer bag and microwave as needed for a quick breakfast or snack.

  1 cup pancake mix or Bisquick
¾ cup skim milk
½ cup low-fat cottage cheese
  1 egg, beaten
  1 teaspoon vegetable oil
¾ cup fresh apple, unpeeled, washed, finely chopped

Coat griddle or skillet with nonstick vegetable spray.

Combine all ingredients, except apple, in a medium bowl until thoroughly moistened. The consistency will be thicker than regular pancake batter. Stir in apples. Heat skillet and use approximately ¼ cup batter for each griddle cake. Cook over medium heat until browned on both sides about 3–5 minutes. Inside texture will remain slightly moist. Top with maple syrup, apple butter, or warm, cut-up fruit or yogurt.

Serves 5 (each serving 2 griddle cakes)

Recipe Option
Add a dash of cinnamon and/or nutmeg to batter.

Nutritional Benefits
Calories   185

Percent RDA for Pregnant Women

Calcium	16 percent
Iron	8 percent
Protein	18 percent
Riboflavin	19 percent

Food Pyramid Servings
Each recipe portion =
2 bread group servings
⅓ milk group serving

Food Mood
Pancakes
Apple/cheese flavor
    combination

Curried Lentil Soup

Soup should be made in large batches so you can freeze it in small containers for later use. Lentils and other dried beans are a great way to add fiber to your diet.

1 pound dried lentils, rinsed
8 cups water
1 cup carrots, sliced
1 cup onion, sliced
1 cup celery, sliced
¼ cup fresh parsley, chopped
1 garlic clove, minced
1 teaspoon salt
3 tablespoons curry powder

Combine lentils and water in a large pot. Bring to a boil and skim off any foam that comes to the surface. Add remaining ingredients and bring to a boil again. Cover and simmer for approximately 30 to 45 minutes or until lentils are tender.

Serves 9 (each serving 1 cup)

Recipe Option
Instead of lentils, use split peas.

Nutritional Benefits
Calories　　　180

Percent RDA for Pregnant Women
Dietary fiber　　20 percent
Folic acid　　　25 percent
Iron　　　　　　15 percent
Protein　　　　18 percent

Food Pyramid Servings
Each recipe portion =
⅓ meat group serving
½ vegetable group serving

Food Mood
Hot, hearty soup
Curry flavor

Baked Onion Soup

We've made this soup in a low-fat version, using just enough cheese to cover the top of the bowl. Paired with a salad, this makes a good, quick dinner.

1 tablespoon olive oil
4 cups onions, sliced
1 teaspoon sugar
½ tablespoon cornstarch
1 13-ounce can reduced-sodium beef broth
3 cups water
½ teaspoon thyme
  Black pepper to taste
4 slices Italian or French bread
3 slices (about 3 ounces) Swiss cheese

Preheat oven to 325° F.

In a large pot, heat oil and cook onions over medium-high heat until soft and lightly browned. This will take approximately 5 to 10 minutes. Stir in the cornstarch, add the broth, water, and seasonings, and bring to a boil. Cover and simmer for 10 minutes.

Meanwhile, lightly brown the bread on both sides under the oven broiler. Ladle the soup into ovenproof bowls, float the bread on top, and lay a half slice of cheese over the bread. Increase oven temperature to 425° F. Place bowls on a baking sheet and bake for 10 minutes or until cheese is bubbly. Be careful removing from the oven.

Serves 6 (each serving 1 cup)

Recipe Option
Instead of Swiss, use Jarlsberg cheese.

Nutritional Benefits

Calories 210

Percent RDA for Pregnant Women

Dietary fiber 10 percent
Calcium 12 percent
Iron 4 percent
Magnesium 9 percent
Vitamin C 15 percent
Zinc 7 percent

Food Pyramid Servings
Each recipe portion =
1 bread group serving
1⅓ vegetable group servings
⅓ milk group serving

Food Mood
Cooked, mild onion flavor
Melted cheese topping

Broccoli Cheese Soup

We've made a low-fat version of a traditionally high-fat soup. You could even use this as a base for a sauce for vegetables and baked potatoes.

1½ teaspoons vegetable oil
 ¼ cup onion, minced
 2 tablespoons cornstarch
 2 cups water
 2 cups skim milk
 1 cup (4 ounces) sharp cheddar cheese, shredded
 ½ teaspoon mustard powder
 ½ teaspoon white pepper
 2 cups broccoli, small flowerets and stalks cut into ½" pieces

In a large pot, heat oil and sauté onions until soft but not browned. Over medium-low heat, stir in cornstarch. Add water, stirring constantly until slightly thickened. Add milk and stir constantly to a slight boil. Reduce heat and whisk in cheese until melted. Add seasonings and broccoli. Turn off heat, cover, and let sit for approximately 10 minutes until broccoli becomes tender. If you like your broccoli very soft, microwave or steam it before adding it to the soup. Be patient and resist the urge to turn up the heat when preparing this recipe; the milk can be easily burned.

Serves 6 (each serving ¾ cup)

Recipe Option
Instead of cheddar, use Colby or any other favorite orange, strong-flavored cheese.

Nutritional Benefits

Calories   120

Percent RDA for Pregnant
Women

Calcium   20 percent
Folic acid   6 percent
Protein   14 percent
Vitamin K   85 percent

Food Pyramid Servings
Each recipe portion =
¾ milk group serving
1 vegetable group serving

Food Mood
Cheese-flavored soup
Broccoli

Corn Zucchini Chowder

This pretty yellow and green soup is a good way to use up extra zucchini growing in the summer garden. Using milk in soups, stews, and chowders is a good way to get calcium for those who don't like to drink milk.

6 cups skim milk
3 cups fresh or frozen, thawed corn
2 tablespoons cornstarch
½ cup onion minced
1 teaspoon ground coriander
½ teaspoon white pepper
¾ teaspoon salt
2 cups zucchini, finely chopped

Combine half the milk and corn and all the cornstarch in a food processor or blender. Process, in batches if necessary, until smooth. Pour into a large pot and add remaining corn, milk, onion, and seasonings. Bring to a boil over medium heat, stirring occasionally. Reduce heat, add zucchini, and simmer another 10 minutes or until vegetables are cooked.

Serves 9 (each serving 1 cup)

Recipe Option
Instead of zucchini, use summer squash, although it won't be quite as colorful.

Nutritional Benefits
Calories   130

Percent RDA for Pregnant Women

Calcium	19 percent
Dietary fiber	8 percent
Magnesium	15 percent
Protein	15 percent
Vitamin C	24 percent

Food Pyramid Servings
Each recipe portion =
¾ milk group serving
1 vegetable group serving

Food Mood
Creamy chowder
Vegetarian soup
Coriander flavor

Salsa and Chips

There's no need to buy tortilla chips when you can make your own low-fat, low-salt version. Keep the salsa in the refrigerator and the chips stored in an airtight container so they're ready for snacking when you are.

  4 6" corn tortillas
  2 cups plum tomatoes (about 5), finely chopped
  3 tablespoons cilantro, finely minced
  1 scallion, finely minced
¼ teaspoon cumin
   Tabasco or other hot sauce to taste

Preheat oven to 425° F.

Stack tortillas and cut into 8 triangles, making 40 chips. Spread out on a baking sheet and bake approximately 5 minutes on each side until stiff and crisp. Remove from oven and let cool

To make salsa, combine remaining ingredients in a small bowl. Cover and refrigerate at least 1 hour to allow flavors to develop.

Serves 4 (10 chips and ½ cup salsa equal 1 serving)

Recipe Option
Instead of scallions, use ¼ cup minced onion.

Nutritional Benefits
Calories   80

Percent RDA for Pregnant Women

Calcium	19 percent
Magnesium	6 percent
Potassium	12 percent
Vitamin K	31 percent
Zinc	2 percent

Food Pyramid Servings
Each recipe portion =
1 bread group serving
1 vegetable group serving

Food Mood
Crisp tortilla chip texture
Spicy tomato flavor

Any Herb Pesto

Pesto is typically made with fresh basil, but sage, parsley, or chives also work great. Use whatever the market or your garden has available. This makes a flavor-intensive spread for grilled meats, to toss with pasta, or to flavor soups.

    2 cups fresh herbs, any combination, washed and dried
    2 tablespoons olive oil
    1 tablespoon walnuts
    ½ cup reduced-sodium chicken broth
    1 tablespoon grated Parmesan cheese

In a blender, process herbs to as fine a consistency as possible. While blender is running, drizzle in oil. Add nuts and broth. Blend until you have a smooth paste. Stir in cheese. You may portion the spread into ice cube trays or wrap into tablespoon-size portions in plastic wrap, then freeze. A tablespoon is enough to season 4 pieces of meat, pasta for 2, or a 6-cup soup recipe.

Serves 16 (each serving 1 tablespoon)

Recipe Option
Instead of walnuts, use pine nuts.

Nutritional Benefits
(Based on 1 tablespoon)
Calories   25

This pesto does not provide any significant nutritional value or pyramid contributions, but is a low-fat flavor enhancer to complement many other nutritionally sound dishes. When used with pasta, you are then getting contributions for the pyramid bread group and when used on meats or poultry, you are getting contributions from the meat group.

Food Mood
Intense herb flavor

Grilled Honey Sandwich

This is based on an old Italian-style recipe Donna's mom always made and it will remind you of French toast. Make them ahead, store in freezer bags, and microwave for a quick breakfast or lunch. Kids really like these, too.

2 teaspoons honey
4 slices whole wheat bread
2 ounces part-skim mozzarella cheese, thinly sliced
1 egg
2 tablespoons skim milk
1 teaspoon butter

Spread honey on a slice of bread, add cheese slices, and top with other bread slice. Repeat to make second sandwich. Beat egg and milk in a small bowl. Dip sandwiches in egg mixture. Melt butter in a skillet and cook sandwiches on both sides until cheese is melted and bread is browned about 5 to 8 minutes.

Serves 2

Recipe Options
Instead of honey, use your favorite fruit jam.
Instead of 1 egg, use 2 egg whites to reduce the cholesterol content.

Nutritional Benefits
Calories   315

Percent RDA for Pregnant Women

Dietary fiber	20 percent
Calcium	29 percent
Folic acid	13 percent
Iron	8 percent
Riboflavin	27 percent
Vitamin K	36 percent
Zinc	15 percent

Food Pyramid Servings
Each recipe portion =
2 bread group servings
¾ milk group serving

Food Mood
Hot sandwich
Stretchy cheese
Something slightly sweet

Ham and Broccoli Calzone

This is another great make-ahead lunch or light dinner. Once baked, these can be frozen, wrapped in foil, and reheated when there's no time to cook.

  1 pound frozen bread or pizza dough, thawed
½ cup part-skim ricotta cheese
  1 cup broccoli, cooked, chopped
  1 cup lean ham, cut into ½" pieces
    Oregano, basil, or Italian seasoning blend to taste

Preheat oven to 425° F. Coat baking sheet with nonstick vegetable spray.

Cut dough into 4 equal parts. Stretch each piece to make a 6" x 6" rectangle. Evenly distribute broccoli and ham over half of each rectangle. Sprinkle on seasonings. Fold over the portion of dough without the ham and broccoli to make a pocket and crimp around the edges with your fingers, making a seal. Place on a baking sheet and bake for 20 minutes or until crust is lightly browned. Do not attempt to cook these in the microwave as the crust will get soggy.

Serves 4

Recipe Options
Use reduced-sodium ham or eliminate ham and replace with cooked mushrooms to reduce sodium content.
Use leftover cooked zucchini, peppers, or onions in filling.

Nutritional Benefits

Calories	400

Percent RDA for Pregnant Women

Folic acid	16 percent
Iron	11 percent
Protein	33 percent
Riboflavin	26 percent
Thiamine	43 percent
Vitamin C	55 percent
Vitamin K	107 percent

Food Pyramid Servings

Each recipe portion =
4 bread group servings
½ milk group serving
⅓ meat group serving

Food Mood

Crusty pizzalike dough
Hot Italian-style sandwich
Creamy cheese filling

Marinated Mozzarella and Tomato Salad

This is on many restaurant menus and it's a cinch to make. Use it as a salad or a snack. Flavorful, ripe tomatoes are a must.

      2 large tomatoes, sliced
      4 ounces part-skim mozzarella cheese, thinly sliced
      2 tablespoons fresh basil, chopped
1½ tablespoons balsamic or red wine vinegar
      1 tablespoon olive oil
         Black pepper, to taste

Using a round, shallow dish, place tomatoes in first, cheese slices next, and basil on top. Drizzle with vinegar and oil, lifting up tomatoes and cheese so marinade runs underneath. Cover and refrigerate for at least 1 hour to allow flavors to develop. Season with pepper.

Serves 4

Recipe Option
Add thinly sliced raw onion.

Nutritional Benefits
Calories   135

Percent RDA for Pregnant
Women
Calcium   17 percent
Protein   15 percent
Vitamin C   21 percent

Food Pyramid Servings
Each recipe portion =
1 vegetable group serving
¾ milk group serving

Food Mood
Fresh tomatoes
Basil flavor
Mild cheese flavor

Honey Dijon Pasta Salad

Use this for lunch, picnics, or as a side dish for dinner. Most of us make macaroni salad the same way for years, so this is a chance to try something different. This mustard version has a tangy flavor.

  ½ cup nonfat plain yogurt
  ½ cup reduced-fat mayonnaise or salad dressing
  2 tablespoons Dijon mustard
  1 tablespoon honey
  ½ pound small pasta shells or elbow macaroni
  2 cups mushrooms, sliced
1½ cup broccoli flowerets, blanched, chopped
  1 cup green pepper, blanched, diced

To prepare dressing, combine yogurt, mayonnaise, mustard, and honey in a small bowl or jar. Cover and refrigerate.

Boil water in a medium pot and cook pasta until done. Drain, rinse with cold water in colander.

Combine pasta and vegetables in a large bowl. Stir in dressing until all ingredients are well coated. Cover and refrigerate for at least 2 hours to allow flavors to develop.

Serves 8 (each serving 1 cup)

Recipe Option
Instead of vegetables listed, use other varieties such as zucchini, peas, and cauliflower.

Nutritional Benefits
Calories   195

Percent RDA for Pregnant
Women
Folic acid   11 percent
Iron   8 percent
Thiamine   24 percent
Vitamin K   106 percent

Food Pyramid Servings
Each recipe portion =
2 bread group servings
1 vegetable group serving

Food Mood
Chilled pasta salad with lots
    of veggies
Creamy, mayonnaise-based
    dressing
Honey mustard flavor

Potato-Crusted Cauliflower Pie

This is a bit like cauliflower au gratin, but lower in fat. Any leftovers are a good carry-along lunch that can be microwaved or eaten at room temperature.

½ tablespoon vegetable oil
½ cup green or red pepper, chopped
¼ cup onion, chopped
 3 cups cauliflower flowerets, cut into small pieces
¾ cup (6 ounces) cheddar cheese, finely shredded
 1 egg
¼ cup skim milk
½ teaspoon mustard powder
 1 cup potato, unpeeled, washed, shredded
 1 egg white, beaten
½ teaspoon paprika
¼ teaspoon black pepper

Preheat oven to 400° F. Coat 9" round pan with nonstick vegetable spray.

Heat oil in large skillet and sauté peppers, onion, and cauliflower about 10 minutes. Place mixture in pan and evenly distribute cheese over top. Whisk egg, milk, and mustard and pour over vegetable-cheese mixture. Combine remaining ingredients in a small bowl and evenly layer on top of vegetables, forming a crust. Bake 35 minutes until top is browned. Cut into wedges to serve.

Serves 6

Recipe Option
Instead of cheddar, use Swiss, Monterey Jack, or another favorite full-flavored cheese.

Nutritional Benefits

Calories 160

Percent RDA for Pregnant Women

Dietary fiber	12 percent
Calcium	19 percent
Folic acid	17 percent
Protein	12 percent
Vitamin C	111 percent
Vitamin K	235 percent

Food Pyramid Servings

Each recipe portion =
1¾ vegetable group
  servings
⅓ milk group serving

Food Mood:

Cheesy flavor
Crusty topping
Baked vegetable dish

White Beans and Greens

The flavors get better as this sits a day or two. This high-fiber dish can be lunch, a main dish, or a side dish. For those who are lactose intolerant or don't like dairy products, this recipe is a good way to get some calcium.

2 slices bacon
1 cup potato, diced
4 cups escarole, chicory, mustard greens, or kale, washed, torn
1 14-ounce can cannellini *or* white northern beans *or* chickpeas, drained
Black pepper to taste

Fry bacon in a large skillet until crisp. Remove and crumble bacon; drain excess fat. Using film of oil left in pan, sauté potatoes, stirring constantly about 2 minutes until lightly browned. Add greens, cover, and heat 3 to 5 minutes until wilted. Stir in bacon, beans, season with ground black pepper, and heat thoroughly.

Serves 4 (each serving 1 cup)

Recipe Options

For a vegetarian version, omit bacon and add 1 teaspoon of olive oil for sautéing potatoes.
Rinse beans to help reduce sodium content.

Nutritional Benefits
Calories   185

Percent RDA for Pregnant
Women
Calcium   17 percent
Dietary fiber   47 percent
Folic acid   63 percent
Iron   12 percent
Potassium   66 percent
Vitamin A   90 percent
Protein   17 percent
Vitamin C   79 percent
Zinc   10 percent

Food Pyramid Servings
Each recipe portion =
⅓ meat group serving
1½ vegetable group
  servings

Food Mood
Hearty bean dish
One-dish meal
Bacon flavor

Tortilla Crusted Chicken

The tortilla crumbs add a nice texture and crunch to the chicken and help keep the meat moist.

  1 egg, beaten
½ cup skim milk
  3 6-inch corn tortillas
  1 teaspoon paprika
¼ teaspoon cayenne pepper
¼ teaspoon cumin
  4 4-ounce chicken breasts, boneless, skinless

Preheat oven to 350° F. Coat baking sheet with nonstick vegetable spray.

Combine egg and milk in a bowl and set aside.

Heat tortillas in the oven or toaster until crisp. Crumble tortillas very finely (using a rolling pin or mortar and pestle) and, on waxed paper, combine with spices. Dip each breast into the egg, then evenly coat with the crumbs. Place on the baking sheet, and bake about 20 to 30 minutes until juices run clear.

Serves 4

Recipe Options
Instead of 1 egg, use 2 egg whites to reduce cholesterol content.
Instead of spices listed, use your favorite Mexican spice blend.
Omit cayenne if it disagrees with you.

Nutritional Benefits
Calories   215

Percent RDA for Pregnant
Women

Calcium	11 percent
Folic acid	7 percent
Iron	11 percent
Niacin	60 percent
Protein	50 percent
Potassium	16 percent
Vitamin B$_6$	35 percent
Zinc	10 percent

Food Pyramid Servings
*Each recipe portion =
1 meat group serving
¾ bread group serving*

Food Mood
Crunchy texture
Mexican-style food
Spicy flavor

Turkey Stir-Fry

If you're in the mood for a Chinese-style stir-fry and want something other than take-out food, try this dish. It's moderate in sodium and low in fat.

Marinade
   3 tablespoons reduced-sodium soy sauce
   2 tablespoons rice wine vinegar
   2 tablespoons water
   1 garlic clove, minced
   1 teaspoon fresh, grated ginger, *or* ½ teaspoon ground
      ginger

Sauce
   ¾ cup orange juice
   2 teaspoons low-salt soy sauce
   1 teaspoon fresh, grated ginger, *or* ½ teaspoon ground
      ginger
   1 teaspoon rice wine vinegar
   1 tablespoon cornstarch, *or* 2 tablespoons flour

   12 ounces turkey breast, boneless, skinless, cut into strips
   2 teaspoons sesame oil
   4 cups Chinese *or* napa cabbage *or* bok choy, shredded
   2 cups yellow squash, sliced
   1 cup scallions, chopped
   2 tablespoons sesame seeds
      Cooked rice, if desired

Prepare marinade and sauce at the same time since they use some of the same ingredients. Combine all marinade ingredients in a shallow dish and add turkey. Cover and refrigerate for at least ½ hour. Set sauce aside.

When ready to cook, heat oil in a very large skillet or wok. Remove turkey from marinade and stir-fry for approximately 1 minute. Remove from pan and stir-fry cabbage, moving it constantly, until partially wilted. Add squash and scallions to pan and continue stir-frying until all vegetables are done. Pour remaining marinade into prepared sauce. Add turkey and sauce to pan and, over high heat, stir until sauce thickens. Sprinkle with sesame seeds prior to serving. Serve over rice, if desired.

Serves 6 (each serving 1 cup)

Recipe Options
Instead of turkey, use chicken.
Instead of vegetables listed, use other varieties such as peppers, snow peas, green beans.

Nutritional Benefits
(*Without rice*)
Calories   160

Percent RDA for Pregnant Women
Folic acid   37 percent
Iron   14 percent
Niacin   35 percent
Protein   39 percent
Vitamin C   65 percent

Food Pyramid Servings
Each recipe portion =
⅔ meat group serving
2 vegetable group servings

Food Mood
Chinese-style food
Soy/ginger flavor
Small amount of meat
Lots of veggies

Pork Rolls Stuffed with Feta Cheese

The cheese and oregano filling is so flavorful you won't need a sauce. Thinly sliced pork loin is sometimes available in the markets. If you cannot buy it presliced, use a pork loin roast and cut your own thin slices. You'll need a total of 16 1-ounce slices.

1 pound lean pork loin, ¼" thick slices, trimmed
½ cup feta cheese, crumbled
1½ teaspoons dried oregano
1 tablespoon vegetable oil

Sprinkle even amounts of cheese and oregano in the center of each slice of pork and roll up with seam side down. Keep cheese in the center of the slice so it won't drip out during cooking. Heat oil in a large skillet and, over medium heat, sauté rolls (seam side down first) on all sides until browned, about 5 to 7 minutes.

Serves 4 (each serving 4 rolls)

Recipe Option
Instead of oregano, use other favorite herbs such as thyme, sage, rosemary.

Nutritional Benefits
Calories   215

Percent RDA for Pregnant
Women
Calcium   12 percent
Protein   39 percent
Thiamine   61 percent
Zinc   17 percent

Food Pyramid Serving
*Each recipe portion =
1 meat group serving*

Food Mood
Small meat portion
Savory, slightly salty feta
    cheese flavor

Apple Raisin Pot Roast

This fruited version is a nice change from the traditional potato and vegetable–style pot roast. The dried fruits contribute fiber and iron to the recipe.

    3 pounds beef rump roast or bottom round roast
    1 cup onion, sliced
    1 cup apple juice
    2 tablespoons brown sugar
    1 teaspoon salt
1½ cups dried apples, chopped
 ½ cup raisins
    Cooked noodles, if desired

Heat a large pot with a tight-fitting cover, add meat, and brown on all sides. Reduce heat and add remaining ingredients except for apples, raisins, and noodles. Cover and cook on low heat for approximately 3 hours or until meat is fork tender. Add apples and raisins and heat an additional 15 minutes. Serve with wide, flat noodles, if desired.

Serves 8

Recipe Option
Instead of apples and raisins, use prunes, apricots, or other favorite dried fruits.

Nutritional Benefits
(*Without noodles*)
Calories   335

Percent RDA for Pregnant
Women
Dietary fiber   10 percent
Iron   9 percent
Niacin   21 percent
Potassium   30 percent
Protein   50 percent

Food Pyramid Servings
Each recipe portion =
1 meat group serving
2 fruit group servings

Food Mood:
Comfort food
Hearty beef dinner
Slightly sweet sauce

Beef Braciola with Rigatoni

A braciola is the Italian name for a seasoned, rolled-up piece of meat, similar to a roulade. This dish is a nice combination of meat and pasta, yet it is fairly quick to make because you use a ready-made marinara sauce.

1 pound flank steak
½ cup parsley, finely chopped
3 garlic cloves, minced
2 tablespoons grated Parmesan cheese
Black pepper to taste
1 cup green peppers, sliced
1 cup onion, sliced
1 teaspoon olive oil
8 ounces rigatoni pasta
1 14-ounce jar marinara-style tomato sauce

Lay steak flat and sprinkle entire surface with parsley, garlic, cheese, and pepper. Roll up, jellyroll fashion, and hold together with toothpicks or tie with thread. Heat a medium skillet on high heat, and brown braciola on all sides. Remove meat from pan, heat oil, and sauté peppers and onion until tender. Return meat to pan, add sauce, cover, and simmer for 15 to 20 minutes.

Meanwhile, boil water in a medium pot and cook pasta until done. To serve remove toothpicks or thread, cut meat crosswise, creating little round slices, with a side of pasta and sauce over top.

Serves 4 (3 ounces of meat and 1 cup pasta per serving)

Recipe Option
Instead of rigatoni, use any favorite pasta.

Nutritional Benefits

Calories   430

Percent RDA for Pregnant
Women

Iron   15 percent
Riboflavin   26 percent
Niacin   52 percent
Thiamine   46 percent
Zinc   39 percent

Food Pyramid Servings

Each recipe portion =
1 meat group serving
2 bread group servings
1 vegetable group serving

Food Mood

Italian-style dinner
Tomato sauce

Basil and Tomato Baked Potato

This is a cinch when you don't feel like cooking. You can vary toppings to suit your fancy, but try to always include the cottage cheese for the calcium. As the cheese melts, it creates a creamy-style topping.

  1 large baked potato
¼ cup low-fat cottage cheese
  2 tablespoons tomato, chopped
  1 tablespoon scallion, chopped
  1 tablespoon black olives, chopped
½ tablespoon dried basil
    Salt and pepper to taste

Bake potato in microwave or oven. When done, slit down the middle and toss with remaining ingredients so cheese gets a chance to melt from the heat of the potato.

Serves 1

Recipe Option
If using fresh basil, increase amount to 1 tablespoon.

Nutritional Benefits
Calories	285

Percent RDA for Pregnant Women
Calcium	6 percent
Iron	10 percent
Magnesium	19 percent
Vitamin C	43 percent
Vitamin B$_6$	35 percent

Food Pyramid Servings
Each recipe portion =
4 vegetable group servings
1 dairy group serving

Food Mood
Quick-fix dinner
Stick-to-your-ribs baked
    potato
Basil and tomato flavor

Fish Sandwich

Use any type of fresh or frozen lean fish fillet to make this sandwich. In warmer months, skip the milk and bread crumbs and simply grill the fish on the barbecue.

3 ounces fish fillet (cod, flounder, mahimahi, snapper)
2 tablespoons milk
1 tablespoon bread crumbs
1 teaspoon vegetable oil
1 ounce provolone cheese, sliced
1 slice of lettuce
1 tomato
1 hard roll

Dip fish in milk and dust with bread crumbs. Heat oil in a small skillet and sauté fish until lightly browned on both sides. Place cheese on top, cover for 1 minute, allowing cheese to melt. Place fish, lettuce, and tomato on a hard roll.

Serves 1

Recipe Options
Instead of provolone, use any favorite cheese.
If grilling, use more firm-fleshed fish varieties.

Nutritional Benefits
Calories   430

Percent RDA for Pregnant Women
Calcium   18 percent
Iron   11 percent
Niacin   20 percent
Riboflavin   23 percent
Thiamine   24 percent

Food Pyramid Servings
Each recipe portion =
2 bread group servings
1 meat group serving
½ dairy group serving

Food Mood
Fish flavor
Melted cheese flavor
Sandwich

Dagwood-Style Sandwich

Pile this high with an assortment of any sliced, raw vegetables such as pepper rings, mushrooms, or radishes, which only adds nutritional value. If you have an urge for something salty, go ahead and use the few potato chips right on the sandwich. It will satisfy the craving and yet you're controlling the amount of chips by putting them on the sandwich instead of on the side.

   3 **slices pumpernickel bread**
   2 **teaspoons mustard**
   2 **ounces sliced deli turkey breast**
   1 **ounce sliced Monterey Jack or provolone cheese**
2–3 **slices of lettuce**
      Tomato, to taste
      Cucumber, to taste
      Onion, to taste
3–4 **potato chips**

Spread mustard on one side of each slice of bread. Assemble the sandwich in any order you wish, adding the potato chips last.

Makes 1 sandwich.

Recipe Options
For a little heat, add hot pepper rings.
Instead of pumpernickel bread, use rye or whole wheat.
To help lower sodium content, eliminate chips.

Nutritional Benefits
Calories   420

Percent RDA for Pregnant
Women
Dietary fiber   10 percent
Calcium   27 percent
Iron   12 percent
Magnesium   21 percent
Niacin   39 percent
Riboflavin   32 percent

This sandwich provides 50 percent of your daily recommended sodium intake, so balance out the day with other foods that are lower in sodium.

Food Pyramid Servings
Each recipe portion = 3 bread group servings
⅔ meat group serving
½ milk group serving
½ vegetable group serving

Food Mood
Everything but the kitchen sink on a sandwich
Salty and crispy

Spaghetti with Shrimp Sauce

If you're in the mood for Italian food and don't feel like going out, this dish may just hit the spot.

½ tablespoon olive oil
 1 pound shrimp, peeled
 1 28-ounce can crushed tomatoes
 2 garlic cloves, minced
 3 tablespoons fresh parsley, minced
 1 teaspoon dried oregano
 1 teaspoon dried basil
 1 pound spaghetti
  Red pepper flakes to taste

Heat oil in a large saucepan. Quickly sauté shrimp for 1 to 2 minutes and remove from pan. Add tomatoes, garlic, parsley, and spices. Bring to a boil, partially cover, and simmer for 20 minutes.

Meanwhile, boil water in a large pot and cook spaghetti until done.

Add shrimp to tomato sauce and remove pan from heat. Drain spaghetti and toss with shrimp sauce. Season with pepper flakes, if desired.

Serves 6 (each serving 1½ cups)

Recipe Options
Instead of shrimp, use firm-fleshed fish such as tuna, cut into chunks.
If using fresh shrimp, save shells to make fish stock and use as a base when preparing seafood chowders.

Nutritional Benefits
Calories   410

Percent RDA for Pregnant Women

Iron	21 percent
Niacin	52 percent
Protein	44 percent
Thiamine	59 percent
Vitamin C	39 percent

Food Pyramid Servings
Each recipe portion = 2 bread group servings
1 meat group serving

Food Mood
Italian-style flavors
Pasta
Tomato sauce

Blue Cheese Drop Biscuits

These can be used with meals, as a snack, or even as a breakfast bread when you crave a savory flavor in the morning. Rich in complex carbohydrates, drop biscuits travel well and can be stored for several days, if lightly wrapped.

 1 cup all-purpose flour
½ tablespoon baking powder
¼ tablespoon salt
 2 tablespoons butter
½ cup skim milk
½ cup blue cheese, crumbled

Preheat oven to 440° F.

Combine flour, baking powder, and salt in a medium bowl. Cut in butter, using two knives or a pastry blender, until mixture is crumbly. Stir in milk and cheese until thoroughly combined. Batter will be sticky. Drop even amounts of batter, about ½ tablespoon each, 1" apart, onto ungreased baking sheet. Bake 12 to 15 minutes until golden.

Makes 9 biscuits.

Recipe Option
Instead of blue cheese, use grated cheddar or Swiss.

Nutritional Benefits
Calories   105

Percent RDA for Pregnant
Women
Calcium   8 percent

Food Pyramid Serving
Each biscuit =
1 bread group serving

Food Mood:
Savory, cheesy flavor
Home-style biscuit
Something starchy

Date Nut Bran Bread

This moist bread travels well and tastes wonderful with a bit of regular or reduced-fat cream cheese. Dates and other dried fruits provide iron, especially important if you don't eat much red meat.

1½ cups all-purpose flour
  2 teaspoons baking powder
 ½ teaspoon baking soda
1½ cups all-bran cereal
  1 cup skim milk
 ¼ cup vegetable oil
  1 egg
 ¼ cup molasses
 ¾ cup dates, chopped, pitted
 ¼ cup walnuts, finely chopped

Preheat oven to 400° F. Coat 9" x 5" loaf pan with nonstick vegetable spray.

Combine flour, baking powder, and baking soda in a large bowl. Set aside.

In another bowl, stir in remaining ingredients, except dates and nuts, until thoroughly blended. Pour wet ingredients into dry and stir until thoroughly blended. Stir in dates and nuts. Pour into loaf pan and bake for 25 to 35 minutes or until inserted toothpick comes out clean. Cool before slicing.

Serves 12

Recipe Option
Instead of dates, use raisins or figs.

Nutritional Benefits
Calories 210

Percent RDA for Pregnant
Women

Dietary fiber	18 percent
Iron	10 percent
Niacin	14 percent
Potassium	21 percent
Thiamine	19 percent

Food Pyramid Servings
*Each recipe portion =
2 bread group servings
½ fruit group serving*

Food Mood
Dark, fruity bread
Slightly sweet molasses
    flavor

Warm Chocolate Sauce

Quickly warm this sauce in the microwave and use it over cut-up fresh fruit, frozen yogurt, ice cream, or sponge cake desserts.

  2 tablespoons cocoa powder, unsweetened
  1 tablespoon cornstarch
  3 tablespoons sugar
⅔ cup skim milk
  1 teaspoon butter

Combine all ingredients except butter in a small saucepan. Bring to a slow boil over low heat, stirring constantly. Remove from heat and stir in butter. Use immediately or cover and refrigerate. Tastes best when slightly heated.

Serves 12 (each serving 1 tablespoon)

Recipe Option
Add ¼ teaspoon of peppermint extract for a chocolate-mint flavor.

Nutritional Benefits
Calories   25

This sauce does not provide any significant nutritional value or pyramid contribution, but is a low-fat treat to complement many other nutritionally sound dishes, especially when used over fruit. You are then getting contributions from the pyramid fruit group.

Food Pyramid Servings
Each tablespoon = a serving from the fats, oils, and sweets category

Food Mood
Warm and gooey
Chocolate flavor
Warm and cold temperature contrast when served over ice cream or frozen yogurt

Maple Cream

This versatile topping can be used as is, refrigerated for a slightly thicker consistency, or lightly heated for a thinner, pouring consistency. Use it over bread pudding, rice pudding, pancakes, waffles, and anything that needs a creamy-style topping.

½ cup low-fat cottage cheese
½ cup part-skim ricotta cheese
  2 tablespoons maple syrup
¼ teaspoon vanilla extract

Combine all ingredients in a food processor on slow speed for 3 to 5 minutes, until the grainy texture of the ricotta is gone and you have a smooth, silky consistency. Cover, if refrigerating.

Serves 16 (each serving 1 tablespoon)

Recipe Option
Instead of vanilla extract, use almond, rum, or other favorite flavored extracts.

Nutritional Benefits
Calories   25

This topping does not provide any significant nutritional value or pyramid contribution in the serving size listed, but is a low-fat treat to complement many other nutritionally sound dishes. Especially when used with carbohydrate-rich items like pancakes, waffles, or bread pudding, you are then getting contributions from the pyramid bread group. If eaten in larger quantities, you are adding calcium to your diet.

Food Mood
Smooth, creamy texture
Creamlike indulgence, but low in fat

Almond Fig Bread Pudding

The sweetness of the figs makes this a suitable dessert and an interesting breakfast. Try it topped with our Maple Cream (page 171).

1 egg
2 egg whites
1 12-ounce can evaporated skimmed milk
1 teaspoon almond extract
2 tablespoons honey
3 cups dry Italian bread, cut in ½" cubes
¾ cup dried figs, chopped

Preheat oven to 375° F. Coat 1-quart casserole dish with nonstick vegetable spray.

Whisk egg, milk, extract, and honey in a large bowl. Stir in bread cubes and figs and let mixture sit for 10 minutes. Pour into casserole and place in a baking pan filled with 1" of water. Bake in the water bath for 45 minutes, until edges are browned. Serve warm or at room temperature.

Serves 6 (each serving ½ cup)

Recipe Option
Instead of figs and almond extract, use pitted prunes and orange extract.

Nutritional Benefits
Calories   200

Percent RDA for Pregnant Women
Dietary fiber   20 percent
Calcium   20 percent
Protein   19 percent
Riboflavin   24 percent

Food Pyramid Servings
*Each recipe portion =
2 bread group servings*

Food Mood
Comfort dessert
Moist texture
Fig flavor

Sweet Polenta

Our adaptation of a traditional Indian pudding uses carrots for added texture, color, and nutrition. The molasses is a good source of iron, especially important for those eating little meat.

 4 cups skim milk
½ cup cornmeal
½ cup carrots, grated
½ cup molasses
 2 tablespoons butter
½ teaspoon cinnamon
½ teaspoon ground ginger
½ teaspoon nutmeg
¼ teaspoon salt

Preheat oven to 325° F.

Stir milk into cornmeal in a large saucepan. Bring to a boil over medium heat, stirring constantly. Reduce heat and simmer for approximately 15 minutes, until thickened. Stir in remaining ingredients and pour into 1-quart casserole. Bake for 30 minutes, stir, and bake an additional 30 minutes. Serve warm or at room temperature.

Serves 8 (each serving ½ cup)

Recipe Option
Use more or less of the spices based on your flavor preference.

Nutritional Benefits
Calories   150

Percent RDA for Pregnant Women
Calcium   24 percent
Iron   12 percent
Potassium   43 percent
Vitamin A   59 percent

Food Pyramid Servings
*Each recipe portion =
½ milk group serving
¼ bread group serving*

Food Mood
Old-fashioned-style dessert
Sweet molasses flavor

Cherry Rice Pudding

This versatile dish, rich in complex carbohydrates, can be eaten as a breakfast cereal, a snack, or even a dessert. It's a good way to use up leftover rice, and it can be baking while dinner dishes are being washed and the kitchen straightened up.

1 egg
1 egg white
1 10-ounce can evaporated skimmed milk
1 teaspoon vanilla extract
⅓ cup sugar
½ teaspoon dried orange peel
⅓ cup dried cherries
1½ cups white rice, cooked
1½ cups brown rice, cooked

Preheat oven to 325° F. Coat 2-quart casserole dish with nonstick vegetable spray.

Combine eggs, milk, vanilla, sugar, and orange peel in a large bowl. Stir in cherries and rice until thoroughly blended. Pour into casserole. Bake for 20 minutes and then increase temperature to 350° F for remaining 20 minutes or until liquid is evaporated. Serve warm or chilled. If desired, pour milk over each portion, which will further boost the calcium value of this dish.

Serves 6 (each serving ½ cup)

Recipe Options
Instead of cherries, use dried blueberries or raisins.
Use all brown rice to increase the fiber content.

Nutritional Benefits
Calories   240

Percent RDA for Pregnant
Women
Calcium   14 percent
Riboflavin   19 percent
Vitamin A   19 percent
Vitamin C   15 percent

Food Pyramid Servings
Each recipe portion =
2 bread group servings
⅓ milk group serving

Food Mood
Comfort food
Mild flavor
Slightly tart cherry flavor

Espresso Cheesecake

This coffee-flavored, no-bake cheesecake requires some advance thought because you need to drain the yogurt overnight. It's worth the effort, since it can feed a crowd and has only 210 calories per serving.

Crust
 ¾ cup graham cracker crumbs (about 4 full squares)
 1½ tablespoons vegetable oil
 2–3 tablespoons water

Filling
  1 cup low-fat coffee-flavored yogurt
  1 cup part-skim ricotta cheese
 12 ounces whipped light cream cheese
 ½ cup low-fat vanilla-flavored yogurt
  2 teaspoons vanilla extract
 ½ cup sugar
  1 teaspoon coffee-flavored extract or liqueur
  1 envelope unflavored gelatin
 ¾ cup espresso coffee or strong-brewed regular coffee,
    room temperature (divided into ½ cup and ¼ cup)
  1 tablespoon unsweetened chocolate, grated or shaved

The night before you make this cake, put the coffee yogurt in a cheesecloth, yogurt funnel, or double-strength paper towels and let it drip over a cup in the refrigerator. The result will be a firm-textured yogurt cheese.

Preheat oven to 350° F.

Combine crumbs, oil, and water in a 10" deep-dish pie pan and, with your fingers, blend until the crumbs hold together. Pat into the bottom of the pan and bake for approximately 10 minutes or until lightly crisped. Cool completely before filling.

To make the filling, process the ricotta in a food processor until the grainy texture is gone. To the processor, add the yogurt cheese, cream cheese, vanilla yogurt, extracts, and sugar, and process until well combined. Meanwhile, in a cup, sprinkle gelatin over ¼ cup coffee and let stand for 2 minutes. Then microwave, on high, for 40 seconds, stir, and let stand for 2 minutes. Alternatively, in a pan, sprinkle gelatin over ¼ cup of coffee, let stand for 1 minute, then slowly heat and stir until gelatin is dissolved. With the processor running, gradually add the gelatin mixture and remaining ½ cup coffee. Pour into pie pan and immediately refrigerate for at least 8 hours or overnight. Cake will firm up as gelatin sets. When ready to serve, dust the top with grated chocolate.

Serves 12

Recipe Option
Instead of grated chocolate, top with sliced strawberries.

Nutritional Benefits

Calories   220

Percent RDA for Pregnant Women

Calcium	10 percent
Protein	12 percent
Riboflavin	11 percent
Vitamin A	21 percent

Food Pyramid Servings
Each recipe portion =
½ bread group serving
½ milk group serving

Food Mood
Creamy, satisfying
   dessert
Coffee flavor

CHAPTER SIX

The Last Three Months: The Home Stretch

You may have thought these last three months would never arrive. Before you're through them, you may begin to wonder if they will ever end. Anticipation of the imminent arrival of baby combined with the increasing awkwardness and discomfort of late pregnancy makes these last several months seem interminable to some women.

But, oh, the excitement! You're probably feeling your baby move more frequently—and more strongly. Those kicks in tender places spur your imagination about just how big that baby is already. And all the preparations during these last few months to make certain everything is ready for your new arrival make it a very busy time, indeed.

Even so, don't let good nutrition take a backseat to the many other things going on right now. Your nutritional needs remain high, and your baby's needs gain momentum. During the last twelve weeks of pregnancy, your baby will more than triple its weight.

You may begin to experience problems you escaped before, such as heartburn, indigestion, or constipation as baby's increasing size weighs heavily on your digestive tract. Or you may experience leg cramps that wake you up in the middle of the night with an excruciating suddenness.

This chapter, like those that precede it, gives you the nutritional insight you need to successfully maneuver through the last trimester of pregnancy. It helps you met the nutritional challenges you face by giving you information, tips, and a variety of wonderfully nutritious and tasty recipes to enjoy. It also looks at an important after-the-baby-comes topic: breast- vs. bottle-feeding.

Nutritional Investments

Nothing significant changes in regard to the Building a Healthy Baby Nutrition Plan during the last trimester. In these last few weeks when baby is growing by leaps and bounds, your need for protein may be at its highest. Ditto for vitamin B_6 since your need for it is determined to some degree by your protein intake. If you're eating according to the Building a Healthy Baby Nutrition Plan for the Second and Third Trimesters, you're covered for these nutrients.

The same holds true for calcium and iron. Most of the calcium your baby will have in his or her body when he or she is born is deposited during the last trimester. Also, getting enough iron remains vital to feeling your best and supplying your baby with the iron it needs to build its blood supply and iron reserves.

Even so, your diet should remain virtually the same as it was in the second trimester. What changes most is which one of you makes the most use of what you're eating. That is, during the first six months of pregnancy, you were gaining the majority of the weight, thereby using the largest part of the calories and many of the nutrients. Now your baby is taking the greater amount of many nutrients.

For example, now is the time when your baby's brain is going through its greatest growth spurt. As a result, your baby needs plenty of calories and protein, which are two nutrients vital to optimal brain development. So even if you have already surpassed your weight gain goal for your entire pregnancy, you shouldn't cut back significantly on how much you eat. It's your baby's turn to gain.

Your need for zinc reaches its highest level during the third trimester. Again, if you've been eating according to the Building a Healthy Baby Nutrition Plan, you're getting plenty of zinc. Read the following section to learn more about this critical nutrient.

Your need for magnesium increased even in the first trimester of pregnancy. We didn't focus on this mineral before because you get plenty if you're eating as advised. But we chose to feature it here to reinforce its importance to this stage of pregnancy. Research shows that many pregnant women fail to get enough magnesium, and getting enough may help reduce your risk of preeclampsia, a problem for some women in the last trimester.

About Zinc

Zinc plays a vital role in two of the processes basic to proper growth: cell division and DNA production. It's also important to digestion, wound healing, healthy skin and hair, and other essential processes.

The RDA for zinc during pregnancy is 15 milligrams per day, 3 mg more than you normally need. Your actual need for the mineral, however, increases only slightly during the first trimester. It rises somewhat during the second three months, and is highest during the last trimester of pregnancy. (The RDA reflects an average guideline for intake during the entire pregnancy to make sure women meet varying needs throughout pregnancy.) The problem is, many women don't get enough zinc even when they're not pregnant.

Taking a supplement isn't usually recommended, however. One study showed an intake of only 18.5 mg a day— just 3.5 mg higher than the RDA for pregnancy—may interfere with absorption of copper, another essential nutrient. Another report suggested a connection between high-dose zinc supplements of 45 mg a day and premature delivery. But if you're taking high doses of iron, you may need additional zinc. Check with your health care provider.

In the United States, we get most of our zinc from animal sources, especially meat. Plant foods also contribute zinc, most of which comes from grains and cereals. Regardless of the source, you aren't likely to find a large amount of zinc in any one food (except oysters—they're a great source). Make certain you get enough zinc every day by choosing good sources, such as:

- Meat and poultry, including liver, beef, veal, pork, and dark-meat turkey and chicken
- Whole grain breads and cereals and some fortified cereals
- Shellfish, especially oysters (but don't eat them raw)
- Dried beans and peas
- Peanuts and peanut butter
- Yogurt
- Eggs

Magnesium Matters

Strong, healthy bones and muscles are just two of the many parts of our bodies that depend on magnesium. Over 300 bodily enzymes need magnesium to work properly. It's a nutrient that performs a variety of functions, but one that we only need in small amounts.

That's fortunate, because magnesium is only found in small amounts in foods. It's also found in foods that many Americans fail to regularly include in their diets. Indeed, in this country, many pregnant women may not meet the RDA for magnesium (320 mg). Studies also suggests diets rich in magnesium may result in less fetal growth retardation, less preeclampsia, fewer premature births, fewer hospitalization, and healthier babies.

We don't know enough about potential dangers of excess

magnesium to recommend that we supplement our diets with magnesium in the form of pills. As a result, our best bet is to make certain we get enough magnesium from the food we eat. If you're careful to eat a diet high in vegetables, whole grains, and legumes, you'll get enough magnesium. Choose some of these foods daily.

- Leafy green vegetables
- Whole grain breads and cereals
- Nuts and seeds
- Dried beans and peas
- Seafood

Surely I Can't Get Any Larger!

While you may already feel quite large at this point, you're still facing a recommended weight gain of about 1 pound a week (more or less if you're over- or underweight) throughout the remainder of your pregnancy. That's at least another 12 pounds.

If you're right on target with your weight gain, just continue doing what you've been doing. If you're inching above the recommended total or you are still having trouble gaining enough, reread page 48 for healthy ideas for keeping your weight in line.

If you've gained too much already, focus on eating healthy, low-fat foods, but don't cut back below the minimum amounts recommended in the Building a Healthy Baby Nutrition Plan. Your baby grows fast and furiously during these last months and needs the nutrition he or she can only get from food you eat.

Inform your health care provider of any sudden weight gains. They may be an indication of fluid retention and potential problems with preeclampsia (see page 117).

Yep, There's a Baby There

At this point, you don't need us to tell you you've got something large growing in your middle. Bouts with heartburn, indigestion, and constipation, along with trouble finding a comfortable sleeping position and the general awkwardness you feel as your stomach really begins to bulge, serve as regular reminders. Baby's increasing weight sits heavily on your digestive tract and can cause all sorts of discomforts.

Review page 56 to learn more about dealing with heartburn and constipation that may result from baby's increasing weight. In general, though, remember that small, frequent meals may be your best approach to calming digestive upsets. Certainly, not eating is *not* a choice. You'll not only deprive your baby, you're undoubtedly pretty hungry much of the time.

Munch on high-fiber, low-fat foods to keep your digestive tract functioning smoothly and efficiently, and enjoy plenty of fluids throughout the day. Remember, the day is not too long away when you'll feel—and be—remarkably lighter.

In Favor of the Breast

Chances are you've already been thinking about how you're going to feed your baby once he or she arrives. Will you breast-feed? Or will you use bottles? Or a combination?

Breast-feeding wins hands down as the method recommended by most nutritionists and other health professionals. Indeed, exclusive breast-feeding is the preferred method for feeding normal, full-term infants from birth to about 4 to 6 months old. The American Academy of Pediatrics also recommends that babies be breast-fed for at least the first full year of life.

That's because breast milk comes ready-made for babies, with the right mix of nutrients we know are necessary to help them thrive. In addition, it's easy to digest and contains substances that help protect your baby against infections. There also is less likelihood that your baby will be allergic to your breast milk.

Breast-feeding helps you, too. Your uterus returns to its normal shape more quickly, and it may help you do the same. What's more, breast milk costs less than formula, even considering the additional food you might need (discussed in Chapter 6).

Further, a recent study of more than 15,000 women revealed that mothers who nursed their infants had an average 20 percent lower risk of getting breast cancer before menopause. The longer the women in the study nursed, the greater the degree of protection. It's not clear why breast-feeding exerts this protective effect. It may be due to hormonal influences or changes in breast tissue, but it appears breast-feeding definitely offers health benefits to mom as well as babe.

If you decide to breast-feed, however, understand the responsibility that comes along with it. While a healthy diet helps ensure an adequate milk supply, you also need to remember the potentially harmful effects of smoking, drinking alcohol, or taking unprescribed drugs. Smoking not only may reduce milk volume, but it can harm you and your child. If you can't stop smoking, at least don't do it while nursing the baby.

Alcohol does not stimulate milk production as commonly believed and is best avoided when breast-feeding. If you do decide to drink, the National Academy of Sciences Subcommittee on Nutrition during Lactation recommends you restrict your intake to no more than 0.5 gram of alcohol per kilogram (2.2 pounds) of your weight. For a 132-pound woman, that's about 2 to 2.5 ounces of liquor, 8 ounces of table wine, or 2 cans of beer.

Stay aware of what's going on around you, too. It's easy

to get caught up in baby and forget about the rest of the world. But if you live in an area in which environmental contaminants such as mercury are a problem, stay on the alert for official advisories about foods or areas to avoid.

While breast milk is considered the best food for a newborn, it doesn't quite meet all needs. All newborns should receive vitamin K immediately after birth, regardless of whether you breast- or bottle-feed. If an infant does not get adequate exposure to sunlight, he or she may also need a vitamin D supplement each day. Fluoride supplements should be given to breast-fed infants if the fluoride content of your household drinking water is low. Follow your pediatrician's advice regarding supplementation.

Getting the hang of breast-feeding can also be difficult for first-time moms. Your nipples may be inverted, you may not hold your baby correctly, or your baby may have difficulty catching on to the whole process. Your nipples may become quite sore at first, too. If you're determined to do it, however, keep trying under the watchful eyes of your health care provider. Lesley, Marsha's daughter, just couldn't seem to latch on when she was first born. But the hospital nurses kept encouraging and guiding Marsha. Soon Lesley had it down—so well, in fact, that she became a constant nurser. But that's another story.

If you are having problems at first, don't be afraid of supplementing with a bottle. While many experts may warn against "confusing" the baby with a bottle, recent reports reveal supplementing with bottles can be crucial to the health of infants whose mothers don't produce enough milk. In such instances, prohibiting the bottle could lead to dehydration, blood clots, brain damage, and even death.

The bottom line: Work closely with your health care provider if you think your breast-feeding isn't going well. Don't delay in bringing your baby in for a checkup if you're not comfortable.

All in all, breast-feeding is a wonderfully satisfying way

to feed your baby physically, and both of you emotionally. We encourage you to give it a try.

Bottle-Feeding Is Fine, Too!

Bottle-feeding ranks as a perfectly acceptable and adequate method to nourish your baby. The time you spend holding your baby during feeding also counts toward building the emotional bond between the two of you, and toward giving your baby a loved, cared-for feeling.

Indeed, as we just discussed, some moms cannot breast-feed for a variety of reasons, such as a physical inability, the fact that Mom has to work and finds breast-feeding inconvenient, or that a mother just plain doesn't want to.

If this is your situation, you can rely on a variety of infant formulas to provide the nutrition your baby needs to get a good start in life outside the womb. Infant formulas are made from cow's milk or soy protein, which is modified to mimic the nutritional profile of breast milk as closely as possible. They come ready to feed or in concentrated liquid or powder forms (the latter is usually the least expensive; ready to feed usually costs the most). Closely follow your pediatrician's instructions for preparing infant formulas to provide your baby with optimal nutrition. Also take care to wash bottles and nipples thoroughly and properly handle and store formula to reduce baby's risk of diarrhea or other stomach upsets due to improperly handled formula.

In the end, the decision whether to nurse or bottle-feed is up to you. Be certain you make the choice based on what *you* want and are able to do, not what someone else pressures you into doing. Either choice can provide the nutrition your baby needs.

*Solving Common Nutrition Problems
During the Third Trimester*

If you need it, copy and tack this chart on your refrigerator for easy reference.

Problem	*Solution*
Gaining too much weight	Check with health care provider that it's not edema. Also alert him or her to any sudden weight gains. If it seems to be an eating problem, keep a diary to determine if and why you are overeating. Eat healthful foods in amounts recommended in the Building a Healthy Baby Nutrition Plan. Choose lean, low-fat, and skim foods whenever possible. Stay active according to advice from your health care provider. *Don't diet.* See a registered dietitian if you need help.
Edema, bloating, or swollen ankles	Sleep and rest several times a day on your left side with a pillow between your legs. Avoid tight shoes. Eat according to the Building a Healthy Baby Nutrition Plan. Continue to use salt in moderation unless your health care provider advises otherwise.

continued

Heartburn	Eat frequent, small meals. Don't overfill your stomach. Drink fluids between meals. Limit spicy and high-fat foods. Wear loose-fitting clothing. Don't lie down immediately after eating or drinking.
Constipation	Eat plenty of fiber and drink 2 to 3 quarts of fluid each day. Never use a laxative without the permission of your health care provider.
Confined to bed	Keep healthy foods close at hand in bedside cooler, if necessary. Buy healthy convenience foods such as frozen "healthy" meals, sandwich fixings, eggs, nuts, low-fat cheeses, and yogurt. Try take-out food, including grilled chicken, vegetable pizza, salads, or bean burritos. Eat plenty of fiber and fluid to avoid constipation.
Leg cramps	Eat according to the Building a Healthy Baby Nutrition Plan. Wear support hose. Contact your health care provider if cramps become problematic.

Special Concerns

I feel so bloated. My ankles have disappeared! Are you sure water pills won't help? As we mentioned before, some bloating (or edema) is a normal part of pregnancy. Your body naturally retains water as part of all the changes that go on during pregnancy. And it just doesn't make sense to try to get rid of the water your body needs. Besides, diuretics (water pills) take more than water from your body. They also cause potassium, an important mineral, to be eliminated. Never take diuretics unless your doctor advises you to.

My doctor has advised me to stay in bed for the rest of my pregnancy. How can I eat healthfully if I can't cook or even shop for food? Bed rest presents several challenges to buying, preparing, and eating healthfully, but it's vital you overcome those challenges. An adequate calorie and nutrient intake is critical for your developing baby.

Start by preparing a list of healthy foods you need for whoever will do your shopping. Include nutritious, low-fat foods that are easy to prepare and eat and that you can enjoy hot, cold, or at room temperature. Consider individual cans, bottles, or boxes of juice, fresh fruit, microwaveable frozen "healthy" meals, sandwiches with low-fat meats on whole grain bread, whole grain crackers, hard-boiled eggs, nuts, low-fat cheeses, skim milk, and low-fat or nonfat yogurt. Keep foods at your bedside for easy access; store perishable items in a cooler.

To keep your time in the kitchen and on your feet to a minimum, don't forget healthy take-out foods such as grilled chicken, vegetable and cheese pizza, salads, and bean burritos.

Because you'll be inactive, you may experience greater problems with constipation. Eat plenty of high-fiber cereals, whole grain breads, and unpeeled fruits and vegetables. Keep a pitcher of water at your bedside to make sure you get plenty of fluids.

To avoid potential problems with heartburn (it can be more of a problem when you lie down right after eating), eat only small amounts at one time. Eat more frequently as you feel hungry.

I have terrible leg cramps. Someone told me they were due to a lack of calcium. Is that true? Muscle cramps plague many women throughout pregnancy, particularly in the last trimester. Theories abound about whether they are related to deficiencies or imbalances of calcium, phosphorus, potassium, or other minerals. To date, no answers are clear. Eating according to the plan provided will give you a balanced intake of nutrients that should ward off such cramps—*if* they're nutrition-related. Wearing support hose during the day may also help.

If you do get a cramp in your calf, slowly flex your toes upward to help relieve it. Don't point your toes; this could make the cramp worse. If it does not go away, contact your health care provider.

Nutrition Checkup for the Third Trimester of Pregnancy
Copy and use this chart often to quickly assess whether you're meeting your nutritional needs during the third trimester of your pregnancy. Then fill in the blanks following each question with strategies for improving your nutritional habits if they need improving (Answer the questions based on how you ate yesterday). Set realistic, small goals for best success. Look back on previous Nutrition Checkups to see how far you've come in meeting some goals. Give yourself plenty of pats on the back for making some important changes.

1. Did you skip any meals?   Yes   No
   How I can improve this habit:

   _____

   _____

continued

2. Did you eat the minimum recommended number of servings from all five food groups (6+ breads and cereals, 5+ fruits and vegetables, 4+ milk, 3+ meat)?

                                  Yes   No

How I can improve this habit:

_____

_____

3. Did you eat several good sources of iron (fortified cereal; clams; oysters; liver; meat; eggs; fruits and vegetables, especially spinach, dried beans, peas, potatoes, raisins, dates, prunes; whole grains)?

                                  Yes   No

How I can improve this habit:

_____

_____

4. Did you eat several good sources of vitamin B_6 (fortified cereal, bananas, poultry, meat, fish, potatoes, sweet potatoes, spinach, prunes, watermelon, nuts)?

                                  Yes   No

How I can improve this habit:

_____

_____

continued

5. Did you eat several good sources of zinc (meat, poultry, seafood, chicken, eggs, whole grain breads and cereals, dried beans and peas, seeds, peanuts, yogurt)?   Yes   No
   How I can improve this habit:

   _____

   _____

6. Did you eat several good sources of magnesium (leafy greens, whole grain breads and cereals, nuts, seeds, dried beans and peas, seafood)? Yes   No
   How I can improve this habit:

   _____

   _____

7. Did you eat a good source of vitamin A (deep or-ange-yellow and dark green fruits and vegetables, fortified milk)?   Yes   No
   How I can improve this habit:

   _____

   _____

8. Did you eat a good source of vitamin C (citrus fruits, green peppers, strawberries, melon, broccoli, cabbage)?   Yes   No
   How I can improve this habit:

   _____

   _____

continued

9. Did you eat at least three servings of whole grain foods? Yes   No
   How I can improve this habit:

   _____

   _____

10. Did you choose more low-fat foods than high-fat items? Yes   No
    How I can improve this habit:

    _____

    _____

11. Did you smoke, drink alcohol, or use an unpre-scribed drug (including self-prescribed vitamin/min-eral supplements)? Yes   No
    How I can improve this habit:

    _____

    _____

12. Did you get plenty of appropriate exercise?
    Yes   No
    How I can improve this habit:

    _____

    _____

Recipe Focus: The Third Trimester

Here you are, going into the seventh month. You may be feeling very fat, worried about weight gain, and not want-ing to eat much. Or you're eating everything that passes in front of you. No matter how you feel, you still need a well-balanced diet as you head into the home stretch. Protein, vitamin B_6, calcium, and iron continue to remain very important in the final stages of development. In addition, you need magnesium and zinc, which are essential for cell division and DNA production in this time when your baby is rapidly growing. Since these nutrients are available in small quantities in foods, eating a good variety of food is especially important to ensure meeting your requirements. The recipes in this section contain many nutrients important during this last trimester. After you've worked so hard to eat right throughout your pregnancy, don't slide now, just because the end is in sight.

Grapefruit-Flavored Pear Juice

This drink contrasts the sweetness of pears with the tartness of grapefruit. It can be made ahead and given a quick shake just before drinking.

½ cup (about 1 small fruit) pear, diced, cored, peeled
½ cup pink grapefruit juice

Puree fruit in a blender until smooth. Add juice and process for another 15 seconds. Drink as is or pour over ice.

Serves 1

Recipe Options
Instead of fresh pears, use canned, drained pears.
Instead of pink juice, use regular grapefruit juice; the flavor will be the same, but the drink will not be as colorful.

Nutritional Benefits
Calories   115

Percent RDA for Pregnant Women
Magnesium	5 percent
Potassium	16 percent
Vitamin C	57 percent

Food Pyramid Servings
*Each recipe portion =
2 fruit group servings*

Food Mood
Sweet/tart flavor contrast
Pretty, pink color

Kiwi Lemonade

If tart flavors quell your nausea, then try this drink. Don't forget that drinking plenty of fluids is important, especially if you're having problems with constipation.

½ cup (about 1 large fruit) kiwi, peeled, cubed
½ cup lemonade

Puree kiwi in a blender until smooth. Add lemonade and process for another 15 seconds. Drink as is or pour over ice.

Serves 1

Recipe Option
Adds 1 teaspoon of sugar for a less tart flavor.

Nutritional Benefits
Calories   90

Percent RDA for Pregnant
Women
Potassium   10 percent
Vitamin C   69 percent

Food Pyramid Serving
Each recipe portion =
1 fruit group serving

Food Mood
Tart flavor
Pleasant, pale green color

Peaches 'n Ice Cream

This takeoff on peaches 'n' cream can either be eaten with a spoon or sipped through a straw. It's somewhere between a dessert and a beverage.

½ cup (about 1 medium fruit) peaches, peeled, cubed
¼ cup skim milk
¼ cup low-fat or fat-free vanilla ice cream
⅛ teaspoon almond extract

Puree peaches in a blender until smooth or leave slightly chunky, depending on the consistency you want. Add remaining ingredients and process for another 15 seconds.

Serves 1

Recipe Option
Instead of fresh peaches, use canned, drained peaches.

Nutritional Benefits
Calories   120

Percent RDA for Pregnant Women
Potassium   16 percent
Vitamin A   12 percent

Food Pyramid Servings
Each recipe portion =
1 fruit group serving
½ milk group serving

Food Mood
Cold, thick, sweet beverage
Fruit and cream flavor

Pumpkin Walnut Waffles

These waffles have a delightful color and texture. Use the leftover canned pumpkin to make quick bread or muffins. Or heat with nutmeg, cinnamon, and a little sugar to serve as a fast dinner side dish.

1 cup pancake or Bisquick mix
¾ skim milk
⅓ cup pumpkin, canned
1 egg
¼ cup walnuts, finely chopped
¼ teaspoon allspice

Coat waffle iron with nonstick vegetable spray and heat.

Whisk together all ingredients in a medium bowl until thoroughly combined. Pour batter into the waffle iron and cook until lightly browned. Top with maple syrup, fruit preserves, or Maple Cream, page 171. If using as a dessert, top with frozen yogurt and Warm Chocolate Sauce, page 170.

Serves 3 (each serving 2 5" x 5" waffles)

Recipe Option
Instead of allspice, use nutmeg, ground cloves, and cinnamon.

Nutritional Benefits
*(Based on 2 waffles,
no topping)*
Calories   300

Percent RDA for Pregnant
Women

Magnesium	16 percent
Thiamine	10 percent
Vitamin A	62 percent
Vitamin B$_6$	10 percent
Zinc	6 percent

Food Pyramid Servings
*Each recipe portion =
2 bread group servings*

Food Mood
Hot breakfast or dessert
Pumpkin flavor
Nutty texture

Homemade Muesli

Making your own muesli allows you to mix and match ingredients you really like. Store this in an airtight container.

4 cups Wheaties or other fortified whole grain wheat flake cereal
1 cup chopped dried dates
½ cup raisins
½ cup sliced almonds

Combine all ingredients in the container or tin you plan to store it in.

Serves 12 (each serving ½ cup)

Recipe Options
Instead of almonds, use your favorite unsalted nuts.
Add a variety of your favorite diced dried fruits.

Nutritional Benefits
Calories　　　　105

Percent RDA for Pregnant
Women

Dietary fiber	10 percent
Folic acid	2 percent
Iron	6 percent
Magnesium	6 percent
Niacin	12 percent
Riboflavin	10 percent
Vitamin A	16 percent

Food Pyramid Servings
Each recipe portion =
1 fruit group serving
⅓ bread group serving

Food Mood
Crunchy texture
Fruit, nut, and grain flavor
　　combination

Breakfast Bagel with Fruit and Veggie Spread

This nutritious and delicious spread can be made in larger quantities, covered, and stored in the refrigerator. Whenever you need something to spread on a cracker, reach for this instead of butter or margarine.

½ cup apple, unpeeled, washed, finely chopped
½ cup carrot, grated
1 tablespoon peanut butter
2 teaspoons honey
2 whole wheat bagels

In a small bowl, mix all ingredients except bagels until thoroughly combined. Toast bagels until crisp and spread mixture on bagels while still warm.

Serves 4 (½ bagel and 1 tablespoon of mixture makes 1 serving)

Recipe Option
Instead of apples and carrots, use diced pears and grated zucchini or any other favorite combinations.

Nutritional Benefits
Calories   210

Percent RDA for Pregnant
Women
Dietary fiber   16 percent
Folic acid   4 percent
Iron   7 percent
Magnesium   7 percent
Thiamine   21 percent
Vitamin A   24 percent
Zinc   4 percent

Food Pyramid Servings
Each recipe portion =
2 bread group servings
½ vegetable group serving

Food Mood
Peanut/fruit/vegetable
    flavor combination

Fruit Cup Omelet

Fruit and eggs are great breakfast foods, so why not combine them? If you're tired of vegetable or herb omelets, give this one a try.

1 egg
1 egg white
1 tablespoon water
¼ cup mixed fruits (banana, melon, peach, grapes, berries), diced

Coat 6" skillet with nonstick vegetable spray.

Whisk egg, egg white, and water in a small bowl. Heat pan, pour in egg mixture, and let it get firm. When still slightly wet on top, add fruit on one half and fold over other side, making a half-moon shape. Cook another minute and remove from pan.

Serves 1

Recipe Option
Instead of fresh fruit, use canned, well-drained fruit.

Nutritional Benefits
Calories   140

Percent RDA for Pregnant Women

Magnesium	3 percent
Protein	16 percent
Riboflavin	24 percent
Vitamin A	12 percent
Vitamin K	32 percent
Zinc	3 percent

Food Pyramid Servings
Each recipe portion =
½ meat group serving
½ fruit group serving

Food Mood
Somewhat sweet breakfast
   omelet

Beef and Mushroom Barley Soup

Soups with barley, pasta, and rice will sometimes get dry, soaking up the broth as they sit. Just add a little water prior to reheating. Adding the vinegar at the end helps reduce the amount of salt needed.

12 ounces beef chuck or other cut suitable for stew, cut into small cubes
½ cup onion, finely chopped
½ cup carrots, finely chopped
6 cups water
⅔ cup pearl barley, rinsed
1 cup mushrooms, sliced
¼ teaspoon salt
1 tablespoon white wine vinegar
Black pepper to taste

Brown beef in a large pot until all sides are evenly browned. Remove beef and sauté onion and carrots for approximately 10 minutes, scraping up any browned bits from the bottom of the pan. Add water and the beef and bring to a boil. Stir in the barley, bring to a boil again, cover, and simmer for approximately 45 minutes. Add mushrooms and salt. Cook an additional 15 minutes or until barley is done. Just prior to serving, stir in the vinegar. Season with black pepper before serving.

Serves 8 (each serving 1 cup)

Recipe Option
Instead of white wine vinegar, use regular white or cider vinegar.

Nutritional Benefits

Calories 150

Percent RDA for Pregnant Women

Dietary fiber	15 percent
Iron	6 percent
Niacin	12 percent
Protein	20 percent
Vitamin A	49 percent
Zinc	25 percent

Food Pyramid Servings

Each recipe portion =
¾ bread group serving
⅓ meat group serving
½ vegetable group serving

Food Mood

Hot, hearty soup
Starchy, filling soup
Small amount of meat

Italian Chicken Soup

If you've just roasted a whole bird, save the carcass and a small amount of white meat to make this soup. You can also use whatever vegetables you have in your refrigerator.

　1 chicken carcass
　6 cups water
½ cup carrots, finely grated
　1 cup onion, sliced
½ cup plum tomatoes, finely chopped
　2 tablespoons fresh parsley, minced
　1 garlic clove, minced
¾ teaspoon dried basil
¾ teaspoon dried oregano
¼ salt
¼ cup orzo pasta
　1 cup chicken meat, finely diced or shredded

Place carcass and water in a large pot and boil. Cover and simmer for approximately 30 minutes, skimming any foam that comes to the surface. Remove the carcass and add the carrots, onion, tomatoes, parsley, garlic, and seasonings. Bring to a boil, partially covered, and stir in pasta. Boil and stir until pasta is cooked, about 7 minutes. Add the chicken just prior to serving.

Serves 6 (each serving 1 cup)

Recipe Options
Instead of orzo, use pastina or any other tiny pasta.
Instead of chicken carcass, use a canned low sodium chicken broth and cook a 4 ounce chicken breast. Add shredded or diced meat to soup.

Nutritional Benefits

Calories 55

Percent RDA for Pregnant Women

Magnesium	4 percent
Niacin	16 percent
Vitamin C	15 percent
Vitamin A	37 percent
Zinc	2 percent

Food Pyramid Serving

Each recipe portion =
½ bread group serving

Food Mood

Starchy soup with a light
   broth
Italian-style flavors

Chilled Cantaloupe Soup

Using chilled fruit soups as a first course is a Scandinavian tradition. This can also be used as a refreshing snack and travels well, if kept cold.

2 cups cantaloupe (about 1 medium melon), peeled, cubed
2 tablespoons lime juice
1 teaspoon honey
3 tablespoons pureed strawberries or raspberries

Puree first three ingredients in a blender until you have a smooth consistency. For a pretty presentation, put soup in a bowl and drizzle pureed berries with a spoon. The color contrast is very striking.

Serves 2 (each serving ¾ cup)

Recipe Option
Instead of cantaloupe, use strawberries, raspberries, honeydew melon, or watermelon

Nutritional Benefits
Calories   70

Percent RDA for Pregnant Women
Potassium   25 percent
Vitamin A   64 percent
Vitamin C   97 percent

Food Pyramid Serving
Each recipe portion =
1 fruit group serving

Food Mood
Cold and refreshing
Smooth consistency
Melon flavor

BLT

Canadian bacon is a lower-fat alternative to regular bacon. However, it is still fairly high in sodium. If that's a problem, try two slices of bacon per sandwich, instead of three. If you need to further reduce sodium, substitute turkey for the Canadian bacon and use one strip of regular bacon, making it more like a pita club sandwich.

2 pieces of whole wheat pita bread
4 ounces Canadian bacon (6 slices)
1 tablespoon reduced-fat mayonnaise
4 lettuce leaves
4 large tomato slices, cut in half

Cut bread in half so you can fill the pockets. In a skillet, heat bacon until browned on both sides. Remove from pan and cut in half. Lightly spread mayonnaise on the inside of all 4 pockets and fill with lettuce, tomato, and bacon.

Serves 2

Recipe Option
Instead of pita, try 2 slices of whole wheat bread.

Nutritional Benefits
Calories   310

Percent RDA for Pregnant
Women
Magnesium   19 percent
Niacin   35 percent
Potassium   22 percent
Thiamine   47 percent
Vitamin C   32 percent
Zinc   13 percent

Food Pyramid Servings
Each recipe portion =
2 bread group servings
⅔ meat group serving
½ vegetable group serving

Food Mood
BLT flavors
Quick sandwich

Lemon-Sage Wild Rice Cakes

Instead of plain rice or potatoes at dinner, try these. They're also quite good for brunch with a little applesauce or a small dollop of sour cream on top.

3 cups water
1 cup brown rice, uncooked
¼ wild rice, uncooked
2 eggs, beaten
¼ cup part skim ricotta cheese
2 tablespoons flour
2 tablespoons lemon juice
1 tablespoon grated lemon zest
2 teaspoons dried sage
½ teaspoon salt

Boil water in a large pot and add both rices. Stir, bring to a boil, cover, and simmer for approximately 50 minutes until rice is cooked. Transfer to a large, shallow bowl and let cool in the refrigerator. This can all be done in advance.

Spray large skillet with nonstick vegetable spray.

Combine all remaining ingredients in a small bowl and stir into rice mixture. Heat skillet, on medium high, and use approximately 1 tablespoon of mixture for each cake. Flatten the cakes with the back of a spatula while cooking. Let the cakes thoroughly brown before turning, otherwise they will fall apart. Brown on other side.

Serves 8 (each serving 2 rice cakes)

Recipe Option
Instead of wild rice, use white rice.

Nutritional Benefits
Calories   140

Percent RDA for Pregnant
Women

Magnesium	12 percent
Niacin	9 percent
Vitamin K	6 percent
Zinc	6 percent

Food Pyramid Servings
*Each recipe portion =
1 bread group serving
½ meat group serving*

Food Mood
Lemon-sage flavor
Crunchy texture of wild
    rice

Baked Cheese and Tomato Nachos

This is much lower in fat than recipes using packaged tortilla chips, which are typically fried. Make this for parties, for your kids, or as a snack for yourself.

1 2-ounce flour tortilla
¼ cup (1 ounce) cheddar cheese, shredded
¼ cup tomato, finely chopped
2 teaspoons picante sauce or salsa

Preheat oven to 350° F. Coat baking sheet with nonstick vegetable spray.

Layer cheese, tomato, and sauce evenly over the tortilla. Cut into 8 triangles. Place on the baking sheet and bake for 10 to 15 minutes, until edges start to brown and nachos become stiff and crisp.

Serves 1

Recipe Option
Add chopped scallions and jalapeño peppers.

Nutritional Benefits		Food Pyramid Servings
Calories	320	*Each recipe portion =*
		2 bread group servings
Percent RDA for Pregnant		*¾ milk group serving*
Women		*½ vegetable group serving*
Calcium	23 percent	
Iron	7 percent	
Potassium	13 percent	**Food Mood**
Thiamine	22 percent	Crispy texture
Vitamin A	16 percent	Spicy cheese nacho flavor
Zinc	9 percent	

Rosemary Roasted Potatoes

Rosemary makes the whole kitchen smell good when you cook with it. These potatoes have so much flavor you won't even miss the fat.

  2 cups potatoes, washed, dried, cubed
  1 cup onion, cubed
  1 tablespoon dried rosemary
  ⅛ teaspoon salt
  2 teaspoons olive oil
    Black pepper to taste

Preheat oven to 400° F. Coat baking sheet with nonstick vegetable spray.

Toss potatoes and onions with seasonings on the baking sheet. Toss with oil to evenly coat mixture as much as possible. Spread out flat on the pan and roast for approximately 20 minutes or until potatoes are cooked.

Serves 4 (each serving ½ cup)

Recipe Option
Instead of dried rosemary, use 2 tablespoons fresh, minced rosemary.

Nutritional Benefits
Calories   120

Percent RDA for Pregnant Women

Dietary fiber	10 percent
Magnesium	9 percent
Potassium	33 percent
Vitamin B_6	15 percent
Zinc	3 percent

Food Pyramid Serving
*Each recipe portion =
1 vegetable group serving*

Food Mood
Strong rosemary flavor
Potato/onion combination

Sesame Noodles with Roasted Vegetables

This dish is served at room temperature or chilled. It's great for feeding lots of people. It can all be prepared ahead and actually tastes better once the flavors have developed overnight.

Sauce
¼ cup sesame oil
⅓ cup reduced-sodium soy sauce
¼ cup water
5 tablespoons sugar
4 tablespoons rice wine vinegar
2 tablespoons fresh cilantro, minced
1 tablespoon fresh ginger, grated
1 dried chili pepper, minced
2 garlic cloves, minced
1 medium eggplant
1 medium red pepper
1 medium green pepper
1 medium summer squash
1 pound angel hair pasta, vermicelli, or thin spaghetti

Preheat oven to 500° F.

Combine all sauce ingredients in a bowl and set aside. Place whole vegetables on bottom rack of oven. As skins begin to blacken, turn vegetables so they char evenly. This should take about 10 to 15 minutes. Remove from the oven and place in a brown paper bag, allowing them to cool and skins to loosen.

Meanwhile, boil water in a large pot and cook pasta until done. Drain and run under cold water in a colander.

To assemble dish, peel skins from roasted vegetables, remove seeds, and cut into strips, catching any juices and pouring them into the sauce. Put pasta into a serving bowl and toss with ½ the sauce. Add vegetables on top and pour remaining sauce over top. If not serving immediately, reserve some sauce to moisten pasta just prior to serving.

Serves 10 (each serving 1 cup)

Recipe Option
Instead of summer squash, use zucchini.

Nutritional Benefits
Calories   270

Percent RDA for Pregnant Women

Magnesium	11 percent
Niacin	24 percent
Thiamine	34 percent
Vitamin A	10 percent
Zinc	4 percent

Food Pyramid Servings
Each recipe portion =
2 bread group servings
½ vegetable group serving

Food Mood
Cold pasta salad
Sesame flavor
Roasted flavor

Moroccan Stew

This is a very hearty one-pot meal that requires long, slow cooking in the oven and can also be made in a crockpot. If stored as a leftover, it will dry up slightly, so just add some water to it before reheating.

½ pound dry lima beans, rinsed
½ pound dry chickpeas, rinsed
½ tablespoon olive oil
2 cups onion, finely chopped
2 garlic cloves, minced
½ pound lamb shoulder, trimmed, diced
2 teaspoons coriander
1½ teaspoons cumin
1 teaspoon paprika
1 cup potatoes, unpeeled, diced
1 cup carrots, cut into ½" pieces
6 cups water
1 lemon
1¼ teaspoons salt
¾ teaspoon black pepper

Put beans and chickpeas in a large pot, add 2" of water, cover, and bring to a boil. Remove from heat, let sit for at least 1 hour, and drain.

Preheat oven to 300° F.

In a large, ovenproof skillet or pan that has a lid, heat oil and sauté onions and garlic until soft. Remove mixture, heat pan again, and brown lamb. Add seasonings, potatoes, carrots, beans, onion mixture, and water and bring to a slow boil. Cover and bake for approximately 1½ hours. Squeeze 2 tablespoons of juice from lemon and reserve half. Cut up squeezed lemon. Remove cover, stir in 1 tablespoon of juice, salt, pepper, and add lemon pieces. Reduce heat to 250° F, cover, and continue baking an additional 3 hours or until water has evaporated and beans have cooked. Check the pan periodically. If mixture appears dry and beans are not yet cooked, add ¼ cup water at a time. When done, stir in remaining lemon juice.

Serves 6 (each serving 1 cup)

Recipe Options
Increase coriander and cumin if you like these flavors.
Omit lamb for a vegetarian dish.

Nutritional Benefits
Calories   520

Percent RDA for Pregnant Women

Dietary fiber	60 percent
Folic acid	62 percent
Iron	22 percent
Magnesium	30 percent
Niacin	23 percent
Potassium	61 percent
Protein	48 percent
Vitamin A	90 percent
Zinc	31 percent

Food Guide Pyramid
Each recipe portion =
1 meat group serving
1 vegetable group serving

Food Mood
Filling, bean dish
Small amount of meat

Jambalaya

We use turkey sausage to reduce the fat content of this one-dish meal. This New Orleans–style dish is very flavorful, but not spicy.

    6 ounces (about 3 links) turkey sausage
    1 pound chicken breasts, boneless, skinless
    1 teaspoon olive oil
    1 cup onions, chopped
 ½ cup green peppers, chopped
 ½ cup red peppers, chopped
    2 garlic cloves, minced
    2 cups plum tomatoes, diced
    1 13-ounce can reduced-sodium chicken broth
1¼ cups water
    1 tablespoon paprika
 ½ teaspoon salt
    1 bay leaf
1½ cups white rice, long grain

Coat large skillet with nonstick vegetable spray. Heat skillet and brown sausage on all sides. Remove from pan and dice. Brown chicken on all sides, remove from pan, and dice. Heat oil and sauté onions, peppers, and garlic until soft. Add tomatoes, broth, water, and seasonings and bring to a boil. Stir in rice, bring to a boil again, and add sausage. Reduce heat to a simmer, cover, and cook for approximately 30 minutes or until rice is tender and liquid has evaporated. If mixture appears too dry and rice has not yet cooked, add a small amount (about ¼ cup) of water. Stir in chicken just before removing from heat.

Serves 6 (each serving 1 cup)

Recipe Option
Instead of turkey sausage, use 4 ounces of pork sausage.

Nutritional Benefits
Calories   275

Percent RDA for Pregnant
Women

Magnesium	11 percent
Niacin	51 percent
Potassium	19 percent
Protein	32 percent
Vitamin B_6	23 percent
Vitamin C	49 percent
Zinc	10 percent

Food Pyramid Servings
Each recipe portion =
1½ bread group servings
1 meat group serving
1 vegetable group serving

Food Mood
One-dish meal
Starchy rice dinner
Small pieces of meat

Tea Smoked Cornish Hens

This cooking method also works great with pork and seafood. It imparts lots of flavor without any added fat. Using a wok is the easiest way to prepare this dish, but any large pot or pan will do.

½ cup reduced-sodium soy sauce
1 tablespoon water
1 tablespoon fresh grated ginger
2 1½-pound cornish hens, skin removed
½ cup loose Chinese tea
1 tablespoon brown sugar, packed
1 teaspoon anise *or* fennel seeds

Combine soy sauce, water, and ginger in a pan big enough to hold the 2 hens. Thoroughly coat hens in the marinade, cover, and refrigerate for at least 1 hour. Line a wok with foil and place tea, sugar, and seeds in the bottom of the foil. Crisscross 4 wooden chopsticks in the wok, making a rack for the hens to sit on. When ready to cook, place the wok on the heating ring, cover, and turn on high heat until you start to see a little smoke. Remove hens from the marinade and place on the wooden rack. Cover and smoke, on high heat, for approximately 20 minutes. Remove hens, place on a baking sheet, and finish cooking in a 350° F oven until juices run clear and meat is no longer pink. (You don't want the hens to get overwhelmed with the smoked flavor; that's why we finish cooking them in the oven.) When done, carve hens in half.

Serves 4

Recipe Option
Instead of Chinese tea, cut open regular or herbal tea bags and use the loose tea.

Nutritional Benefits
Calories   150

Percent RDA for Pregnant
Women
Iron   16 percent
Magnesium   11 percent
Niacin   66 percent
Protein   50 percent
Vitamin B$_6$ 35 percent
Zinc   6 percent

Food Pyramid Servings
Each recipe portion =
1½ meat group servings

Food Mood
Oriental flavors
Smoked flavor

Herbed Pork Loin

Nothing could be easier than this dish, which can be cooked outside on the grill or in the oven. While a pork loin may seem an expensive cut of meat, there's no fat or bone, so there's absolutely no waste.

12 ounces boneless pork loin
 1 teaspoon Dijon mustard
$\frac{1}{2}$ teaspoon dried sage
$\frac{1}{2}$ teaspoon dried rosemary
$\frac{1}{4}$ teaspoon dried thyme
$\frac{1}{4}$ teaspoon onion powder
$\frac{1}{4}$ teaspoon garlic powder
$\frac{1}{8}$ teaspoon black pepper

Preheat oven to 350° F.

Place pork loin on a baking sheet and, with the back of a spoon, rub mustard over the meat. In a small bowl, combine the remaining ingredients and pat on the meat. Roast for approximately 15 minutes until center is cooked to desired doneness, at least medium. Remove from oven and let rest for 5 minutes before slicing.

Serves 4 (each serving 3 ounces)

Recipe Option
Mix and match other spice and herb combinations such as cumin and coriander or tarragon and parsley.

Nutritional Benefits
Calories   150

Percent RDA for Pregnant Women

Magnesium	7 percent
Niacin	31 percent
Protein	37 percent
Vitamin B$_6$	25 percent
Zinc	15 percent

Food Pyramid Servings
*Each recipe portion =
1$\frac{1}{3}$ meat group servings*

Food Mood
Lean, roasted pork
Herb flavor

Tangerine Beef

Fruit and meat make a wonderful combination. This recipe can be done outside on the grill or in your oven broiler, and it goes nicely with rice pilaf.

  1 cup orange juice
  2 teaspoons honey
  1 pound beef top round, cut into ½" cubes, trimmed
1½ cups red onion, cut into small cubes
  2 tangerines, peeled, sectioned, pits removed
     Black pepper to taste

Combine orange juice and honey in a shallow bowl. Add beef, cover, and refrigerate for 1 to 2 hours. When ready to cook, alternate pieces of beef, onion, and tangerine onto 8 wooden or metal skewers. Season with pepper, if desired. Grill on high heat or in oven broiler for approximately 5 to 7 minutes until meat is cooked.

Serves 4

Recipe Option
Instead of tangerines, use orange sections.

Nutritional Benefits
(Based on 2 skewers)

Calories   200

Percent RDA for Pregnant Women

Magnesium	12 percent
Niacin	31 percent
Potassium	20 percent
Protein	45 percent
Vitamin B6	25 percent
Zinc	32 percent

Food Pyramid Servings
Each recipe portion =
1 meat group serving
½ fruit group serving

Food Mood
Small amounts of meat
Grilled or broiled meat
Citrus flavor

Veal Paprika Stroganoff

This simple dish serves two, but can easily be doubled for four servings. The cholesterol content is slightly high due to the egg noodles and veal, so consider it a bit of a splurge.

6 ounces veal shank, trimmed, cut into small cubes
½ cup onion, diced
1 cup water
½ tablespoon paprika
¼ teaspoon salt
⅛ teaspoon black pepper
4 ounces egg noodles, dry
½ teaspoon cornstarch
¼ cup light sour cream
Fresh parsley, if desired

In a medium saucepan, brown the veal on all sides. Remove the meat and sauté onions in the film of fat left in the pan. Return meat to pan, add water and seasonings, and cover. Simmer for approximately 1½ hours until meat is fork-tender. Shortly before serving, boil water and cook noodles until done. Mix the cornstarch with a tablespoon or two of water and stir into the meat mixture until thickened. Stir in sour cream and remove from heat. Portion noodles into shallow soup bowls or plates and top with stroganoff. Garnish with fresh parsley or other green herb.

Serves 2 (1 cup noodles, ¾ cup meat/sauce equals 1 serving)

Recipe Option
Instead of egg noodles, use small pasta such as bow ties or ziti to reduce the cholesterol.

Nutritional Benefits
Calories   440

Percent RDA for Pregnant
Women

Folic acid	7 percent
Iron	12 percent
Magnesium	20 percent
Niacin	69 percent
Protein	73 percent
Thiamine	45 percent
Zinc	35 percent

Food Pyramid Servings
Each recipe portion =
2 bread group servings
1 meat group serving

Food Mood
Traditional, stroganoff-style
   dish
Creamy sauce

Fish Under a Meringue Blanket

Here's a different way to serve baked fish. We usually think of meringue as being on desserts, but why not use it at dinner? The meringue coating keeps the fish from drying out and makes a pretty presentation.

1 cup nonfat plain yogurt
2 teaspoons prepared horseradish
$\frac{1}{2}$ teaspoon garlic powder
2 egg whites
$\frac{1}{2}$ teaspoon sugar
4 4-ounce flounder fillets or other white-fleshed, mild-tasting fish
Dill, parsley, chervil, *or* other green herb to taste

Place yogurt in a cheesecloth or strong paper towels and suspend over a cup, allowing it to drip for 6 hours in the refrigerator. The result is a firm-textured yogurt cheese.

Preheat oven to 425° F. Coat baking sheet with nonstick vegetable spray.

Combine yogurt cheese with horseradish and garlic powder in a medium bowl. In a separate bowl, beat egg whites to soft speaks, add sugar, and continue beating to stiff peaks. Gently fold the egg whites into the yogurt mixture until all ingredients are combined. Spread mixture over fillets. Bake for approximately 10 minutes until meringue is lightly browned. Remove from oven and sprinkle with chopped dill, parsley, or your favorite green herb.

Serves 4

Recipe Option
Instead of horseradish, use Dijon mustard.

Nutritional Benefits

Calories 155

Percent RDA for Pregnant Women

Magnesium	22 percent
Niacin	14 percent
Potassium	24 percent
Protein	50 percent
Zinc	6 percent

Food Pyramid Servings

Each recipe portion =
1⅓ meat group servings

Food Mood

Seafood

Strong, savory horseradish
flavor

Bouillabaise

The rich flavor of this soup is enhanced simply by using the shrimp shells to make the stock.

½ pound shrimp, shells on
 6 cups water
 1 bay leaf
 1 cup onion, diced
½ cup celery, diced
 1 cup plum tomatoes, diced
12 ounces swordfish, cut into bite-size cubes
 1 teaspoon dried thyme

Peel shrimp and put peels, water, and bay leaf in a large pot. Bring to a boil, partially covered, and simmer for 30 minutes. Using a strainer, strain broth to get it as clear as possible. Put broth into a clean pot and add onion, celery, and tomato. Partially cover and simmer for 15 minutes until vegetables are tender. Add fish, shrimp, and thyme, cover and turn off heat. Let sit for 5 to 8 minutes until seafood is cooked. Serve in bowls.

Serves 4 (each serving 1½ cups)

Recipe Option
Instead of swordfish, use halibut or other favorite firm-fleshed fish.

Nutritional Benefits
Calories   190

Percent RDA for Pregnant
Women
Iron	6 percent
Magnesium	17 percent
Niacin	60 percent
Potassium	30 percent
Vitamin B$_6$	20 percent
Vitamin K	23 percent
Zinc	11 percent

Food Pyramid Servings
Each recipe portion =
1⅓ meat group servings
1 vegetable group serving

Food Mood
Light, clear broth
Seafood soup

Spinach Fettuccine with Clam and Parsley Sauce

Clam sauce is often made with lots of oil, but not this version. It's a colorful, filling dish with big flavors.

1 6½-ounce can clams, chopped, with juice
1 cup chicken broth, reduced-sodium, canned
⅔ cup fresh parsley, minced
½ cup red pepper, diced
1 teaspoon dried basil
2 garlic cloves, minced
12 ounces spinach fettuccine
2 tablespoons grated Parmesan cheese

Combine all ingredients except fettuccine and cheese in a medium saucepan. Simmer for 15 minutes.

Meanwhile, boil water in a large pot and cook pasta until done. Drain and portion into 4 bowls or plates. Evenly divide sauce over each portion, tossing to coat pasta. Sprinkle cheese over top.

Serves 4 (each serving 1½ cups)

Recipe Options
Instead of spinach, use plain fettuccine.
Instead of dried basil, use fresh basil and increase to 1 tablespoon.

Nutritional Benefits
Calories   310

Percent RDA for Pregnant Women

Magnesium	25 percent
Protein	30 percent
Riboflavin	27 percent
Thiamine	27 percent
Vitamin C	50 percent
Zinc	12 percent

Food Pyramid Servings
*Each recipe portion =
3 bread group servings*

Food Mood
Pasta
Strong (clam, cheese)
    flavors

Double Cornbread with Chives

This goes well with soups, as a snack, or enjoy a square for breakfast. The corn kernels provide texture while the chives add a nice touch of color.

1¼ cups all-purpose flour
¾ cup yellow cornmeal
2 tablespoons sugar
1½ teaspoons baking powder
1 egg, beaten
2 tablespoons vegetable oil
¾ cup fresh or frozen, thawed corn
2 tablespoons chives, minced

Preheat oven to 400° F. Coat 8" square pan with nonstick vegetable spray.

Combine flour, cornmeal, sugar, and baking powder in a medium bowl. Stir in remaining ingredients, except chives, until well moistened. Stir in chives last and pour into pan. Bake for 30 to 35 minutes or until golden. Let cornbread cool slightly before cutting.

Serves 9

Recipe Option
Instead of chives, use scallions.

Nutritional Benefits
Calories   170

Percent RDA for Pregnant Women

Dietary fiber	10 percent
Magnesium	4 percent
Riboflavin	12 percent
Thiamine	15 percent
Zinc	2 percent

Food Pyramid Servings
*Each recipe portion =
2 bread group servings*

Food Mood
Crumbly, cornbread texture
Slight chive flavor

Irish Soda Bread

This crusty-topped bread has lots of flavor with little fat. You may have already removed your rings during this pregnancy, due to puffy fingers. If not, you'll certainly want to take off your rings before starting this recipe as the dough is extremely sticky.

    4 cups all-purpose flour
    2 tablespoons sugar
    1 tablespoon baking powder
 ¾ teaspoon baking soda
 ½ teaspoon salt
    2 tablespoons butter, softened
    1 egg, beaten (1 tablespoon reserved)
1¾ cups low-fat buttermilk
    1 cup raisins
    1 tablespoon caraway seeds

Preheat oven to 357° F. Coat 1-quart casserole or 8" round pie pan with nonstick vegetable spray. Heavily flour countertop.

In a large bowl, combine first 5 ingredients. Cut in butter with 2 knives or pastry blender until crumbly. With a wooden spoon, stir egg and buttermilk into dry mixture. Add raisins and caraway seeds. Dough will be very sticky. Turn dough onto floured countertop and knead a few times. Shape into a ball and place in the casserole and, with a knife, cut a cross on top. Brush reserved egg on top. Bake for 40 minutes, reduce heat to 350° F, and bake an additional 30 minutes or until skewer inserted in the center comes out clean. Cool before slicing.

Serves 16

Recipe Option
Omit caraway seeds if you don't like them.

Nutritional Benefits
Calories   175

Percent RDA for Pregnant Women
Calcium	8 percent
Iron	5 percent
Magnesium	4 percent
Niacin	1 percent
Thiamine	18 percent
Zinc	2 percent

Food Pyramid Servings
Each recipe portion =
1½ bread group servings
½ fruit group serving

Food Mood
Traditional Irish bread
Raisin/caraway flavor

Apricot Upside Down Cake

Here's a new twist on the traditional pineapple version. We've reduced the fat and used whole wheat flour to boost the fiber content. Substituting apricots for pineapple increases the vitamin A content of the recipe.

1 tablespoon butter
2 tablespoons brown sugar, packed
1 17-ounce can apricot halves, juice pack, drained (reserve juice)
1 cup all-purpose flour
2/3 cup whole wheat flour
1/2 teaspoon baking powder
1/2 teaspoon baking soda
1/3 cup sugar
1/4 teaspoon ground ginger
1/4 teaspoon cinnamon
1 cup skim milk
1 egg, beaten
1/2 cup reserved apricot juice
2 tablespoons vegetable oil
1 teaspoon vanilla

Preheat oven to 350° F. Coat 10" cast-iron skillet with non-stick vegetable spray.

Melt butter and brown sugar in the skillet over low heat. Spread the mixture over entire surface and lay apricot halves, round side down, in skillet. Set aside.

Combine all dry ingredients in a large bowl. Combine wet ingredients in a small bowl. Stir wet ingredients into dry until thoroughly combined. Evenly pour batter over fruit in skillet and bake for approximately 40 minutes or until golden. Remove from oven, slightly cool, and loosen edges of cake from pan. Place a large plate over the skillet and invert cake onto plate. If some fruit or cake sticks to skillet bottom, carefully remove and place it where it belongs.

Serves 8

Recipe Option
Instead of apricots, use peach halves.

Nutritional Benefits
Calories   200

Percent RDA for Pregnant
Women
Dietary fiber   10 percent
Magnesium   7 percent
Vitamin A   15 percent
Vitamin K   13 percent
Zinc   4 percent

Food Pyramid Servings
*Each recipe portion =
2 bread group servings*

Food Mood
Sweet, traditional-style
    cake
Brown, sugary coating
Apricots

Plum Crumble

The crumble topping makes this dessert seem rich and decadent, but it's really low in fat. Substitute any mixture of seasonal fruit except citrus.

2 cups fresh purple plums, pitted, cubed
2 cups Granny Smith apples, unpeeled, cubed
2 tablespoons all-purpose flour
2 tablespoons sugar

Topping
½ cup whole wheat flour
½ cup all-purpose flour
½ cup sugar
1 teaspoon orange peel
1 teaspoon cinnamon
½ teaspoon nutmeg
1 tablespoon margarine, softened
½ tablespoon vegetable oil
3 tablespoons skim milk
1 teaspoon vanilla

Preheat oven to 350° F.

Place fruits, flour, and sugar in a 10" deep-dish pie pan. Toss until thoroughly combined and spread out.

In a medium bowl, combine all dry ingredients for topping and cut in margarine with 2 knives or pastry blender.

In a cup, combine oil, milk, and vanilla, and stir into topping with a fork until crumbly. Spoon this over fruit mixture. Bake for 50 to 60 minutes until fruit is bubbly. Slightly cool before serving.

Serves 10

Recipe Option
*Instead of fresh plums, use drained, canned plums packed
in water or light syrup.*

Nutritional Benefits
Calories   150

Percent RDA for Pregnant
Women

Dietary fiber	10 percent
Magnesium	4 percent
Niacin	6 percent
Potassium	8 percent
Riboflavin	7 percent
Zinc	2 percent

Food Pyramid Servings
Each recipe portion =
¾ fruit group serving
½ bread group serving

Food Mood
Comfort dessert
Crunchy, crumbly topping
Soft, cooked fruit filling

Oatmeal Raisin Chocolate Chip Cookies

Because these cookies are so low in fat, they have a soft, chewy consistency as compared to a crisp cookie texture. Since low-fat baked goods dry out more quickly, store them in an airtight container.

1 egg
½ cup low-fat vanilla-flavored yogurt
1½ tablespoons vanilla
¼ cup vegetable oil
½ cup brown sugar
¼ cup sugar
1 cup old-fashioned oats
1½ cups cake flour
1 teaspoon baking soda
1 teaspoon cinnamon
¼ teaspoon nutmeg
¼ teaspoon ground cloves
½ cup raisins
⅓ cup semisweet chocolate chip mini-morsels

Preheat oven to 350° F. Coat baking sheet with nonstick vegetable spray.

In a small bowl, whisk the egg, yogurt, and vanilla and gradually whisk in oil. In a large bowl, combine all remaining ingredients except raisins and chocolate chips. Stir the wet ingredients into the dry, using a wooden spoon, until thoroughly combined. Stir in raisins and chocolate chips last. Using approximately ½ tablespoon for each cookie, drop dough onto the baking sheet. Bake for 10 to 12 minutes or until bottoms are lightly browned. Don't expect the cookie tops to brown a great deal. Check the bottom of the cookies to determine when they're done. Remove from pan and cool on wire racks.

Makes 5 dozen cookies.

Recipe Option
Omit chocolate chips and increase raisins.

Nutritional Benefits
(Per cookie)
Calories   50

These cookies do not provide any significant nutritional contribution on a per serving basis, but are a good source of complex carbohydrates. Moderate in calories and low in fat, they are a healthful sweet treat for you and your family.

Food Pyramid Servings
Each recipe portion = ½ bread group serving

Food Mood
Low-fat cookie
Raisin/chocolate chip flavor

CHAPTER SEVEN

One-Handed Living

How many times did baby wake up last night? When Marsha's daughter, Lesley, was born, she slept like a dream, regularly snoozing through the night at seven weeks old. Jake, Marsha's second child, started with colds and ear infections at two weeks old. Marsha and her husband gave up sleep for the next two years—and that was just the nighttime activity! It's trite but true: Once you have children, your life is never the same again.

Of course, it's not all drudgery by any means. Those first sweet smiles (or was that gas?) and gurgles warm even the most tired parent's heart. And when your child begins to know who you are . . . well, there's no doubt you'd never choose to go back to things the way they were.

If this is your first child, you may feel like you just enrolled in a crash course in parenting. You're busy learning technical details—how to nurse or bottle-feed and burp your baby, change diapers, bathe him, clip nails, dress her comfortably—the list goes on. You're probably also spending a lot of time running back and forth to the bassinet or crib to make certain your child is still breathing. Yes, we all do that.

If you have other children, you're hard at work fitting the needs and demands of your new baby into an already hectic and overloaded schedule. Regardless of your specific situation, you likely share one problem common to many post-partum moms. That is finding the time to take care of yourself while you take care of everyone else.

We've written this chapter to help you do just that. We guide you in meeting your nutritional needs during this time and outline a sensible approach to managing postpartum weight worries. We also include more information about feeding your baby, in preparation for when you begin to introduce solid foods. Finally, we've developed especially easy yet nutritious recipes that you can cook with one hand. It's an art all moms find useful.

Nutritional Investments

Certainly you face tremendous demands on your time and energy during the first few months after birth (and later). That means good nutrition is as important now as it ever was. Without a solid foundation of nutrient-rich foods to sustain you, you just won't have the get-up-and-go you need. In addition, if you're breast-feeding, you still need to choose your diet wisely to make certain you get the nutrition both you and your baby need.

If you're not breast-feeding, your nutritional needs return to normal. You can go back to a minimum of two servings from the milk group each day (if you're twenty-four years of age or younger, you need at least three servings a day). You'll probably need fewer calories than when you were pregnant, too; we'll discuss that in the next section. The rest of your diet remains essentially the same. Eat a wide variety of foods as outlined in the Food Guide Pyramid (see page 17) to get the nutrition and energy you need. It's important, too, to get plenty of rest to keep yourself going.

If you are breast-feeding, your requirement for several nutrients increases. That makes sense since you'll produce about a pint of milk a day at first, which will increase to about a quart a day as your baby grows and needs more. To make this milk and stay healthy yourself, you need a diet brimming with essential nutrients. By no means does this mean your diet has to be perfect in order for you to feed your baby well. To a large extent, nature guarantees breast milk will supply an infant with the nutrition he or she needs for proper growth, even if the mother does not eat well. Necessary nutrients are simply drawn from the mother's body. But these aren't excess nutrients stored in your body in case you need them some time in the future—they are stores you need right now for healthy bones, teeth, organs, your whole body. To stay healthy yourself, you must get these extra nutrients from the foods you eat.

You also need more calories (again, we'll get to that later) and fluid when you're breast-feeding. Drink often, and be certain to drink whenever you are thirsty. Don't forget calorie-free water—it's a great thirst-quencher.

Meeting these increased nutrient needs remains relatively simple, however. Just eat according to the Building a Healthy Baby Nutrition Plan for Breast-feeding Moms that follows. Copy it and post it on your refrigerator for quick and easy reference. It emphasizes eating enough to ensure a healthy supply of milk along with a healthy you. It also pays special attention to several nutrients experts have singled out for concern in a breast-feeding woman's diet. That's because many American women just don't get enough of these vitamins and minerals, whether they are breast-feeding or not.

The nutrients include calcium, zinc, magnesium, vitamin B_6, and folic acid. They're mighty important. For example, as we mentioned above, if you don't get enough calcium in your diet when you're breast-feeding, it's pulled from your bones to guarantee enough in your breast milk. That puts you at a higher risk for osteoporosis, a crippling disease that affects many women in later life. Review the sections on these nutrients in previous chapters to make sure you know how to choose foods to meet your need for these important nutrients.

The Building Your Baby Nutrition Plan
for Breast-feeding Moms

As before, the Food Guide Pyramid continues as your basic guide. Review the information on pages 16–21. Then:

- Eat a wide variety of nutrient-dense foods from the five food groups each day. Review Choosing Smart from Each Food Group on page 23.
- Consume four or more servings each day from the milk group. If you don't, eat more high-calcium foods (see page 113). You also may need supplements of calcium and vitamin D. Talk with your health care provider.
- Eat at least three servings each day from the meat group (7 to 8 ounces total).
- Eat plenty of whole grain breads and cereals (especially fortified cereals) and deep yellow-orange and green vegetables. Try leafy greens, cantaloupe, carrots, sweet potatoes, green peppers, and winter squash.
- Eat at least 1800 calories a day to help maintain milk production and supply your baby and yourself with important nutrients. Avoid weight loss diets; let your hunger guide you in how much you eat.
- Choose low-fat and lean items from each group to keep fat intake moderate.
- Drink plenty of fluids—you need more when you're breastfeeding. Try water, milk, juice, and soup.
- Limit coffee and other caffeinated beverages such as cola to no more than 1 to 2 cups daily. Caffeine passes into the milk.
- Do not drink alcohol. Beer does *not* help you produce more milk.

continued

- When your health care provider says it's okay (usually not before 4 to 6 weeks postpartum), continue following the activity program you followed while you were pregnant.
- Get plenty of rest.

If I Eat Like This, Will I Ever Return to My Normal Size?

After years of dieting, the automatic inclination for most American women whenever they feel too fat is to cut back drastically on how much they eat. But now is definitely *not* the time to go on a diet (if there ever *is* a time to go on one). You may worry about those extra inches around your waist, but give yourself a break. Your body can return to almost normal without any extreme measures on your part.

We say *almost normal* because women average a permanent gain of about two pounds with each pregnancy. And many women testify that their bodies were never the same again after pregnancy. The changes aren't necessarily gigantic—it may be that your stomach is never quite as flat as it once was or your breasts don't resist gravity quite as much. But these changes appear final, which indicates the smart course probably is to accept it and go on with your life.

Of course, that doesn't mean you need to carry around an extra ten, twenty or more pounds just because you had a baby. While some women don't lose weight, and even gain it postpartum, that may be more due to lifestyle and behavioral issues rather than any physiological change in their bodies. When baby arrived, they may have cut out their regular exercise classes or formed new eating habits such as eating whenever baby eats, which resulted in too many calories.

You can lose most of the extra pounds and inches by following a sound approach, which is a weight management principle that applies regardless of your situation, i.e., whether you're pregnant, breast-feeding, or your usual self. That approach reduces down (pun intended) to sensible eating, which means not starving yourself and eating foods you like as well as particularly healthful foods, learning how to cope with your emotions in ways other than eating, and staying active.

Above all, resist the temptation to compare yourself to your friends, especially those who seemed to regain their figure immediately after they gave birth. For most women, it's a slow process that doesn't happen overnight. Instead, it's a gradual loss of pounds and inches that may take months. It can be helped, but not necessarily speeded up, with healthy eating and exercise.

Putting Your Body Back Together: Tips for
Bottle-feeding Moms

If you're not breast-feeding, your calorie needs drop by about 300 calories a day compared to your pregnancy requirements. But don't start counting calories. Follow the prime directive: Pay attention to what your body is telling you. If you feel hungry, eat. (Be certain, however, that it's hunger gnawing at your stomach instead of anxiety, anger, or other emotions.) Trust your body to find its own way back to normal. The following tips will help.

- Continue to choose smart from the Food Guide Pyramid, eating no less than the minimum recommended servings each day. Let your hunger guide how much more you eat.
- Limit the number of high-fat foods you eat. Remember, it may be important *not* to eliminate such foods. By prohibiting them, you may find yourself wanting—and eating—them even more.

continued

- Remember to eat at least three meals a day, starting with a hearty breakfast. Whole grain cereals and bread, skim milk, and fresh fruit or juice give you a healthy, hearty, and quick start for a busy day.
- Snacks can be important, too. A planned snack between meals can help curb your hunger to ward off random snacking on high-fat foods and overeating at regular mealtimes. Keep it simple for convenience' sake.
- Stay active. Many of the limitations that applied during pregnancy remain four to six weeks postpartum. Reread the section on page 50 to refresh yourself about safe exercise, and check with your doctor. Resume your prepregnancy exercise routines gradually and only with your doctor's permission.
- If you've struggled with your weight in the past and/or feel tempted to drastically diet, reread the section on managing weight when you're pregnant (see pages 45–47). The basic principles apply whether you're pregnant or not. Or seek the help of a registered dietitian who specializes in helping people manage weight without dieting.

You're Not Done Yet:
Tips for Breast-feeding Moms

While breast-feeding can be a messy situation at times, there are plenty of silver linings in the process. Just one of them—and a minor one, at that—is the fact that some breast-feeding women may lose more weight than women who choose to bottle-feed. It seems the hormone prolactin, which regulates milk production, may also assist in weight loss. A recent study showed women who breast-fed during their child's first year lost about four pounds more on average than moms who bottle-fed. Other studies, however, reveal little difference in the weight losses of nursing or nonnursing moms. Some even indicate up to 20 percent of breast-feeding women maintain or gain weight.

These conflicting findings point to something experts have known about weight management for some time. What works for some people has no effect for others. It's all highly individual.

We are certain, however, that now is *not* the time to consider a diet. Here's some information to help you heed that advice. It can also increase the likelihood you'll be a part of the 80 percent of nursing moms who lose at least some of the extra weight they gained when they were pregnant.

continued

- Breast-feeding women typically lose weight at the rate of about 1 to 2 pounds a month during the first six months after birth (that doesn't include the weight lost during the first month—it's usually at a much higher rate). If a breast-feeding mom is overweight, she may lose up to about 4 pounds a month without adversely affecting her milk production, but she should stay alert for any signs that her child's appetite is not being satisfied. If you were underweight before pregnancy, check with your health care provider if you continue to lose past your prepregnancy weight. After the first month postpartum, any woman losing more than 4.5 pounds a month may not produce enough milk to satisfy her infant.

- To ensure healthy nutrition for you and your baby, eat according to the Building a Healthy Baby Nutrition Plan for Breast-feeding Moms. Eat according to your hunger level, but don't eat less than is recommended. Most women who breast-feed can eat more calories than they did before they were pregnant without gaining weight.

- Your nutritional status may affect your child's nutrition, growth and development, and incidence of illness. Studies indicate you may risk inadequate intakes of important nutrients such as calcium, zinc, magnesium, vitamin B_6, and folic acid on diets that contain less than 1500 calories a day. Further, to help ensure adequate milk production, you need to eat at least 1800 calories a day. Don't begin to obsess on, or even regularly count, calories, but if you feel you need a quite estimate, check page 20 for the average calorie content of foods in the different food groups.

continued

- Limit the number of high-fat foods you eat. Remember, it may be important not to eliminate such foods. By prohibiting them, you may find yourself wanting—and eating—them even more.
- Remember to eat at least three meals a day, starting with a hearty breakfast. Whole grain cereals and bread, skim milk, and fresh fruit or juice give you a healthy, hearty, and quick start for a busy day.
- Snacks can be important, too. A planned snack between meals can help curb your hunger to keep you from random snacking on high-fat foods and overeating at regular mealtimes. Keep it simple for convenience' sake.
- Stay active to help keep your calorie requirements above the number of calories you eat. That's the only way you'll lose weight as time goes on. You can gain benefits from regular exercise without affecting the quality or quantity of your breast milk. But many of the limitations that applied during pregnancy remain four to six weeks postpartum. Reread the section on page 50 to refresh yourself about safe exercise, and check with your doctor. Resume your prepregnancy exercise routines gradually and only with your doctor's permission.
- If you've struggled with your weight in the past and/ or feel tempted to drastically diet, reread the section on managing weight when you're pregnant (see pages 45–47). The basic principles also apply when you're breast-feeding. Or seek the help of a registered dietitian who specializes in helping people manage weight without dieting.

Look Who's Coming to Dinner

By now you've probably already made your decision whether to breast-feed. Depending on when you read this chapter, you may be well established on either course. The questions and answers at the end of this chapter cover a few of the concerns that may arise as you breast-feed.

We've devoted this section to giving you vital information about the next step in feeding your baby. First, however, there are a couple of things you need to know about adequately feeding your baby before he or she starts eating solid foods. Number one, if you are breast-feeding, the American Academy of Pediatrics recommends you supplement your baby's diet with vitamin D and fluoride starting at birth, and with iron starting at about four months of age. Your pediatrician will prescribe supplements in amounts that are right for your baby. Iron can be obtained either through supplements (again, use a prescribed supplement) or with iron-fortified cereal.

If you are feeding your baby by bottle, use iron-fortified formula. Fluoride supplementation may also be necessary if your water supply is not fluoridated.

At about four months, your baby is also ready for solid foods, which provide other important nutrients not found in breast milk or formula, such as zinc and copper.

You'll know it's time to start solid foods when you see your baby:

- Has doubled his or her birthweight
- Nurses eight to ten times a day or drinks more than 32 ounces of formula
- Is six months old
- Has greater physical control over his or her body and seems to be seeking new sensory experiences, such as exploring her hands or putting teethers and toys in his mouth

Dining with Baby

- Start with soft, smooth foods that require no chewing. Try single-ingredient items such as iron-fortified infant cereals and strained vegetables and fruits in very small amounts (one teaspoon).

- Mix cereal with breast milk or formula to a very thin consistency at first. As your baby becomes more experienced, make cereal thicker to both encourage her development and provide more food.

- Offer new foods one at a time, then wait about one week before introducing another new food. Watch for symptoms of food allergies such as gas, diarrhea, colic, wheezing, or skin rashes. Most common food allergens are egg whites, peanut and other nut butters, citrus, dairy products, wheat, fish, and chocolate. If your child seems to react to any food, contact your pediatrician.

- Expect initial refusal of new tastes and textures. Keep offering new foods along with familiar items.

- Start with one feeding of solid foods a day, and work up to your family's meal schedule by baby's first birthday. Plan on snacks to get him through the long period between meals—he can't eat a lot at one time.

- Avoid foods such as hot dogs, peanuts and other nuts, grapes, raw carrots, apple pieces, raisins, seeds, and round, hard, or sticky candies that may cause choking in infants and young children. Nuts and seeds are not recommended for children younger than four years of age. Even plain peanut butter can be hard for some children to swallow; dress it up with jelly or mashed bananas. Also stay away from honey and corn syrup; they can contain botulinum spores that are harmful to infants.

continued

- Do not add salt or sugar to commercial or home-prepared food.
- Encourage self-feeding as times goes on. Start with easy-to-handle, bite-size foods such as Cheerios.
- Store unopened jars and packages of commercial baby food and juices in a dry, cool spot. Pay attention to the date stamped on the package. Store opened jars covered in the refrigerator, and use them within two to three days.
- Make mealtimes pleasurable. Remember that food supplies more than nutrition—it's also a source of enjoyment. Be careful not to pressure your child. Make certain there are plenty of nutritious foods available, but let her decide how much she will eat. Children have great internal regulation systems that work well to provide them with good nutrition if the proper food is available. If you try to force a child to eat, you may set up a situation in which he rebels, turns mealtimes into nightmares, and may eventually develop disordered eating habits.
- Give vitamin/mineral supplements as prescribed by your pediatrician. In particular, your child needs a source of fluoride to build strong teeth and bones, whether it be fluoridated water or supplements.

Now is also the time to set the stage for a lifetime of healthy eating for your child. As she grows older, feed her according to the Food Guide Pyramid. Offer her plenty of whole grain foods, beans and other legumes, fruits and vegetables, and moderate amounts of dairy foods and meat, poultry, or fish. *Do not limit fat intake for children under two years of age*. They need a certain amount of fat in their diets for proper development.

Children love sweets, and don't feel as if you need to eliminate them from your child's diet. Sugars alone provide calories and little else nutritionally, but many children need the extra calories. Foods such as oatmeal cookies, frozen yogurt, and presweetened breakfast cereals can satisfy a child's sweet tooth while providing other important nutrients. Of course, offer these foods as part of a well-balanced diet that includes all the food groups in the Food Guide Pyramid.

Lest this seems like nutritional heresy, rest assured that sugars do not cause most of the problems they've been accused of in the past. Take the most common one, hyperactivity. A recent study showed children whose parents believed they were negatively affected by sugar actually reacted no differently when the children ate higher than normal amounts of sugar compared to when they ate diets low in sugar. In fact, this and other research suggests sugars may have the opposite effect. Eating sugars and other carbohydrates tends to calm both children and adults. This effect could go unnoticed, however, due to other influences. For instance, birthday party excitement could override the calming effect of sugars eaten.

Sugars, like other carbohydrates, including starches, do play a role in dental decay, however. Regular dental care that includes brushing after meals and snacks, flossing, fluoride, and dental checkups helps reduce that problem.

Research shows, too, that people who eat moderate amounts of sugar (as opposed to high or low amounts of sugar) tend to have diets that are lower in fat while still containing plenty of essential vitamins and minerals. That means sugar may play an important role in helping us eat healthfully by providing good taste without negative effects.

If your child tends toward overweight, encourage increased activity (limit the number of hours watching television), and talk with a registered dietitian who specializes in working with overweight children. Don't prohibit foods or place undue limits on how much your child eats. Let him decide. If you try to tightly control your child's eating behaviors, you may find him sneaking food or otherwise developing unhealthy attitudes about food and eating.

In the end, you and the members of your immediate family set the best examples for your child. He or she will eat as you do. Stay with the healthy eating habits you established during pregnancy and urge the rest of your family to examine—and improve, if necessary—what they eat, too.

Special Concerns

I'm not sure I'm producing enough milk. It seems like my baby wants to nurse all the time, and she's smaller than my neighbor's bottle-fed baby who is about the same age. First of all, check with your health care provider if you have any concerns about whether your baby is getting enough milk. You may want to take him in for a checkup, too, rather than just discussing it over the telephone, to let your health care provider do a thorough exam. Some moms do not produce enough milk and may seriously risk their babies' health as a result.

If all seems fine with your baby, consider the following to calm your concerns about how often your baby nurses. To establish an adequate milk supply, you need to let your child nurse as often as he or she wishes. But in general, in the first few weeks, infants should nurse at least eight times a day. Some may nurse fifteen or more times a day. (Marsha felt like she spent most of her time nursing both her kids when they were first born.) After the first month, infants fed on demand usually nurse five to twelve times per day. Your baby will also want to nurse more when he or she starts a growth spurt. This will increase your milk supply to give your baby the nutrition he or she needs.

You may need to wake infants who sleep more than three or four hours at a time to feed them if they are not gaining weight. On average, however, after the first few months, breast-fed infants gain weight more slowly than those fed formula. Slower weight gain does not necessarily mean you need to supplement your baby's diet with formula, but you should check with your pediatrician to make certain. By the way, women of all sizes successfully breast-feed, whether they are thin, normal weight, or overweight. Undernourished moms (those eating too little), however, may produce less milk. Vigorous exercise does not affect the volume or composition of your milk.

I've got the opposite problem. My baby is getting so fat! Could she be nursing too much (or drinking too much formula)? If you're breast-feeding, it's unlikely. And it's a real comment on our times when moms worry so much about how fat their infants are. What's worse, it doesn't just come from mom. There are plenty of concerned glances and comments from relatives and friends when they see what seems to be an overly chubby baby. The fact is, how much a baby weighs has no relationship to what he or she will weigh when older, so relax, and let your baby satisfy her appetite. Don't start trying to limit how much he eats now (or ever). You'll only make both of you miserable, and you may lead him down the path to eating disorders later in life. If she drinks formula, don't fall into the trap of trying to get her to finish the bottle. That *can* lead to unnecessary pounds. Let her decide when she's full.

Should I take vitamin or mineral supplements now that I'm breast-feeding? The best way to get the nutrition you need continues to be through a healthy diet, such as that outlined in the Building a Healthy Baby Nutrition Plan for Breast-feeding Moms. The only exception is iron if you have iron-deficiency anemia. In particular, if you experienced heavy blood loss during delivery, you may benefit from supplements of iron, zinc, and copper.

Still, as we've said before, there is little risk from a supplement that doesn't exceed 100 percent of the Recommended Dietary Allowance (RDA) for vitamins and minerals during breast-feeding. And there may be benefits. If you were taking a supplement prescribed during pregnancy, you may want to continue with it. Check with your health care provider.

Also, if you find you are consistently unable to eat as recommended, a vitamin/mineral supplement is probably a good idea. Again, check with your health care provider and only take supplements as recommended or prescribed.

There are also special situations in which your need for a supplement is almost certain. If you are a strict vegetarian who avoids all animal foods, including meat, fish, dairy products, and eggs, you need a regular source of vitamin B_{12}, such as a daily supplement that contains 2.6 micrograms of B_{12}. If you can't tolerate milk or other high-calcium dairy foods, and you don't eat other sources of calcium, you may need a supplement of 600 milligrams of calcium a day. See pages 111–113 to learn more about calcium sources. If you don't drink milk or eat fortified cereal and aren't out in the sunlight very much, you also need a source of vitamin D. If these situations describe yours, check with your health care provider.

I work, and when I get home, all my time is devoted to my baby. I just can't find the time or energy to prepare well-balanced meals. Healthy eating doesn't have to be an effort. A simple sandwich of sliced turkey or even peanut butter on whole grain bread makes a great entrée for a healthy meal. Top it off with a few carrot sticks or other vegetables you've picked up from the grocery salad bar or produce section, and enjoy it with a glass of milk. Then munch fresh fruit for dessert, and you've put together a meal that satisfies your needs for nutrition and convenience.

Of course, you won't be happy with a peanut butter sandwich every night, so look for other convenient yet healthy meals. Many stores now offer rotisserie chicken along with a variety of fresh salads. Study the frozen food section. There are plenty of healthy frozen dinners and even varieties of pizza that can make the beginnings of a great meal. Round them out with extra vegetables, bread, and a beverage to make the meal substantial enough for you and the rest of your family.

If you work outside the home, think about making lunch your main meal of the day. You can then take advantage of company cafeterias or local restaurants for a hot meal, and leave dinner for simple fixings. Marsha sometimes enjoys whole grain breakfast cereal with milk and a piece of fruit at the end of a long and busy day. Even more important, her children love it, too. Her husband? He's always easy to please (thank goodness). Reread the section on page 121 for information about healthy eating when dining out.

My baby has colic. Will cutting out foods like milk help?
The only way you can know for certain if your child is reacting to a food you eat is through an oral-elimination challenge. This involves eliminating suspected foods from your diet to see if your infant's symptoms disappear. Then, under careful medical supervision, the foods are again introduced one at a time to determine if the symptoms reappear. If they do, steps should be quickly taken to treat negative reactions. If the test indicates you should eliminate a major nutrient source from your diet (such as milk), carefully plan your diet to provide these important nutrients in other ways, or consider nutrient supplementation.

Nutrition Checkup for Breast-feeding Moms

Copy and use this chart often to quickly assess whether you're meeting your nutritional needs when breast-feeding. Then fill in the blanks following each question with strategies for improving your nutritional habits if they need improving. (Answer the questions based on how you ate yesterday.) Set realistic, small goals for best success. Look back on previous nutrient checkups to see how far you've come in meeting some goals. Give yourself plenty of pats on the back for making some important changes.

continued

1. Did you eat the minimum recommended number of servings from all five food groups (6+ breads and cereals, 5+ fruits and vegetables, 4+ milk, 3+ meat) and at least 1800 calories?   Yes   No
   How I can improve this habit:

   _____

   _____

2. Did you eat several good sources of folic acid (fortified cereal; green leafy vegetables; green beans; broccoli; brussels sprouts; asparagus; okra; corn; lentils; black beans; peanuts; almonds; liver; fruit such as oranges, grapefruit, strawberries, and cantaloupe)?   Yes   No
   How I can improve this habit:

   _____

   _____

3. Did you eat several good sources of vitamin B_6 (fortified cereal, bananas, poultry, meat, fish, potatoes, sweet potatoes, spinach, prunes, watermelon, nuts)?
                                   Yes   No
   How I can improve this habit:

   _____

   _____

4. Did you eat several good sources of zinc (meat, poultry, seafood, eggs, whole grain breads and cereals, dried beans and peas, peanuts, seeds, yogurt)?
                                   Yes   No

continued

How I can improve this habit:

_____

_____

5. Did you eat several good sources of magnesium (leafy greens, whole grain breads and cereals, nuts, dried beans and peas, seafood)?   Yes   No
How I can improve this habit:

_____

_____

6. Did you eat a good source of vitamin A (deep orange-yellow and dark green fruits and vegetables, fortified milk)?   Yes   No
How I can improve this habit:

_____

_____

7. Did you eat a good source of vitamin C (citrus fruits, green peppers, strawberries, melon, broccoli, cabbage)?   Yes   No
How I can improve this habit:

_____

_____

8. Did you eat at least three servings of whole grain foods?   Yes   No
How I can improve this habit:

_____

_____

continued

9. Did you drink plenty of fluids (water, milk, juice, soup; no more than two servings of coffee or other caffeinated beverage)?   Yes   No
   How I can improve this habit:

   _____

   _____

10. Did you choose more low-fat foods than high-fat items?   Yes   No
    How I can improve this habit:

    _____

    _____

11. Did you smoke, drink alcohol, or use an unpre-scribed drug (including self-prescribed vitamin/mineral supplements)?   Yes   No
    How I can improve this habit:

    _____

    _____

12. Did you get plenty of appropriate exercise?
                                                Yes   No
    How I can improve this habit:

    _____

    _____

Recipe Focus: One-Handed Cooking

Now that the baby is here, time is very precious and you will, almost literally, learn to cook with one hand. The recipes in this section are designed for the ultimate in ease and convenience. But just because you've delivered doesn't mean nutrition goes out the window. This is especially true if you are breast-feeding. Breast-feeding requires a good supply of many nutrients including folic acid, calcium, vitamin B_6, magnesium, and zinc to make sure you stay healthy while feeding your baby. The recipes in this section reflect the nutritional needs for breast-feeding moms, which are higher than for women who are not breast-feeding. If you are not breast-feeding, these recipes will contribute even more of your daily requirements. Whether you're breast- or bottle-feeding, taking care of yourself nutritionally is very important to help you through the physical, emotional, and mental demands you now have in your life.

Ricotta Toast

This recipe is for a single serving, but make up a larger batch simply by increasing the ingredients in the same proportions. Once you've put the ricotta spread on the toast, you can make it even creamier by putting the whole thing under the broiler for a minute.

2 tablespoons reduced-fat ricotta cheese
1 teaspoon brown sugar
  Sprinkle of cinnamon
1 slice whole wheat toast

In a small bowl, combine ricotta, brown sugar, and cinnamon. Spread on the toast.

Serves 1

Recipe Option
Instead of brown sugar, use white sugar.

Nutritional Benefits
Calories   100

Percent RDA for
Breast-feeding Moms
Calcium   4 percent
Dietary fiber   10 percent
Iron   7 percent
Riboflavin   9 percent
Thiamine   7 percent

Food Pyramid Servings
Each recipe portion =
1 bread group serving
¾ milk group serving

Food Mood
Quick toast
Creamy texture
Sweet ricotta flavor

Morning Yams

Hash browns in the morning aren't considered unusual, so why not sweeter-tasting yams? If you've baked yams or sweet potatoes for dinner and have any left over, this makes a quick breakfast the next morning.

1 small baked yam or sweet potato, scooped out of skin
$\frac{1}{2}$ banana, sliced
$\frac{1}{2}$ cup skim milk
2 tablespoons Grape-Nuts
1 teaspoon sugar

Put all ingredients in a small bowl, sprinkling the cereal and sugar on top. Microwave for 1 to 2 minutes to create a warm, potato-fruit cereal.

Serves 1

Recipe Option
Add cinnamon and nutmeg for more flavor.

Nutritional Benefits
Calories   260

Percent RDA for
Breast-feeding Moms
Calcium   14 percent
Dietary fiber   22 percent
Folic acid   9 percent
Iron   16 percent
Potassium   44 percent
Vitamin A   64 percent
Vitamin B$_6$ 30 percent

Food Pyramid Servings
Each recipe portion =
$1\frac{1}{2}$ bread group servings
$\frac{1}{2}$ milk group serving
$\frac{1}{2}$ fruit group serving

Food Mood
Warm, soft cereal
Yam/banana flavor

Cranberry Muffin Cake

We've used this muffin batter to make a single cake because it's faster than filling individual muffin cups. When turned upside down, this breakfast cake looks festive and stays moist when covered.

⅔ cup cake flour
⅔ cup whole wheat flour
½ cup sugar
2½ teaspoons baking powder
½ teaspoon baking soda
½ teaspoon nutmeg
½ teaspoon cinnamon
1 egg
¼ cup vegetable oil
¾ cup skim milk
1 16-ounce can whole cranberry sauce

Preheat oven to 400° F. Coat 9" to 10" round quiche or cake pan with nonstick vegetable spray.

In a large bowl, combine all the dry ingredients. In a small bowl, combine wet ingredients except for cranberry sauce. With a wooden spoon, stir wet ingredients into dry until thoroughly combined. Spread cranberry sauce on bottom of baking dish. Pour batter over top. Bake for 30 to 35 minutes until done. Remove from oven and let cook for 5 minutes. Loosen sides of pan and invert onto a plate.

Serves 12

Recipe Option

To make muffins instead of a cake, coat muffin pan with vegetable spray and place 1 tablespoon of cranberry sauce into the bottom of each cup before pouring in the batter.

Nutritional Benefits
Calories   225

Percent RDA for
Breast-feeding Moms
Iron   10 percent
Magnesium   6 percent
Niacin   9 percent
Riboflavin   6 percent
Vitamin K   9 percent

Food Pyramid Serving
Each recipe portion =
1 bread group serving

Food Mood
Sweet/tart flavor
    combination
Gooey topping

Cereal-to-Go

These granolalike bars are packed with nutrition and are perfect if you don't have time or don't like to eat breakfast before leaving the house in the mornings. Or pack one as a snack. Do not use jelly in the recipe; it won't provide a smooth consistency.

    3 cups Total or other fortified wheat flake cereal
    5 tablespoons raspberry jam or preserves
1½ tablespoons peanut butter, chunky *or* smooth
    2 tablespoons orange juice concentrate

Preheat oven to 325° F. Coat 9" x 9" square pan with non-stick vegetable spray.

In a small bowl, crush cereal with your hands. In a cup, using a spoon, combine the jam with the peanut butter until well blended. Stir in juice concentrate. Stir jam mixture into the cereal until sticky. Spread cereal mixture into the pan, patting down with the back of a spoon. Bake for 20 to 25 minutes until slightly crisp. Remove from oven, cut into 9 squares, and let cool.

Serves 9

Recipe Option
Instead of raspberry jam, use other dark-colored fruit jams such as strawberry or boysenberry.

Nutritional Benefits
Calories   95

Percent RDA for
Breast-feeding Moms
Folic acid   59 percent
Iron   47 percent
Niacin   40 percent
Riboflavin   37 percent
Thiamine   36 percent
Vitamin A   44 percent
Vitamin B_6 37 percent
Vitamin C   34 percent

Food Pyramid Serving
Each recipe portion =
½ bread group serving

Food Mood
Granola bar–type food
Portable snack
Peanut butter/fruit flavor
    combination

Breakfast Grits

If you like hot cereal in the mornings, try grits instead of oatmeal. Using milk, instead of water, helps boost the calcium value.

¾ cup skim milk
3 tablespoons quick grits
¼ cup (1 ounce) shredded reduced-fat cheese
1 teaspoon sugar
½ teaspoon butter

In a 2-cup bowl, stir together milk and grits. Microwave on high for 3 to 4 minutes or until thickened. Stir in remaining ingredients.

This can also be made on the stove. Heat the milk to a boil, stir in grits, cover, and cook over medium-low heat for 5 to 7 minutes.

Serves 1

Recipe Option
Instead of sugar, use a few drops of Tabasco if you prefer a spicy rather than a sweet flavor.

Nutritional Benefits
Calories   165

Percent RDA for
Breast-feeding Moms
Calcium   22 percent
Protein   16 percent
Riboflavin   22 percent
Thiamine   9 percent

Food Pyramid Servings
Each recipe portion =
1¼ milk group servings
1 bread group serving

Food Mood
Hot cereal
Smooth, creamy texture
Mild cheese flavor

Banana Corn Cakes

These toaster-style corn cakes make an extremely fast and tasty breakfast.

2 toaster corn cakes
1 large banana, cut in half and lengthwise
1 tablespoon orange marmalade

Heat oven or toaster oven to broil setting.

Place corn cakes on a baking sheet or piece of foil. Lay sliced banana on top and spread marmalade over top of banana. Broil for 2 to 3 minutes, on middle rack of oven (so marmalade will melt and cakes won't burn), and serve warm.

Serves 2

Recipe Option
Instead of marmalade, use your favorite jam or preserves.

Nutritional Benefits
Calories   225

Percent RDA for
Breast-feeding Moms
Dietary fiber   12 percent
Potassium   15 percent
Riboflavin   10 percent
Vitamin B_6 17 percent

Food Pyramid Servings
Each recipe portion =
1 bread group serving
1 fruit group serving

Food Mood
Cornbread flavor
Crumbly texture
Warm fruit

Shrimp Soup

This light soup can be eaten as lunch, or when served with a salad or half a sandwich, can also be dinner. The carrots really bump up the vitamin A value.

1 15-ounce can reduced-sodium chicken broth
1 garlic clove, *or* ¼ teaspoon garlic powder
1 slice fresh ginger, *or* ¼ teaspoon ground ginger
1 cup carrots, long thin slices (done with a vegetable peeler)
½ cup scallions, thinly sliced (green part only)
1 5-ounce bag tiny frozen shrimp, thawed

In a medium pan, heat broth, garlic, and ginger to boiling. Add carrots and scallions, cover, and reduce to a simmer for 10 to 15 minutes. If shrimp is frozen, place in a colander or strainer and run cold water over it for a few minutes until thawed. Add shrimp to pan and heat for 1 minute. Remove garlic clove and ginger slice before serving.

Serves 4 (each serving ¾ cup)

Recipe Option
Instead of shrimp, use leftover diced white chicken meat or a combination of both to total 5 to 6 ounces.

Nutritional Benefits
Calories   55

Percent RDA for
Breast-feeding Moms
Niacin   7 percent
Protein   13 percent
Vitamin A   67 percent
Vitamin C   10 percent

Food Pyramid Servings
Each recipe portion =
⅓ *meat group serving*
¾ *vegetable group serving*

Food Mood
Clear, light broth
Mild, slight ginger flavor

Split Pea Soup

Lean Canadian bacon is added for flavoring instead of a ham bone or bacon, which are often used in split pea soup.

1 pound yellow or green split peas
2 quarts water
2 cups frozen carrots, diced
4 ounces (about 4 slices) Canadian bacon, diced
½ teaspoon salt
Black pepper to taste

Put peas in a large pot and cover with 2" of water. Cover and boil for 2 minutes. Remove from heat and let sit for 1 hour. Drain and add 2 quarts of water. Bring to a boil. Add carrots and bacon, cover and simmer for 1 to 1½ hours or until peas are tender. Stir in salt and pepper.

Serves 8 (each serving 1 cup)

Recipe Option
Instead of carrots, use frozen peas and carrots or mixed vegetables.

Nutritional Benefits
Calories   230

Percent RDA for
Breast-feeding Moms
Dietary fiber   15 percent
Folic acid   56 percent
Iron   18 percent
Protein   26 percent
Thiamine   32 percent
Zinc   10 percent
Vitamin A   50 percent

Food Pyramid Servings
Each recipe portion =
½ meat group serving
½ vegetable group serving

Food Mood
Hearty, filling soup
Small amount of meat

Chili Soup

By adding enough water, a thick chili can easily become a soup. Heat plain corn tortillas in the oven until crisp, and crumble them on top of the chili, as though they were crackers. This adds crunch and color.

½ pound lean ground beef
2 cups water
1 15-ounce can kidney beans, drained
1 cup onion, diced
1 cup tomato, diced
1 tablespoon (about ½ envelope) chili seasoning mix

In a large pot, brown meat and drain any excess fat. Add all remaining ingredients and heat to boiling. Reduce heat, cover, and simmer for 15 minutes.

Serves 5 (each serving 1 cup)

Recipe Option
Instead of kidney beans, use pinto beans.

Nutritional Benefits
(*Without tortilla*)
Calories   180

Percent RDA for
Breast-feeding Moms
Dietary fiber   18 percent
Folic acid   13 percent
Iron   14 percent
Protein   21 percent
Vitamin B$_6$ 10 percent
Zinc   13 percent

Food Pyramid Servings
Each recipe portion =
⅔ *meat group serving*
½ *vegetable group serving*

Food Mood
Hearty, meat-based soup
Chili flavor

Frosted Grapes

This no-fat snack will please the entire family all summer long. On a hot day, frozen grapes are a refreshing and cool treat to pop in your mouth.

2 cups seedless white or red grapes, washed and dried

Lay grapes flat in a shallow bowl or tray and freeze.

Serves 4 (each serving ½ cup)

Nutritional Benefits
Calories   50

Percent RDA for
Breast-feeding Moms
Potassium   3 percent
Vitamin B$_6$ 2 percent

Food Pyramid Serving
Each recipe portion =
1 fruit group serving

Food Mood
Icy cold
No-fuss snack

Stuffed Celery

This highly nutritious dish provides enough calories and protein to serve as a quick lunch. Your older kids will love it, too.

2 tablespoons peanut butter
4 larger celery stalks, washed and dried
2 tablespoons raisins

Spread peanut butter down the middle of the celery. Top with raisins.

Serves 1

Recipe Option
Instead of raisins, use diced dried apricots, apples, or pears.

Nutritional Benefits
Calories   275

Percent RDA for
Breast-feeding Moms

Dietary fiber	24 percent
Folic acid	30 percent
Iron	11 percent
Magnesium	22 percent
Niacin	25 percent
Protein	15 percent
Vitamin B6	16 percent
Vitamin K	18 percent

Food Pyramid Servings
Each recipe portion =
2 vegetable group servings
1 fruit group serving
⅓ meat group serving

Food Mood
Crunchy texture
Peanut flavor

Vegetable Dip

When hunger pangs hit, just dip a few carrot or celery sticks into this tasty dip.

1 cup nonfat plain yogurt
1 cup reduced-fat sour cream
1 cnvelope vegetable soup and recipe mix
  Black pepper to taste

Combine all ingredients in a bowl. Cover and refrigerate for at least 1 hour to allow flavors to develop.

Serves 8 (each serving ¼ cup)

Recipe Option
Use as a topping for baked potatoes.

Nutritional Benefits
Calories   40

Percent RDA for
Breast-feeding Moms
Calcium   7 percent

Food Pyramid Serving
Each recipe portion =
¼ milk group serving

Food Mood
Creamy texture
Savory vegetable flavor

Peach Yogurt Topping

This recipe can be made with various flavors of yogurt and complementary fruits. Use it to pour over plain cake or as an accompaniment to muffins and breakfast breads.

 1 cup low-fat peach yogurt
¼ cup peaches, fresh or canned, juice packed, drained, finely diced

Pour yogurt into cheesecloth or strong paper towels. Let it drain into a cup in the refrigerator overnight, resulting in a firm-textured yogurt cheese. Stir in peaches.

Serves 3 (each serving ¼ cup)

Recipe Option
Instead of peach yogurt, use any other favorite fruit variety.

Nutritional Benefits
Calories   60

Percent RDA for
Breast-feeding Moms
Calcium   11 percent
Magnesium   5 percent
Potassium   7 percent

Food Pyramid Serving
Each recipe portion =
⅓ milk group serving

Food Mood
Creamy texture
Fruity flavors

Eggcellent Salad

Removing the yolks from two of the four eggs helps reduce the cholesterol content of this recipe. The Dijon mustard provides a tangy flavor and added color.

4 eggs
¼ cup celery, finely diced
½ tablespoon Dijon mustard
½ tablespoon reduced-fat mayonnaise

In a medium saucepan, boil water and hard-boil the eggs. Drain, rinse with cold water, and peel. Remove and discard two yolks and mash remaining eggs in a bowl. Stir in remaining ingredients.

Serves 3 (each serving ⅓ cup)

Recipe Option
Instead of celery, used shredded carrot.

Nutritional Benefits
Calories   80

Percent RDA for
Breast-feeding Moms

Folic acid	7 percent
Potassium	5 percent
Protein	13 percent
Vitamin K	27 percent

Food Pyramid Serving
Each recipe portion =
⅓ meat group serving

Food Mood
Egg salad
Slight mustardy flavor

Cucumber and Onion Salad

This cool, refreshing salad is ideal for summer, especially if the garden is producing lots of cukes. Regular sour cream is okay since there's no other source of fat in the recipe.

2 cups cucumbers, sliced
1 cup red onion, halved and sliced
¼ cup nonfat plain yogurt
2 tablespoons sour cream
1 teaspoon white vinegar
1 teaspoon sugar
¼ teaspoon salt
White *or* black pepper to taste

In a shallow bowl or plate, toss cucumber and onions. In a small cup, combine remaining ingredients and mix with vegetables. Cover and refrigerate for 1 hour to allow flavors to develop.

Serves 6 (each serving ½ cup)

Recipe Option
Add fresh or dried dill for flavor and color.

Nutritional Benefits
Calories   30

Percent RDA for
Breast-feeding Moms
Folic acid   2 percent
Potassium   5 percent
Vitamin C   4 percent

Food Pyramid Serving
*Each recipe portion =
1 vegetable group serving*

Food Mood
Crunchy, crisp vegetables
Creamy-style dressing

Chilled Rice and Vegetable Salad

This salad travels well, making it perfect for picnics, potluck suppers, or as a bring-along lunch.

2 cups instant cooked rice
2 cups frozen mixed vegetables
½ cup fat-free red wine vinaigrette *or* Italian bottled dressing.

Combine cooked rice and frozen vegetables in a bowl. Toss with ¼ cup of dressing. Cover and refrigerate for at least 2 hours, so rice will cool and vegetables will thaw. Toss with remaining dressing prior to serving.

Serves 4 (each serving 1 cup)

Recipe Options
Instead of frozen vegetables, use a mixture of lightly steamed fresh vegetables.
If you have leftover rice from another meal, use that instead of instant rice.

Nutritional Benefits
Calories   325

Percent RDA for
Breast-feeding Moms
Dietary fiber   20 percent
Iron   6 percent
Niacin   7 percent
Potassium   14 percent

Food Pyramid Servings
Each recipe portion =
1 bread group serving
1 vegetable group serving

Food Mood
Starchy salad
Chilled dish
Italian dressing flavor

Raspberry-Orange Mold

Gelatin salads are still a great standby as a side dish, snack, or dessert. This can be set up in a bowl or, for a fancier look, poured into a 2-cup mold. There's a scant amount of fat that comes from the walnuts.

1 3-ounce package sugar-free raspberry gelatin
1 orange, peeled, finely chopped
¼ cup walnuts, finely chopped

In a bowl, stir 1 cup of boiling water into gelatin until dissolved. Add 1 cup of cold water and refrigerate until slightly thickened (about 30 to 45 minutes). Stir in remaining ingredients and let set until firm.

Serves 4 (each serving ½ cup)

Recipe Option
Use any flavor combinations of gelatin and fresh or canned fruit (except fresh pineapple or kiwi) that are available.

Nutritional Benefits
Calories   40

Percent RDA for
Breast-feeding Moms
Folic acid   7 percent
Potassium   5 percent
Vitamin C   36 percent

Food Pyramid Serving
Each recipe portion =
½ fruit group serving

Food Mood
Old-fashioned gelatin salad
Smooth gelatin texture
    contrasted with bits of
    fruit/nuts

Glazed Carrots

This quick vegetable dish is packed with vitamin A. If you have leftovers, the orange flavor makes this a tasty cold snack.

4 large carrots, cut in half and lengthwise
1 tablespoon orange juice concentrate

In a large, shallow pan, add ½" water and bring to a boil. Add carrots, reduce to a simmer, and cover. Cook for 10 minutes or until carrots are tender. Drain water, leaving a scant amount in the pan. Alternatively, microwave carrots on high for 3 to 4 minutes. Stir in juice concentrate and thoroughly coat carrots.

Serves 4

Recipe Option
Instead of orange juice, use apple juice concentrate.

Nutritional Benefits
Calories   35

Percent RDA for
Breast-feeding Moms
Dietary fiber   8 percent
Vitamin A   155 percent
Vitamin C   12 percent
Vitamin K   14 percent

Food Pyramid Serving
Each recipe portion =
1 vegetable group serving

Food Mood
Orange-flavored vegetable

Baked Spinach Tomatoes

This is a good way to get kids to eat their spinach, and you'll love it, too. It's very colorful and takes just a minute to put together.

1 box frozen chopped spinach, thawed, squeezed dry
1 cup (4 ounces) shredded reduced-fat cheddar cheese
4 large tomatoes, washed, cut in half horizontally

Preheat oven to 350° F.

If the spinach is still frozen, run under cold water in a colander or strainer, and squeeze very dry. Combine spinach and cheese and top each tomato half with equal amounts. Place on a baking sheet and bake for 20 minutes until tomatoes are heated through and cheese has melted.

Serves 4

Recipe Option
Instead of reduced-fat cheddar cheese, use reduced-fat Jarlsberg or Swiss.

Nutritional Benefits
Calories   110

Percent RDA for
Breast-feeding Moms
Calcium   23 percent
Dietary fiber   10 percent
Folic acid   26 percent
Magnesium   13 percent
Vitamin A   41 percent
Vitamin C   31 percent

Food Pyramid Servings
Each recipe portion =
3 vegetable group servings
¼ milk group serving

Food Mood
Slightly cooked tomatoes
Spinach

Creamy Garlic Mashed Potatoes

Make this when the oven is already being used to cook something else. It requires only one bowl and an electric beater. Leaving the skins on increases the fiber value.

4 large baking potatoes, washed and dried (about 2 cups cubed)
½ bulb garlic, wrapped in foil
1 cup skim milk
½ teaspoon salt

Preheat oven to 350° F.

Bake potatoes and garlic for approximately 45 to 60 minutes or until done. Remove from oven, cut potatoes in half, and let cool slightly until you can handle them. Cut into cubes and put into a bowl. The garlic cloves will be very soft. Squeeze the garlic out of the skins into the bowl. Gradually add milk and whip potatoes until creamy. Stir in salt. Because the skins are in there, these will not be as smooth as regular mashed potatoes, but they taste great.

Serves 8 (each serving ½ cup)

Recipe Option
Instead of garlic, use a small onion.

Nutritional Benefits
Calories   120

Percent RDA for
Breast-feeding Moms
Dietary fiber   10 percent
Iron   9 percent
Potassium   19 percent
Vitamin B$_6$ 17 percent
Vitamin C   14 percent

Food Pyramid Serving
*Each recipe portion =
1 vegetable group serving*

Food Mood
Comfort food with a new
    flavor twist
Creamy texture
Spuds

Mixed Fruit Stuffing

Use this for stuffing a bird or as a baked side dish when serving poultry, pork, or ham. The dried fruits really boost the fiber value of this dish.

1 6-ounce bag mixed dried fruit bits or a mixture of
    minced dried fruits
1½ cups water
4 cups (about 8 slices) dry whole wheat bread, cubed
½ cup onion, diced
1 cup orange juice
2 tablespoons sugar
1 teaspoon allspice
½ teaspoon salt

Place fruit and water in a shallow dish and microwave on high for 3 minutes. Alternatively, heat fruit and water to boiling, reduce heat, and simmer for 15 minutes. Drain all but ½ cup of water from the fruit. Pour fruit, water, and remaining ingredients into a 2-quart casserole pan that has been coated with a nonstick vegetable spray. Toss until bread is well moistened. Cover and bake at 350° F for 40 to 45 minutes.

Serves 8 (each serving ½ cup)

Recipe Option
Instead of mixed fruit, use prunes, raisins, dried apricots, or pears.

Nutritional Benefits

Calories 125

Percent RDA for
Breast-feeding Moms

Dietary fiber	18 percent
Folic acid	11 percent
Iron	9 percent
Magnesium	6 percent
Niacin	6 percent
Potassium	10 percent
Vitamin C	13 percent

Food Pyramid Servings

Each recipe portion =
1 bread group serving
¾ fruit group serving

Food Mood

Starchy side dish
Slightly sweet side dish

Baked Butternut with Cheese Filling

Use this as an entrée when you're just not in the mood for meat. I've even heated up leftovers for breakfast.

1 medium butternut squash, halved and seeds scooped out
1 cup low-fat cottage cheese
2 tablespoons jam or preserves, any flavor

Preheat oven to 350° F. Coat baking sheet with nonstick vegetable spray.

Place squash halves, cut side down, on baking sheet. Bake for approximately 30 minutes.

Meanwhile, thoroughly combine cottage cheese and jam. Turn squash right side up and fill cavities with cheese mixture. Bake an additional 15 minutes until cheese is hot and creamy. If you enjoy eating the skin, which is a good source of fiber, make sure you washed and dried the squash prior to cooking.

Serves 2

Recipe Option
Instead of butternut squash, use hubbard or acorn.

Nutritional Benefits
Calories   220

Percent RDA for
Breast-feeding Moms

Dietary fiber	20 percent
Folic acid	19 percent
Iron	10 percent
Magnesium	10 percent
Protein	24 percent
Vitamin A	111 percent
Vitamin C	32 percent

Food Pyramid Servings
Each recipe portion =
2 milk group servings
2 vegetable group servings

Food Mood
Soft texture
Mild, almost-sweet flavor
Vegetarian meal

Mushroom, Onion, and Salsa Pie

This is similar to a quiche, but without a crust and with a larger proportion of vegetables to the egg in the filling. To keep it simple, we don't sauté the vegetables first, which gives them a slight crunch in the finished dish.

2 cups mushrooms, sliced
2 cups onion, sliced
1 cup (4 ounces) shredded reduced-fat cheese
3 eggs
1 egg white
1 cup skim milk
1 tablespoon salsa or picante sauce

Preheat oven to 350° F. Coat 9" quiche or tart pan with nonstick vegetable spray.

Place mushrooms and onions in pan. Sprinkle cheese over top. In a small bowl, beat eggs, egg white, milk, and salsa. Pour into the pan. Bake for 45 to 50 minutes or until egg filling is firm. Serve warm or chilled.

Serves 8

Recipe Options
Instead of eggs and an egg white, use an egg substitute product to reduce the cholesterol content.
Instead of salsa, use a variety of dried herbs.

Nutritional Benefits
Calories　　　90

Percent RDA for
Breast-feeding Moms

Calcium	22 percent
Folic acid	7 percent
Riboflavin	23 percent
Vitamin K	10 percent

Food Pyramid Servings
Each recipe portion =
½ vegetable group serving
⅓ milk group serving
⅓ meat group serving

Food Mood
Quiche-style dish
Salsa flavor

Homemade Fried Rice

If there's no time for take-out food, and you have leftover rice in the refrigerator, whip up this dish in a jiffy. You can dice up any leftover vegetables and throw them in, too. You'll find that this version is significantly lower in fat than any restaurant version.

> 1 teaspoon vegetable oil
> 1 egg, beaten
> 3 cups cooked white rice
> 1 cup leftover white chicken meat, diced
> 1 cup scallion, thinly sliced
> ¼ teaspoon garlic powder
> 1½ tablespoons reduced-sodium soy or tamari sauce
>   diluted in ¼ cup water
>   Red pepper flakes to taste

In a large skillet, heat oil and quickly scramble egg. Remove egg from pan. Put cooked rice in pan and stir. Over high heat, add remaining ingredients, stirring so rice takes on a light brown color from the soy sauce. Break scrambled egg into small bits and stir into rice.

Serves 10 (each serving ½ cup)

Recipe Option
If you made Shrimp Soup on page 268 and have any tiny shrimp left over, add them to the rice.

Nutritional Benefits
Calories   110

Percent RDA for
Breast-feeding Moms
Iron   7 percent
Niacin   19 percent
Protein   14 percent
Thiamine   6 percent
Vitamin B$_6$ 9 percent

Food Pyramid Serving
*Each recipe portion =
1 bread group serving*

Food Mood
Chinese-style food
Lots of rice
Small amount of meat

Creamy Penne Pasta

The ricotta cheese melts nicely over the hot pasta creating a creamy-style tomato sauce. Leftovers, cold or heated, make a great packable lunch.

1 pound penne pasta
1 15-ounce jar marinara-style spaghetti sauce
¾ cup reduced-fat ricotta cheese

In a large pot, boil water and cook pasta until done.

Meanwhile, heat sauce in a small pot or microwave. Drain pasta and toss with sauce. Portion pasta onto plates and top with 2 tablespoons of ricotta per serving. Ricotta will begin to melt and mix in as you're eating.

Serves 6 (each serving 1½ cups)

Recipe Option
Instead of penne pasta, use ziti.

Nutritional Benefits
Calories   370

Percent RDA for
Breast-feeding Moms
Calcium   7 percent
Dietary fiber   16 percent
Magnesium   13 percent
Riboflavin   16 percent
Thiamine   24 percent
Vitamin B$_6$ 9 percent

Food Pyramid Servings
Each recipe portion =
3 bread group servings
½ vegetable group serving
¼ milk group serving

Food Mood
Pasta
Creamy tomato sauce

Chicken Cacciatore

The red wine in this recipe blends nicely with the peppers and onions. Keep some crusty Italian bread on hand for dunking in the delicious sauce.

1/2 tablespoon olive oil
 1 pound skinless split chicken breasts, with ribs
 1 15-ounce can whole tomatoes and juice
1/2 cup dry red wine
 1 tablespoon dried basil
1/2 teaspoon garlic powder
1/2 teaspoon red pepper flakes
 2 cups green peppers, sliced
 2 cups onions, sliced

In a large skillet, heat oil and brown chicken on both sides. Add the tomatoes and their juice, wine, basil, garlic powder, and pepper flakes. Bring to a boil. Add green peppers and onions and bring to a boil again. Reduce to a simmer, cover, and heat for 15 to 20 minutes or until vegetables are tender.

Serves 4

Recipe Option
Instead of chicken, use veal cutlets.

Nutritional Benefits
Calories   270

Percent RDA for
Breast-feeding Moms

Dietary fiber	15 percent
Folic acid	13 percent
Iron	16 percent
Magnesium	18 percent
Protein	45 percent
Vitamin B$_6$	46 percent
Vitamin C	130 percent

Food Pyramid Servings
Each recipe portion =
3 vegetable group servings
1 meat group serving

Food Mood
Italian-style flavors
Lots of veggies
Wine-flavored tomato sauce

Ted's Marinated Chicken

Donna reduced the amount of fat in this marinade her husband, Ted, has been making for years. This recipe makes enough to marinate 1 pound of boneless chicken, turkey or fish. Increase the proportions, depending on how much you're cooking.

¼ cup reduced-sodium tamari or soy sauce
  1 tablespoon rice wine vinegar
  1 tablespoon olive oil
  1 garlic clove, minced
  1 pound boneless, skinless chicken breasts

Combine all ingredients except chicken in a shallow dish or pan. Add chicken and turn over so both sides are moistened. Cover and refrigerate for at least 1 hour. Grill or broil in the oven until done.

Serves 4

Recipe Options
Instead of fresh garlic, use ¼ teaspoon garlic powder.
Instead of olive oil, use sesame or peanut oil.

Nutritional Benefits
Calories   160

Percent RDA for
Breast-feeding Moms
Iron   7 percent
Niacin   59 percent
Potassium   10 percent
Protein   54 percent
Vitamin B$_6$ 24 percent

Food Pyramid Servings
Each recipe portion =
1 meat group serving

Food Mood
Tamari or soy flavor

Stuffed Turkey Peppers

Instead of the traditional ground meat and rice filling, we've used turkey sausage for a change of pace. We cut down on time and effort by filling the peppers with uncooked ingredients so you don't dirty an extra pan. And although there's a long cooking time, it's very short on prep time.

4 large green peppers
8 ounces (about 4 links or patties) turkey sausage
2 cups frozen corn
1 8-ounce can tomato sauce
1 tablespoon Italian seasoning blend

Preheat oven to 400° F.

Cut tops from peppers and remove seeds. Stand peppers upright in a 9" x 12" baking dish. Fill pan with 1" water, cover with foil, and bake for ½ hour.

While the peppers are partially cooking, prepare the filling. In a bowl, squeeze the turkey from its casing (if using links) and combine remaining ingredients (you may chop up the pepper tops and add them in, too). Remove peppers from oven and fill. Cover and bake an additional 1 hour.

Serves 4

Recipe Option
If you do not have Italian seasoning blend, use equal amounts of basil, oregano, and garlic powder to total 1 tablespoon.

Nutritional Benefits
Calories   265

Percent RDA for
Breast-feeding Moms

Dietary fiber	25 percent
Folic acid	27 percent
Iron	18 percent
Niacin	28 percent
Potassium	37 percent
Protein	26 percent
Zinc	12 percent

Food Pyramid Servings
Each recipe portion =
3 vegetable group servings
⅔ meat group serving

Food Mood
Comfort food
One-dish meal

Beef and Beer

This one-pot dish is so simple. Just put all the ingredients in at once and let it cook. The beer provides a subtle flavor and liquid needed for tenderizing this cut of meat. With such prolonged cooking, the alcohol has just about all cooked off. If you prefer not to use beer, our recipe option calls for using nonalcoholic beer.

 1 pound chuck steak, boneless, trimmed
 1 cup onions, sliced
 ½ can light beer
 ½ cup water
 1 teaspoon dried thyme
 ½ teaspoon garlic powder
 ½ teaspoon black pepper
 2 cups cooked rice

In a large skillet, on high heat, brown meat on both sides. Add all remaining ingredients except rice, and bring to a boil. Reduce heat, cover, and simmer for 1 to 1½ hours or until meat is fork-tender. Divide meat and rice into portions and spoon sauce over rice.

Serves 4

Recipe Options
Instead of chuck, use round or other less tender meat cut. Instead of light beer, use nonalcoholic beer.

Nutritional Benefits
(including rice)
Calories   315

Percent RDA for
Breast-feeding Moms

Iron	22 percent
Magnesium	6 percent
Protein	44 percent
Vitamin B$_6$	14 percent
Zinc	47 percent

Food Pyramid Servings
Each recipe portion =
3 meat group servings
1 bread group serving

Food Mood
Moist, pot roast–style meat
Beer flavor

Peppered Meat Loaf

Leftover meat loaf makes a great sandwich. Use a dash of ketchup or mustard on your sandwich bread for added flavor and moisture.

1½ pounds ground meat loaf (packaged as beef, veal, pork combination)
  1 cup onions, finely chopped
 ½ cup plain bread crumbs
  1 egg
  2 tablespoons ketchup
  5 tablespoons hot pepper rings, jarred, finely diced

Preheat oven to 375° F.

Mix all ingredients except ketchup and 1 tablespoon of diced pepper rings thoroughly in a large bowl. On an ungreased baking sheet, shape the meat mixture into a loaf shape. Combine reserved peppers and ketchup and spoon or brush over top and sides of meat loaf. Bake for approximately 1 hour. Remove from baking sheet with spatula and let rest for a few minutes before slicing.

Serves 6 (each serving 3 ounces)

Recipe Options
If the ground meat loaf combination is unavailable, use equal amount of lean ground beef, pork, and veal to total 1½ pounds.
Use a total of 3 tablespoons of peppers for a less spicy flavor.

Nutritional Benefits

Calories	250

Percent RDA for
Breast-feeding Moms

Folic acid	5 percent
Iron	13 percent
Magnesium	7 percent
Niacin	20 percent
Protein	35 percent
Vitamin B_6	14 percent
Zinc	23 percent

Food Pyramid Servings

*Each recipe portion =
3 meat group servings*

Food Mood

Comfort food
Hot, spicy flavor

Lemon-Caper Tuna and Pasta

Send hubby outside to grill the tuna while you boil the spaghetti and heat up the sauce. This dish will taste like you spent lots of time with it, but it's really quick.

1¼ pound fresh tuna, cut into 6 portions
  1 pound spaghetti or other long pasta
  1 15-ounce can reduced-sodium chicken broth
 ½ cup scallions, sliced (green part only)
  2 tablespoons capers
  1 tablespoon olive oil
  2 tablespoons lemon juice
  3 tablespoons grated Parmesan cheese
    Black pepper to taste

Grill tuna until no longer pink in the center, about 5 to 7 minutes. Set aside.

Boil water and cook pasta until done.

While pasta is cooking, heat broth, scallions, capers, and oil in a small pan. Add lemon juice just prior to serving. Drain pasta and portion into individual bowls. Top with tuna steak and pour sauce over top. Sprinkle with cheese.

Serves 6 (1½ cups pasta, ⅓ cup sauce, ½ tablespoon cheese per serving)

Recipe Option
Instead of tuna, use swordfish or other firm-fleshed fish that will not fall apart on the grill.

Nutritional Benefits

Calories   400

Percent RDA for
Breast-feeding Moms

Iron	29 percent
Magnesium	10 percent
Niacin	73 percent
Protein	46 percent
Riboflavin	53 percent

Food Pyramid Servings

*Each recipe portion =
3 bread group servings
1 meat group serving*

Food Mood

Seafood and pasta dish
Lemon/caper flavor
Clear, brothlike sauce

Gingerbread with Lemon Frosting

Gingerbread pairs with this lemon yogurt topping to make a low-fat and delicious dessert.

1 cup nonfat lemon yogurt
1 box gingerbread cake and cookie mix
2 teaspoons grated lemon zest

Pour yogurt into a cheesecloth or strong paper towels. Let it drain over a cup for approximately 6 to 8 hours in the refrigerator, resulting in a firm-textured yogurt cheese.

Bake gingerbread according to directions in a 9" square pan or as cupcakes. Cool gingerbread completely.

Stir lemon zest into yogurt cheese and evenly spread over cake.

Serves 9

Recipe Option
Instead of lemon yogurt, use orange yogurt and orange zest or lime yogurt and lime zest.

Nutritional Benefits
Calories   180

Percent RDA for
Breast-feeding Moms
Calcium   8 percent
Iron   5 percent
Potassium   6 percent

Food Pyramid Servings
Each recipe portion =
1½ bread group servings

Food Mood
Old-fashioned ginger flavor
Tart lemon flavor

Chiffon "Ice Cream" Cake

Most supermarkets sell prepackaged chiffon cake in the bakery department. Any flavor will do, although we particularly like orange chiffon with chocolate frozen yogurt. This dessert gets only 20 percent of its calories from fat.

1 10" orange chiffon cake
2 cups chocolate low-fat frozen yogurt
1½ cups frozen nondairy whipped topping, thawed

Slice cake in half lengthwise to make 2 layers. Spread frozen yogurt on bottom layer (this works best if yogurt is not really hard). Put top layer on and cover top and sides of cake with whipped topping. Freeze for at least 1 hour. Slice just before serving. If refreezing leftovers, loosely cover with plastic wrap to prevent cake from drying out.

Serves 18

Recipe Options
Use any flavor combination of cake and frozen yogurt that is available.
Top cake with shaved chocolate.

Nutritional Benefits
Calories   200

Percent RDA for
Breast-feeding Moms
Niacin   4 percent
Riboflavin   5 percent
Thiamine   5 percent

Food Pyramid Serving
Each recipe portion =
1 bread group serving

Food Mood
Ice cream cake

Baked Apples

You can make this dessert while the oven is on cooking dinner. We also like this dish for breakfast.

   2 tablespoons Grape-Nuts
1 1/2 tablespoons brown sugar
   1/2 tablespoon maple syrup
   1/2 teaspoon cinnamon
   2 large apples, washed, dried, cored
   1/2 cup water

Preheat oven to 350° F.

Combine first 4 ingredients in a small bowl. Fill the cavity of the apples with this mixture. Place stuffed apples in a pie pan or small baking dish. Pour water over top of apples and into pan. Bake for approximately 1 hour. Tastes best when served warm.

Serves 2

Recipe Option
Instead of apples, use fresh pears.

Nutritional Benefits
Calories   150

Percent RDA for
Breast-feeding Moms
Dietary fiber   12 percent
Iron   9 percent
Potassium   9 percent
Thiamine   10 percent

Food Pyramid Servings
*Each recipe portion =
2 fruit group servings*

Food Mood
Warm, baked fruit
Struesel topping flavors

Poached Wine Pears

These can be kept in the refrigerator and used as a quick snack or dessert. Use any variety of pears in season.

3 medium pears, washed, dried, halved, cored
½ cup chardonnay, sauvignon blanc, or chablis wine
2 tablespoons sugar

In a large, shallow pan, add ½" of water and bring to a boil. Add pears, reduce to a simmer, and cover. Poach for 5 to 8 minutes until pears are slightly soft. Place pears in a shallow dish and discard the water. In the same pan, over medium heat, stir wine and sugar together. Heat 5 minutes. Pour sauce over pears. Cover and refrigerate for at least 1 hour.

Serves 6

Recipe Option
Instead of white wine, use nonalcoholic wine or white grape juice.

Nutritional Benefits
Calories   80

Percent RDA for
Breast-feeding Moms
Dietary fiber   9 percent
Potassium   5 percent

Food Pyramid Serving
*Each recipe portion =
1 fruit group serving*

Food Mood
Chilled fruit
Soft texture
Wine flavor